LUDMILLA PETRUSHEVSKAYA

Kidnapped:

A STORY IN CRIMES

Translated by Marian Schwartz

DEEP VELLUM PUBLISHING

DALLAS, TEXAS

Deep Vellum Publishing
3000 Commerce St., Dallas, Texas 75226
deepvellum.org · @deepvellum

Deep Vellum is a 501c3 nonprofit literary arts organization
founded in 2013 with the mission to bring
the world into conversation through literature.

Originally published as *Нас украли. История преступлений* by Издательство "Э"
in Moscow, Russia, in 2017

First US Edition, 2022

LIBRARY OF CONGRESS CATALOGING-IN-PUBLICATION DATA

Names: Petrushevskaia, Liudmila, author. | Schwartz, Marian, 1951–
translator.
Title: Kidnapped : a story in crimes / Ludmilla Petrushevksaya ; translated
by Marian Schwartz.
Other titles: Nas ukrali. English
Description: First US edition. | Dallas, Texas : Deep Vellum Publishing,
2022.
Identifiers: LCCN 2022034786 | ISBN 9781646052042 (trade paperback) | ISBN
9781646052301 (ebook)
Subjects: LCGFT: Satirical literature. | Novels.
Classification: LCC PG3485.E724 N3613 2023 | DDC
891.73/44--dc23/eng/20220721
LC record available at https://lccn.loc.gov/2022034786

ISBN (TPB) 978-1-64605-204-2 | ISBN (Ebook) 978-1-64605-230-1

Cover design by Natalya Balnova

Interior layout and typesetting by KGT

PRINTED IN CANADA

1

THE TWENTY-FIRST CENTURY

The Boys' Departure

THE BOYS' MOTHER took them to the airport.

"So, Seryozha. Look after Osya, make sure he doesn't lose anything. Osya, wake up, get your backpack. Here are your passports and tickets. Call me the minute you land. Two prearranged calls every day: in the morning the moment you wake up, and in the evening. So I don't lose my mind. Seryozha, make sure this happens. Each of you call me separately. If you don't call, just in case, I'm going to the embassy."

"Mama! Isn't that going overboard? The embassy. Really. Are we little kids? It's not like this is the first time."

"We don't know who's waiting for you. Osya, where are you off to now?"

"Check-in. We're late."

"You'll go in a second. I can't talk to you in line."

"What, we're being followed?"

"I can't rule that out."

"Mom! Is this some kind of whodunit?"

"No, Osya, it's a soap opera. The Missing Boy-Twins! Ma, that's it, we're late."

"Seryozha, don't joke. I repeat, we don't know who's waiting for you."

"Our father, that's who."

"Fine. Here's the deal. You'll each call me separately, don't forget! Morning and evening. The secret word when we say goodbye is *tse*."

"Tse."

"Tse."

"And don't tell a soul."

2

What the Historians Will Write

THE FRENETIC NINETIES, if you bother to look. When Russian ships insured by Lloyd's carrying ferrous metal were lost at sea, when billions, let's just say, of union assets—meaning sold-off schools, factories, management's private homes, dispensaries, sanatoriums, hospitals, kindergartens, nursery schools, and training courses, and Party and Young Communist buildings—vanished into offshores, when entire Style Moderne and Empire palaces in Moscow, which had belonged, by tradition, to the district and municipal Party committees, were sold for a song. When abandoned factories fell into the hands of people speculating with those worthless pieces of paper called vouchers. When the proprietor of a billion-ruble business could be approached with an offer to give it all away, and after his categorical refusal, that same summer, during dacha season, at the reservoir where the proprietor's huge dacha stood on the shore, two divers were sent down. His bodyguards were grilling shashlyk, glancing over at their boss, who'd gone to cool off from the heat—and drowned in one second flat. Dragged down by his feet.

Oh well, the historians will write about it one day.

3

Next Stop, Montegasco

TWO YOUNG MEN with backpacks, whispering back and forth, boarded a plane from Moscow to Montegasco.

While outside, by the way, it was already the first decade of the twenty-first century.

Two handsome brunets with the classic profiles of those heroes-in-tiger-skins Moscow patrol cops were hell-bent on hassling but whose passports for some reason they were less than eager to check. Who wants to go looking for trouble with foreigners? Dagos, they looked like. Especially because their backs were too straight, and even though they had bodybuilder shoulders, their legs were a little long for young toughs from some Lyubertsy or Solntsevo gang. And look at those toothpaste grins. Different teeth, too. Not ours, for sure.

You know. Theirs.

There was just one thing. Galya, who was working the check-in counter at Sheremetyevo-2, looked at the second passport and blinked: these guys had two identical passports in a row. Their full names coincided exactly, even the dates of birth were one and the same. Twins? But their names were identical, too. That doesn't happen in real life! What should she do?

All right, fine. This is above your pay grade, as military intel would say. Why raise a stink? You'll catch hell for holding up the plane and get fired for cause. Different photographs. They didn't look alike.

So the boys breezed onto the plane, spent the allotted time in it, and exited at Montegasco's international airport.

Where a driver, Nikolai, Uncle Kolya, was waiting for them in the greeting line holding a sign: "Sergei Sertsov."

Two boys who looked like they were from the Caucasus approached him.

Approached, mocking someone quietly to each other. He understood. They saw him. They clammed up.

"You waiting for Sergei Sergeyevich Sertsov?" one asked.

The other one guffawed again.

"That's us," the first one again explained.

They exchanged smiles.

As if their being met was a practical joke. Not taking it seriously.

Not so much as a hello. Here people said hello even in the hotel elevator, and when his boss had visitors, Kolya got them settled himself.

Even Kolya had grown used to civility.

Everyone here smiled at each other, just in case—but don't look them in the eye, they won't understand.

No staring.

But these two weren't looking at him, just at each other.

Kolya asked, "Which one of you is Sergei Sergeyevich Sertsov?"

"We both are," one boomed.

They guffawed again.

They'd come here to make jokes.

"Then I'll ask for your passport," Kolya said, surprising himself. He was responsible for meeting a son, after all! Not two!

They showed them.

Everything in the passports coincided except for the numbers. He had no choice, he had to take them in the Bentley.

They swiveled their heads, exchanged more smiles (he was watching them in the rearview mirror), and looked nothing like his boss.

Caucasus faces, for sure. Swarthy skin, big noses.

They didn't even look like each other, for that matter.

They were murmuring something. Guffawing quietly.

He was driving them through neighborhoods where only billionaires lived.

Walls, trees, houses.

Villas, really! Past fences and parks. Just like our place. You'll see.

"Waldis Wembers's house," Kolya said.

Both made a face. Chances were they didn't know who that was.

"The tennis player," Kolya explained. "Ranked fifteenth in the world."

They goggled like morons. Their jaws dangled.

They looked amazed.

And guffawed again.

"Came in third at Wimbledon and the Australian Open."

"Impossible," one said.

The other one blinked and curled his mouth into a tube.

Morons.

Moscow riffraff, the driver decided.

Ignorant, they didn't know the first thing about what was going on here in Europe.

The driver always pointed out Wembers's house to all his boss's guests so they'd know they were on their way to see someone who lived next to Wembers.

"He and his girlfriend drive around in a Ferrari," the driver explained.

Both these clowns started winking at each other, jaws hanging.

Then Kolya waxed enthusiastic. "And a banker lives right here, a billionaire. With ten wives, who all wear paranjas when they go to the jeweler's."

He said it and didn't even look in the mirror to see what they were up to there in the back seat, making stupid faces and clapping.

At the entrance the driver clicked the remote to open the gate and drove them down the driveway toward his boss's villa, past his own so-called gatehouse (the door was shut; his wife must have been busy either in the garden or in the villa).

Gatehouse or no, Uncle Kolya noted to himself, it was nearly two stories.

And on top Kolya had done something mansard-ish with particleboard walls so his little girl, Angelka, would have a place to play.

It looked like a shipping crate, his wife said, plywood everywhere.

Put something up yourself then.

The boss was waiting for his son, and now (the driver cursed silently) there were two, two con artists.

The boss didn't have twins, let alone with the exact same name!

His boss would be worked up, understandably so, but he had no suspicion what kind of scam they'd cooked up for him.

These two brother acrobats. Then Nikolai calmed down. He knew Daddy Sertsov.

It was okay, he'd shake out this scam fast. He'd dealt with worse.

Kolya took unfailing pride in his boss.

Kolya had been his driver before, back under Soviet power, but not always. Back then, there'd been two cars for the whole department, and Kolya mostly drove the chief around. At the time, his own boss, Sertsov, was a flunky and so didn't often get to take the black Volga.

Kolya may have driven the chief around then, but later Sertsov figured out what was what, got himself into the Soviet of People's Deputies, and took Kolya along. Then came the good life, access to consumer goods, perestroika and guns blazing, and his boss laid his hands on a whole lot of something—three factories, actually, and two ships of scrap copper that they sank off the coast of Nigeria but that were well and duly insured. "Loyt," it was called. His boss "drowned," too, basically got the hell out of Russia before the investors could investigate. Two of them went on television and spoke at rallies, too, two clowns.

His boss had done the right thing.

4

THE TURN OF THE TWENTY-FIRST CENTURY

Kolya's Story

WHEN KOLYA LOST his job and went back to live with his parents in Tula Province, they leased three hundred hectares, a farm, basically.

But the calf-shed, garage, and all their equipment were torched. They knew who had done it—men from the next village, because his father was leasing their fields.

That land hadn't been plowed or sown in so long that it was all grown up in aspen, but the locals took the lease as an affront.

His father had gone to their village and asked them to come work for him, promised good pay. They'd turned him down.

They thought he wasn't offering enough, and everyone wanted to know how much they were paying in Moscow. Right. How much they were paying in Moscow to work in an Arbat calf-shed.

But what do you expect from boozers?

His father hired refugees from Kyrgyzstan, ethnic Russians returned to the fatherland and waiting for their Russian citizenship. His father bought them three abandoned huts.

They'd only just started settling in when three guys with scythes paid them a visit and said they were going to slaughter and set fire to everyone—this isn't your land, it's ours.

They were so small-time, these guys, as one old lady said later, they were mowing other people's grass on the plots of those deserted huts.

They drove people out over a lousy stack of hay.

But then they burned down his father's calf-shed and whole equipment yard.

People just can't stand anyone making more money than them.

Oh well, Kolya and his parents got the hell out.

The collective farmers promised to burn down his father's house. Even though they'd lived there longer than anyone could remember, so his father settled them next to his grandfather's place, on his land.

Both old folks were still living in that house. That's where they always took us for the summer, Nikolai recalled in fury.

And we come from there!

It was all very simple: two villages, ours and theirs, forever at war.

Once upon a time, they'd lost an entire field to our people at cards. Well, not they themselves but their landlord, when they'd had one. And they just couldn't forget it.

So the young men would form a solid wall around the club during dances.

They'd always knife one of ours in the forest on St. Ilya's. St. Ilya's Day used to be our church holiday, and they always celebrated it in our forest, in the Maples. And they'd range around us.

They'd sneak up on our guys, leap out onto the paths, and attack.

One of our girls hanged herself. Then our guys went there to kill whoever they happened to come across and burn down their houses. So Kolya, his father, and his mother had to run away, joined his mother's sister in Moscow, who worked in management at a high-rise and got his mother a job there as a dispatcher.

They got a room in a dorm, in the basement, with the Moldovan and Ukrainian janitors.

They all had families joining them, the more the merrier.

There was no squeezing into the kitchen.

After that his mother quickly scoped out what was what. Her sister had everything lined up, his mama helped out and eventually got a new job as a housing manager in a new district.

They got his father a supervisor job in a garage and gave them an official one-room apartment on the first floor for the time being, but the kitchen there was twelve square meters, so Kolya put a cot in the kitchen. Someone had carried out a brand-new one to a doorway around Patriarch Ponds, and Kolya was driving by in his father's van, a Gazelle—the people had moved, maybe, or it didn't fit, or someone had died, his mother went back and forth.

Kolya soured on discos and mixing with Moscow girls. They got right down to brass tacks ("Are you from Moscow?" "Yes." "Where in Moscow?") and wormed it out of him that he didn't have two kopeks to rub together, was working in a garage, and officially lived in the countryside.

No one would even go to McDonald's with him.

For New Year's, Nikolai decided to visit his grandfather, and on December 31, at loose ends, went to the disco in his large exurban settlement.

Rather than sit around with his grandfather and listen to all the same war stories.

When his grandfather got snockered, he would start in. Usually he was reluctant to reminisce and never did, because you shouldn't, but he couldn't help himself then, and his old buddies would show up from the next world as alive as you or me.

At the disco, Kolya met two girls, who got Kolya to take them home in his Gazelle. Home turned out to be nearby, but one more girl squeezed into the car behind them—a chubby girl from the disco, a real skank, you could tell right off. Jumped inside when it was practically moving.

The others started swearing.

They got to their house and she plunked herself down in Kolya's lap, started kissing him, fondling him wherever.

The girls pretended they'd never seen her before and tried to run her out.

So Kolya drove her home, and she invited him in, but no one was there, her mother had gone to visit family for a couple of days, she said.

The girl was fun and straightforward, didn't try to put on airs like those Moscow girls.

She said, "I wasn't the only one turning tricks in the field."

"What's that?" Nikolai asked, panting.

"Nothing, knock on wood," replied the girl who had given herself to Nikolai, no questions asked.

She even joked.

"Soup's on. Chicken tabaka."

Which is to say, she didn't give a damn.

Every word out of her mouth was a swear word.

Kolya was loaded, cutting loose, having a ball after a long drought.

The girl didn't object, either, you could tell this wasn't her first time. It felt like she was getting back at somebody.

And she suited Nikolai to the ground. A fine girl, it turned out, pretty even—when he got a good look at her later, on the couch.

After it was over she lay there undressed. She'd dropped all her clothes on the floor.

He actually asked, "What's your name, beautiful?"

"You forgot?"

She answered with her full name, and as for her age added: almost seventeen. So still in high school.

How's about them apples.

But she looked twenty. Because she was fat.

He could go to jail for this. That's why it's called jailbait.

All the village boys knew about it and worried about underage girls' parents taking revenge and forcing them to get married.

But all the girls in the village that summer (they were from the city, spending the summer with relatives) laughed at the word. Not a one of them wanted to get married.

In the winter, there were nothing but old women left in the village. Nearly all the old men were dead from one thing or another. Only Kolya's granddad was still hanging on.

When he was saying goodbye to this new girl, he helped her get dressed, buttoned her up the back, and she asked him for his phone number.

And in February she phoned: she was pregnant. And she wouldn't be seventeen until April.

Kolya freaked out. She said he hadn't used anything, after all. Hadn't protected her in any way. And she was a virgin.

"What do you mean a virgin?"

"Just what I said."

"I didn't notice anything."

"I hid it. I was embarrassed to be a virgin. Sixteen and you were my first. My girlfriends would have made fun of me. But I knew all about it. I watched videos."

"What kind?"

"Porn, that's what kind."

"For crying out loud." Nikolai was stunned.

"Yeah, I noticed you at the disco. You danced with me, remember?"

"No!"

"You were drunk. A whole bunch of us were partying hard. And I followed you when I saw they were taking you away. I know them. Group sex. They'd call in even more boys. I followed you to the neighbor's especially, I realized who they were and where they were sending your Gazelle, they were grown girls, they'd come from Tula to see her, the niece. They were all twenty, if not more. That wasn't the first time I'd seen them here. And then I jumped into your Gazelle, too. The faces they made! They swore at me and shoved, pinched me! But they didn't scare me. I got there and sat down at their table as if you were my boyfriend. They weren't sure who was with who. I started making out with you right away. I did everything under the table. Then I put on my coat and led you away. They went out of their minds over you leaving."

"Imagine that," Nikolai marveled, like an idiot.

"But you were the one who said, 'Let's go to your place.' You!"

"I don't remember," Nikolai, the future father replied apropos of nothing, gobsmacked.

"You agreed to it. Do you think I'm going for an abortion in high school? So I can be a cripple my whole life? And kill my own child?"

Kolya went over to try to talk her into it, but her enraged mother was home, and she said right off that they'd put him in jail.

And they had his passport info, don't you know.

So here's the deal.

If need be, when the baby was born they'd do a paternity test in Tula.

Everything started spinning and fast. Her mother worked at a department store, she had everything you need for a wedding, including German china, and she bought all the booze, Nikolai organized the refreshments through his mother-in-law, she took the order, and his grandfather provided from his own barrels, he was always pickling cabbage and cucumbers and sousing apples, and he donated a sack of potatoes.

They got married.

His parents approved his choice of a Tula girl.

Kolya got a job in Moscow and rented a one-room apartment. Galina found work as a cleaning lady in a daycare center, even though she was four months pregnant.

She was so heavy anyway, no one noticed anything until the seventh month, at which point she could go on maternity leave.

Galina was put on bed rest at the maternity hospital because of some bad tests.

Then Angelka was born, prematurely, and now they could pay Galina less for her maternity leave than she'd been counting on.

Galina cried at the maternity hospital, tied herself in knots. Angelka was underweight, but lots are born like that nowadays, skinny, the doctor told Kolya when he went to find out why they'd taken Galina to examine her for some reason, this was in the ninth month, the doctor from Khimki used the hook, and that night her water broke.

The doctor said it was a routine examination, and you had to be prepared for anything during a birth.

And that was it. All this was quickly forgotten, though, because when Galina, Angelka, and Kolya had been living in their one-room for a month, Kolya's mama got a three-room apartment through her job.

And at that point his parents invited the three of them to move in!

Kolya was happy, went nuts buying and installing fixtures, whipped the apartment into shape. They'd been given bare walls!

He got tiles from a construction site, bought them from Tajiks, installed them all himself, and bought a kitchen, not a new one, but in good condition.

Life began, Angelka was already wanting to run around the apartment, and Galina wasn't working and stayed home with her.

They bought themselves a foldout bed and started sleeping with Angelka, since they hadn't bought a child's bed yet. Money was tight.

And all of a sudden, one fine day, his mother barged into their room in the middle of the night, without knocking, black as a storm cloud, and said, "Get out, all of you."

What? How's that? Kolya had no effing idea what she was talking about.

Galina, who after the birth had gone on a diet subsisting on kefir and groats, always wanting to slim down, told Kolya how his mother had been mean to her.

That supposedly Galina had eaten something from the fridge that wasn't hers.

But Galina would rather choke than eat their food. Kolya knew her.

His wife could be pretty mean herself.

She answered his mama tit for tat, cursing a blue streak. His mama had the last word.

Tula females don't kid around.

Afterward, Galina added that Irina Ivanovna had really ticked her off, she hadn't wanted to complain for a long time.

Implying Angelka isn't yours.

Implying I'd tricked you by saying I was sixteen. Sure, I did trick you after the disco, I was a good twenty already, and I was working as a cleaner in my mother's store. What, I'm going to tell your mama how I tricked you? It's not like you were going to marry someone older, a cleaner, and fat on top of everything else. I went to work for my mother because we knew she was going to die soon, I was helping her, the loaders were swindling her, and there wasn't a salesclerk job open.

After mama, I'd have become manager, I did graduate from trade school, after all, and I had a high school education. At the disco I liked you, you were totally different, not like our local boys, and I wanted a child by you, and that's why I got into your car with those sluts. I lied, I told you I was sixteen, and when you fell asleep I wrote down your passport info. And took your phone number, so when I found out I was pregnant, I decided to fight for you. And when we filed at the registry office, you didn't see what I wrote for my year of birth. I had to preserve our family. My mother kept crying, she wanted me to get an abortion, and she was planning to hire a hit man to take you out. Five hundred dollars, hell, a hundred would have done it. There are numbskulls like that. Your mama may judge me, but Angelka is your daughter. I'm fat and older than you. I'm a cleaner. I'll leave, so be it.

Kolya sat on the ottoman as if he'd been hit over the head.

Find another apartment! But he had no money!

Kolya loved his parents very much. Especially his mama.

And now he understood her and his father. Even his older sister was against Galina. But Galina was his wife, Angelka was his daughter, he was used to them. He'd raised his daughter since she was six days old.

Galina watched him spitefully, blubbering. As if she'd proven something.

So she left to live with her mother in her village. She took all her personal belongings.

He drove her, and Galina didn't say a word. Like she was hurt.

Good thing it was April already, so it looked like his wife and child were going to the dacha.

He stayed on with his parents, only on weekends he cleared off to see his family. Without a word to his mama, let alone his father.

They didn't say anything either, didn't ask about their granddaughter.

Their own granddaughter!

Oh, how life had turned upside down, everyone now enemies. Galina was hurt that he didn't go to live with her. But where could you find work in the countryside?

It's burying yourself alive in a strange settlement, and she had a brother, too, a drinker and a brawler, as she said. He even came especially from Tula to rumble.

Over the summer, Kolya saved some money to rent a one-room apartment.

So they could move in the fall. But Galina wouldn't let him get close to her. When he came he slept on the floor.

His whole life was ruined!

It was at this very moment that he got the signal from Sergei Ivanovich Sertsov, his former boss.

Somehow, through channels, he'd found his phone number, and some guy called and said Sertsov needed a driver and assistant in a certain country. The address was a secret.

"Thank you," Kolya replied. He was thrown and didn't understand what was going on. "I have a wife and daughter now and I can't come alone, probably."

He said "probably" because he didn't know how it was all going to go between him and Galina.

What if she'd already found herself someone in the village?

Her old boyfriend? She'd had someone before Kolya.

It was true, Angelka didn't look at all like her father.

Both he and Galina were fair-haired, whereas the little girl was dark and curly.

His mother had been hinting at exactly that. That was probably the reason for all of it.

But Sertsov didn't know about Kolya's life now. He thought he was a free-ranging Cossack, like before. But Kolya was banned from travel now. He couldn't even imagine leaving to make money at this moment.

Galina was the only thing Kolya could call his own. His mother also had a favorite daughter, Kolya's sister, who had a college education and an apartment, rich, too.

But Kolya—what was Kolya? Her son, who'd barely graduated from high school with mediocre grades.

They'd always considered Kolya backward.

"I'll get back to you," the guy said over the phone, and indeed, he did.

"Dictate all their info to me. Your wife and child's passports. They'll send an invitation to your address. It's not a bad living situation for a family, there's a separate gatehouse on the grounds."

The gatehouse turned out to be a two-room house in a park!

His wife started helping the gardener, and now she was content. Everything in their life had changed. ·

Her memory of childhood, when her mother made her till the garden, something Galina hated at the time, came in handy now.

Galina was a real trooper, she mastered the gas mower, he showed her once and that was it.

She even managed to plant her own Tula flowers. In front of their gatehouse.

Her mother sent seeds from their village, and in early spring Galina propagated seedlings.

Here, in Montegasco, no one had ever seen fragrant tobacco, or phlox, or asters, or gladioli, or dahlias. People in this village didn't know anything about them. Or coneflowers!

The boss, who himself had grown up in his grandmother's village, said right away that she'd had a front garden at her house, and now he was proud of his own unusual flowerbed.

A native Russian—here, where it was solid lawns. He would sit there in a rocking chair under the awning.

The boss's wife made fun of that flowerbed.

Galina grew cucumbers, too, and tomatoes, and dill and coriander! It was hot here, water it and it would pop up.

The boss liked crunching from a vegetable garden without nitrates and pesticides. No comparison to store-bought! Galina pickled and marinated store-bought produce for the pantry because there wasn't that much she grew, just enough for salad.

A plot the size of a handkerchief.

The next winter the boss thought it over, treated himself to Galina's pickled squash and eggplant, and then set aside room in the back for her for a vegetable plot.

And very late one night, Galina said to Kolya, "Make no mistake, Angelka is your daughter, her little fingers are exactly like yours, long and curling, and her nails are like yours, pretty. My fingers, just look, they're different, peasant.

"It's just my father was curly and dark, I guess my granny hooked up with a Romanian, they had all kinds of Romanians stationed in the village during the Occupation. My father was born after them. My grandfather never came back from the war or he would have driven her and her little Gypsy out, that's how they talked in the countryside.

"She gave birth to him late, after her due date. And his mother left with her fella, they signed up for a construction brigade at Shaturtorf. They left him at an orphanage for a while. A bitter cup! And all because of the color of his skin. My Gypsy father didn't take me for his own daughter, either, I'm so blonde," Galina said, and she suddenly started crying. "That's where my whole curse comes from. Everything that's happened to me."

She was smart, she understood everything that Kolya's mother had said about her.

And that Kolya had heard more than once.

"It happens, it's fine, we're over it," Kolya said, and he kissed her short puffy fingers. "Since I've got two Romanians, let's go somewhere. Everything's close here. When the boss and his wife are away."

5

Kustodiev

KOLYA THE DRIVER'S wife, Galina—sometimes called Kustodiev for reasons to be explained—finding herself suddenly abroad, had two choices: remain Mrs. Russia with measurements of 98-60-98, where the first number was her weight in kilos, the second was her leg measurements at the capital, if you think of a leg as a column, and the third her waist measurement—in centimeters.

Or, the second possibility, Galina could wind up being like all the female service staff here, all those Ukrainians, Thais, and Poles, and the young women "from Moscow."

That is, dry up like a hag, let your face darken, and learn to fake a smile in response to any gaze. Smile politely, no grinning.

Not only that, all those women spoke Montegascan, they'd got the hang of it somehow. English, too.

Kustodiev had had no ear for languages, even in school.

Her German teacher had passed her only because Galina's mother gave her access to where she wasn't supposed to go, the back storeroom.

Where her mother worked.

Even in school, Galina had known she was going to do the same thing, sell in the same kind of store. She used to get her girlfriends what they needed through her mother.

Not for free, though. She earned enough for her makeup.

In their house in the village they had everything—Chaliapin wallpaper, white Romanian Louis XIV furniture, a Czech Cascade chandelier, china sets, a Ruby television—and her mother bought all kinds of imports for her and her brother Yuri, only there were problems with Galina, who was a plump little girl and so foreign lands didn't have her sizes.

Her mother bought her short boots (the tall ones wouldn't go above her ankles) and tights, but Galina couldn't wear them, they were all too tight.

Her father had been a driver, but he'd had his license taken away because of his drinking, so in the summer he worked at the boating station, but in the winter he stayed home.

With nothing to do, her father drank and beat her mama when she wouldn't give him money, and one time he put little Yuri's six-year-old head on a stool while holding an axe and started screaming, "I'm going to chop his head off if you don't give me money again! I might as well croak." Her mother screamed, "I'm begging you, let him go, you're out of your mind."

But he waved the axe over the kid's head and held Yuri's shoulders to the stool.

Her mother started crying and gave him some money, and later Yuri screamed bloody murder when they tried to put him to bed.

When her father ran out, her mama hid the axe under her mattress.

And when her father dragged himself back, drunk, and fell asleep on the ottoman in the kitchen as he was, having pissed himself, Galina's mother woke her up and they wound her father up in sheets.

He woke up early in the morning and started hollering and cursing, "Untie me! I'll kill you all and Galka, too, if you don't get me the hair of the dog."

Then her mother stood over him holding the axe and said, "Now I'm going to give you the death penalty." He started cursing even more, writhed like a fish, but her mother sat on him and then said, "I'm punishing you for Yuri and for Galina, you bastard, for what you did to her."

He understood exactly what she meant and started shouting, "I didn't do anything to her, she was the one who wiggled her ass, she was asking for it."

And in this reedy voice, "Help me."

Yuri had woken up and stood in the kitchen doorway, but no one noticed, and as if that business with the axe weren't enough, he saw the axe again, only now in his mother's hand.

She noticed Yuri, though, and told Galina to take him away and then sent her to get a towel, while her father kept whining, and then her mother covered her father's head with the towel, put the axe down, grabbed the handle, and struck the swaddled father in the neck as hard as she could.

He fell silent instantly, as if he'd choked, and when her mother pulled back the towel, he wasn't even breathing.

They unwound the towel and her mother called an ambulance. She wept. Galina wept, too.

The sheets wound around had left some marks, but the doctor didn't even look at him under the blanket, squeamish, there was the stink of vomit and plenty else. Her father often pissed himself.

But nothing happened to her mama, the patient infarcted while in a state of alcoholic intoxication, and after the autopsy they also found end-stage cirrhosis.

Her mother asked how long he would have lasted, and the doctor couldn't say, cases like that sometimes lived a year, sometimes longer.

Fine, then, the sufferings are on your head, say thank you. After all, Galina hadn't told her mother what her father'd done to her. He'd always said, "I'll kill your mother if you talk. You're no daughter to me, your mother's a f–ing whore."

Galina was a plump little girl, and pretty. It took him hours to come, the pig.

But Galina had to pick up Yuri at daycare by seven, and her mother didn't get home until nine.

To this day Galina couldn't bear the smell of a man who smoked and drank or any of the stuff that comes out of him.

That nothing came of anything with her husband wasn't her fault.

She had a daughter. But her husband drank beer when the weekend came and he smoked and you couldn't tell him anything.

Her daughter, Angelka, was Galina's sole happiness and great pride. At six, the girl started going to the local school and was immediately chattering away in their language. A skinny little girl, with black curls, just like a local, and long-legged, and you could already tell she was going to be a beauty.

Galina's husband Kolya was as sweet as a calf and loved her.

And every night he labored hard, panted away. But no dice.

Plus, Galina was afraid of everything in the world and wouldn't leave Angelka with him.

But then she started noticing that the girl was embarrassed when her mother picked her up at school and couldn't say word one.

So Angelka would translate, for instance, that tomorrow she had to pick her up earlier, not like today.

Then Galina did something: she got a job in the local supermarket's storeroom for the morning shift, from nine to twelve.

She couldn't learn the language at home since neither the boss nor Kolya could speak Montegascan.

Moreover, the boss's wife, herself stick-thin, she knew all the languages, but she couldn't stand Galina and called her "Kustodiev, basically" with a laugh and nodded at the bookshelf. Galina checked there on purpose, went to considerable effort, and finally spotted a book, *Kustodiev.*

Trembling all over, she started looking at the pictures. And yes, she did look like one woman there.

Later, Galina deliberately brought a loveseat into the bathroom as if she were going to wash it, scrub it, got undressed, and turned on the water. And sat down in the altogether. No one was home anyway. The boss's wife had had a mirror installed the full length of the wall.

No, the Kustodiev female in the picture was worse than Galina. Galina's face was better, her mouth was better, all of her was prettier.

She was an old bag, thirty or so. But everything on Galina was firm, her breasts and belly, and her waist was narrower.

Not for nothing had Galina been laboring in the orchard and garden, bending over with all her might. In rubber gloves and overalls. They showed ones like that on TV here, as if they were riding and plowing on these tiny tractors.

Galina had never been able to stand working in the garden and orchard, but her mother had made her, and rightly so. It came in handy here and was as good as a gym.

In phys. ed. at school she'd pretty much been embarrassed, the kids from her class guffawed at her when she jumped over the bar. Cow, they said.

Where were they now, the boys from her class? Some locked up, some taken to drink, and those so-called businessmen, they had stalls selling used spare parts, they looked like women themselves now, with bellies and tits.

Russian beauties, Kustodiev.

So what happened was, Galina started working there in the super market and immediately figured out who's who, as her boss, Sergei Ivanovich, liked to say.

She carried a case of bottles from the van into the storeroom herself.

By the time they'd driven the car up, it was over. They laughed and slapped her on the shoulder.

If anyone got her the job there, it was this one woman, Galina'd met her in the supermarket actually, she was stocking shelves and they all spilled, and the woman started swearing and Galina helped her.

She turned out to be a compatriot, from Perm.

After that they talked often. Shared experiences.

This compatriot, Rimma, laughed as she told her about her former boss, an elderly Englishman who had gone to Moscow and wanted to marry at sixty and had heard on TV that Moscow was full of beauties, and there he met a young woman, Nelya, who herself came from Frunze and was earning her living as a nanny.

How they met—Nelya herself told the tale. John was visiting the people Nelya worked for, and she was invited to the table, too. Nelya was her own person in the house and was learning English and she sat and heard everything about how tomorrow he was going to have tea at the National Hotel at five o'clock, and if anyone wanted to join him, please do.

Her boss immediately translated this for his wife, but she said she was busy.

And that evening at five o'clock, this Nelya, taking along the little girl she was supposed to be watching at this time and giving lessons, went to the National, burst into the restaurant with the child, and said she had an appointment. The guard went to find out, and John himself jumped up and was very surprised but asked her to join him. Evidently, Nelya had already struck a chord with him.

True, later she learned that he'd already been introduced to someone. In Moscow a certain family from the Caucasus had made a play for him, they had a twenty-six-year-old daughter, not very pretty, but at least she didn't have a mustache, as Nelya's employers said. They'd introduced them sort of as a joke.

So Nelya correctly calculated that if she was a young woman with a child—that is, not a prostitute—they'd let her into the National. She drank tea with this Mr. John for two whole hours, John ordered ice cream for the little girl, something she never got to have, especially in winter, and by seven the girl's parents were out of their minds, and they kept ringing Nelya, but she didn't pick up.

Well, just as she'd hoped, John took an interest, left for Montegasco, and sent this Nelya an invitation—she'd asked for six months but he sent her one for four. Naturally, she, Nelya, was immediately fired from her job looking after the child.

But she quickly got her visa and was off. And she started living here, with our John, but my visa is good for six.

But later, one night, she called the police to say she was being sexually abused. He was making her dance until dawn for him in just her stockings.

And she left the house with the police, taking all her presents, he'd even bought her a fur coat, this was in March, when the apricot trees here are already in blossom.

And this Nelya lived somewhere else for another three and a half months, but not in Montegasco.

Rimma never ran across her again.

Here the police come right away. Not like at home, there's no point waiting there, they only come for murder, this Rimma said.

Galina already knew that. How many times had her mother called, and they never came. They'd say, "Everyone's on a murder."

Galina coped with the language in fits and starts, and in six months she was understanding everything and saying what needed saying.

And they immediately took her off loading and onto shelving, like her Perm compatriot.

After all, the whole time her father was gone and little Yuri had grown up and run off with his buddies, Galina had been hanging around her mother at the store.

From the salesclerks, Galina picked up the kinds of words and expressions Angelka could not have learned at her school.

They told her where the boss was buying his produce and dairy. Meat, too. This came in handy as well, and now she and her husband Kolya no longer bought their groceries at the supermarket for fantastic sums, she now knew about cheap farms and she and Kolya would buy up food there, they'd drive all over the district, and as for receipts and labeled packages—she'd scoop them up at the supermarket.

Their boss didn't check every item, he just looked at the total and paid the bill.

The boss lady scorned prepared foods, ate her own food, various brans, artificial milk, various effing proteins and amino acids.

In the morning, Galina would cook and serve her daughter and husband breakfast at seven thirty—then she'd go off on her bicycle, drop her daughter at school, and then go to her job.

In the mornings, the boss's wife ate only her own stuff, out of jars. Maintaining her eternal youth. Gluten-free.

The boss got up closer to one in the afternoon. He watched videos on the internet every night, porn.

And Galina served him lunch.

Just one thing hit her hard: the death of family members.

A year before, her brother Yuri had gone out on the balcony to smoke, the investigator said, but Yuri'd had too much to drink, that was the conclusion, and they found him on the pavement under the balcony. His cigarette was swimming in his blood.

His former wife immediately showed up to exercise her rights, saying she was the heir. But Yuri had managed to get a divorce, and his mama had given him the money for the apartment, and she'd kept all the documents and Yuri's receipt. His mother must have looked in a crystal ball and seen that this woman with a child would come and latch on to the apartment since she'd remarried a drinker and unemployed epileptic.

Yura had met her not just anywhere but in her stall one night, she was doing business there, and right on cue there he was, in his old crate. His mother had bought him a scooter because you didn't need a license.

He was constantly zooming off to Moscow to see some friend, he'd call him and say, "I'm on my way, let's make some noise and get pissed in your neighborhood," and he found this bimbo in a stall holding a box, like she wanted to lift the box up. He'd stopped by for cigarettes, actually, but it turned out to be a vegetable stand.

That's okay, though, he loaded the box up, lifted it off the floor onto the counter, and later she kept saying how considerate he was!

She invited him behind the counter, treated him to a banana and her own infusion out of a jar, it was cold there, and it kept her warm at night.

They hit it off right away, he said. He stayed with her until morning, ate what he wanted, bananas, oranges, drank her infusion.

She worked around the clock in Moscow, rented a room with a pal, so when one left the other slept. Now she took him to her empty bed.

She and Yuri got married fast, went down to the registry office, but Yuri wouldn't register her at his apartment, he listened to his mother.

They held out the prospect of residency for her only after three years. She waited a year and then hooked up with one of her customers, an old veteran who used to visit.

So that's how it was, but the most terrible thing was that right before his death, as it turned out, Yuri had sold his one-room apartment to the owner of that round-the-clock stall. But Yuri lived out his days in that apartment—the guy said he was giving him another two weeks before he started renovations, while an estimate was being drawn up. The guy showed him all the documents.

By that time Yuri's apartment was a total wreck. His mother never visited, it was too far, and he was incapable of anything. No floor, no walls, the bathroom smashed up, the toilet on its side.

As they say, buy your son an apartment—bye-bye son, bye-bye apartment. But his mama was done with him, she'd raised a second father. He raised his hand to her.

The stall owner said maybe Yuri had wanted to use the apartment money to win big on some exchange. But a fool's a fool, God rest his soul.

There wasn't any money left in the apartment. The stall owner kicked him out, naturally. Why would he, though, if all the documents were in order?

His mother was not in her right mind to understand what had happened. Galina flew in, Angelka under her arm, to bury him, dug through her brother's poverty, pulled everything apart thread by thread. Nothing.

She'd had the idea they'd killed Yuri for his money. There wasn't a kopek left. But the apartment door, when the investigator arrived, was locked from the inside, on a chain. They tried to open it, but the residents had long since glassed in their balconies above and below so there was no access to Yuri's up or down via the balconies.

But people these days, they pay mountain climbers to rappel from the roof, after all Yuri's balcony wasn't glassed in, they could tip the sleepy drunk over the railing, take the money, put on the chain, back up they go, and that's that.

Galina had to stay with her mama, who lost her marbles and passed away two weeks later.

While her mother was still breathing, Galina plucked up her courage and asked her to find out from Yuri in the next world where he'd put the money. "And then you can come to me in a dream," Galina said.

Whether her mama heard, who can tell, but ever since, after she went back to Montegasco, Galina would tell Kolya all her dreams at breakfast in hopes he'd find some clue.

Kolya always chewed for a long time, like a calf, and now he would just eat, his eyes focused on his plate, and he never once noticed anything suspicious.

"Okay now, I'm telling you. I'll tell you my dream. The things you dream, you can't tell what it's about. So here it is. So like I'm walking over the ground, and it's really black, like it's coals, and hot. And there's stairs going up. And my mama's, like, standing on the stairs. I want to go up to her, the ground's hot, burning my feet. Picture it, and there's these, like, very low clouds. Gray-black, too, like ashes. And suffocating. No air to breathe. And Mama's going up the stairs, and there, at the top, my father has the axe, can you imagine? So I put my foot on a step, and the step, imagine, it's super-hot! How is Mama standing on it? Mama, Mama, come down to me! I look and she's not standing there but, like, floating. Her feet aren't touching the steps. And I'm suffocating. And then it's all over and I'm lying there with a blanket on my face. It was hot last night."

Kolya mumbled something. He was eating.

"I want to be understood in my personal life," Galina said, and finally, after those long months, she could unwind and have a good cry.

Kolya went "mm, mm" again. What a dolt.

Galina and Angelka were away for six weeks, and maybe he'd lost touch, but the fact that his wife had breast reduction surgery (down four sizes) and lipo-pack-suction, lipo-cap-suction, or whatever you call it, on her belly—he didn't notice.

Galina, actually, had saved a lot of money. In Tula things were a hundred times cheaper, people even went there from Moscow.

But you can't tell your husband that sort of thing if he's clueless anyway. Like, it would take too long to explain.

Back in Tula Galina had met a woman, a funeral agent. She'd taken out two coffins in a month, after all.

And she liked that woman, and as soon as her mother passed away, this time Galina didn't even open the door to the other agent who'd rushed to her door the minute the ambulance pulled away. She called Venera.

Venera was there in a flash, they had a good sit and a drink, and Venera revealed that they had their own person stationed day and night monitoring the ambulance radio. The second an ambulance alerted the police about a death, they were required to tell them first, they gave them the address, and then that radio monitor would call the agent, in the dead of night, it didn't matter, with the address and name, and the agent would run to the address and ring the doorbell first. Even before the cops. While they were still radioing around, our man was already at the door. Accept my sincere condolences at Ivan Petrovich's passing. I can help you. Sometimes at night, people won't have come to their senses yet, they'll sign anything.

Venera promised to find Galina a job in their system if need be.

Venera had already found a job for her husband, Rustam, who was ten years younger, at the morgue as an orderly. Relatives passed out a lot of money there, and she herself wanted to take a course so she could be the one standing by the coffin with the ribbon saying, "And now, family and friends, the time has come to say goodbye." Like that.

Galina was interested, but Venera told her that with her size chest they wouldn't take her at the crematorium. They had strict standards.

Galina found a clinic in Tula through them, too, and quickly had two operations done, which took care of her belly and breasts.

She also rented out her mother's house and all its contents. The same Venera had pointed her in the right direction, to her brother, Edik. Venera had got him a job as a realtor in an agency.

Galina had zero interest in what happened to the house inside, all that furniture, she just took some photographs and two sets of china, a tea service, and a Madonna. For her, it had been a terrible house.

Now, every month, the rent money got added to her bank book, thank you very much.

It all went into the pot.

And she asked Edik to find buyers for the house. And extracted a promise from her husband, Kolya, not to believe any of his boss's promises about giving them a Moscow apartment on the Ring Road, not to sign anything, not to accept presents or money from his boss, because he could immediately go to the police and say his employees had robbed him and give them the banknotes' serial numbers. He had it all written down.

There'd been a case like that. A horrifying thought.

One time his boss sent Kolya to a neighboring country on an assignment from Moscow and sent his wife to some clinic in Israel while he sat at home watching endless videos, porn.

Usually he watched them at night, but now he'd slipped his chain.

Bought new ones or something. Japanese.

One day Galina came back from the supermarket and was making him breakfast.

Going back and forth, she saw all those images out of the corner of her eye. And heard obvious sounds.

That is, he'd sniff and sniff, even snort-laugh kind of, and then say, "Have a seat, quit your running around."

Galina said, "Wait a minute."

"Forget wait a minute, have a seat. I bet you can't do it like this, have a look-see at what she's pulling off, eh, Kustodiev?"

She just had to ignore him. She set the table and shuttled between the kitchen and the living room.

While the boss told her stories, laughing:

"Once we were in Japan and wanted to get some Japanese prostitutes, so they took us. We go in and who's sitting there but Katya, Masha, and Dasha. Oh, they shouted, ours have come! We go to another place, and sitting there again are Katya, Masha, and Dasha. Where are you from? They're all from Khabarovsk and Vladivostok. By the time we find locals, the mood's passed. What's the matter, not interested?"

Then Galina took off her apron and gloves (he kept grunting, looking at her, and slapping the couch next to him), turned around, and left altogether.

She went to her house, where she started crying.

Here we go again.

She stood eating Angelka's ice cream straight from the fridge and crying, wiping her tears with a kitchen towel.

Right then he burst into the house and before she could turn around he grabbed her from behind, jerked her to the floor by her braid, the pig, hit the back of her head hard with something, his fist, probably, as hard as he could, and started pawing at her, and grumbling, "Kustodiev, where's your stinking bush, Kustodiev."

And she gave in—he could maim her. Her papa's lessons stood her in good stead, she'd learned how to spread out so she didn't get mutilated.

But the boss didn't make it even two minutes and let her go.

And retreated to his lair, saying as he went, "You fucking stupid cow."

Galina was so insulted! She would call the police, if that's how it was going to be.

They arrived quickly and she said she'd been attacked from behind and didn't see who'd done it.

She wasn't crying but she was trembling.

They wrote everything down, took photographs, and took Galina to the station and then to the hospital, where they swabbed her for tests.

The boss wouldn't open the door to the police, pretended he wasn't home.

His Bentley wasn't in the garage either, they poked their noses in there.

Kolya was using it.

They asked her where her boss was and she said, "I don't know."

"Noll sa."

But she knew very well he was sitting in his bathroom listening to what was happening on the grounds. He definitely heard the siren. Naturally, he got scared—because of what he'd done and Galina calling the police.

What happened after that was this. Galina got washed, brought Angelka home on her bicycle, and sat with her until Kolya arrived that evening.

In the morning, Galina went into the house as if nothing had happened, opening the door with her keys, and cooked her boss breakfast.

He crawled out of his bedroom holding an envelope and with a nasty smile on his ugly face.

"Well then, we'll be saying goodbye. You're not going to want to work for me after that. That's what I think. And I've lost interest. As a result of your behavior."

Galina said, "You aren't getting off that easy. The police have your smear. They swabbed me for testing."

"What the hell?"

"Just that. You'll go to prison for thirty years."

"Oh ho. You're getting ahead of yourself. You're all clearing out of here today. Here's your money, now get lost"—and he cursed. "The prime minister's my friend."

"That's there. This is here."

"And I'll tell Kolya you were always spreading your legs for me. And you decided to blackmail me when I said I don't want to anymore and this is the last time."

"Tell Kolya whatever you want. The police have it all recorded and on video, that my furniture was turned over and I have a bruise on the back on my head. And they found hair pulled out of my braid on the floor by the door."

"You pulled the hair out yourself, you cunt! And gave yourself the bruise on the door! I never trusted you, you cunt, you spread your legs for me! Who's been wiggling her ass?"

(The same old story. Just like her father.)

"They're going to put you in prison. In Russia lots of people would like you to do time there, not here."

"Oh ho! Aren't you the one! Fine, then. Kustodiev, why are you so mad? Okay, I lost control. But you're such a beauty! Wiggling around here. It's enough to try a saint! Especially me, who never gets any."

He chickened out. Well and truly spooked. And the whole time holding out the envelope, as if protecting himself with it.

"Kustodiev, what do you need? Citizenship here? For all of you?"

"You can't buy me off. You'll be doing time in a labor camp."

"I'm not buying anything. I haven't offered you any money yet. Maybe you want an apartment in Moscow? I've got four there. On Sadovo-Spasskaya, on Sivtsevy Vrazhek, and two in a high-rise on Vosstaniya."

"Sit down."

"Aren't you the nasty one. I'll draw up the papers for you today for a one-hundred-twenty-square-meter apartment and they'll send me the papers by plane."

"You'll be doing time in the Komi Republic. In a maximum-security camp with the most dangerous criminals. The commissary once a week. And no one's going to be sending packages. You'll be a goddamn pariah there. I'll make sure of that."

"Pleased with yourself, Kustodiev? How do you know all that?"

"You'll be doing hard time."

"I bow down at your lovely feet, Kustodiev. Save me from prison. The rose in your bush is very fine, Kustodiev! Can't get it off my mind! Shall we go to my room? No rush, as they say."

"Fat chance."

"I'd give you money right now, fifty thousand euros, but I can't take it from my account. The police would suspect right away I was being blackmailed. This is blackmail, right? Why were you twirling your ass in front of me?"

"Me? In front of you?"

"Hey, come to my room. I can't stand it anymore."

"That's it, I've served your breakfast. I'm in a hurry." And it was good she didn't take the envelope.

It probably contained marked bills, and he would have gone to the police and said he'd been robbed.

But she didn't go home.

Kustodiev squeezed into an opening under the veranda and sat there on a wooden pallet, in a space where some air vent forgotten by the builders came out—straight from the kitchen.

Angelka had discovered it, she'd crawled in there, the way all kids explore everything, and her mother had searched for her for a long time, going crazy, and Angelka shouted "cuckoo" when Galina was about to call the police from the kitchen and her mother heard that "cuckoo" very nearby. As if someone had said it right next to her. She ran out of the house and figured out where the kitchen had to be, and there, under the veranda, you could crawl between the posts, and Angelka answered her shout.

After that, Galina would crouch her way into the hiding place, where she fit nicely, sitting.

She eavesdropped on everything, all the conversations and negotiations, all the scandals between husband and wife. The wife wanted the boss to adopt her thirty-year-old son.

According to Montegascan law, estates transfer first to the children, not the wife. The boss asked her whether she wanted to be his widow. I have my own son, he said, I don't give a fuck about your little bastard.

Right now the boss was on the phone.

"So the deed for the apartment on Vosstaniya. I'll dictate the name and address to you in a minute . . . Wait up, I'll call you back."

Galina quickly climbed out of the hidey-hole and ran home. She was caught by her cell phone ringing: "Kustodiev! Look here, text me your address and passport info."

Galina didn't answer, she was running.

"Why don't you say something? Scared? I've been needing you for a hundred years. You were the one wiggling your ass, you were asking for it."

"Stop it!" She was already on her veranda and could speak freely. "I don't know anything and don't want to. You're going to prison."

"Fine, then, I'll come over myself."

He came to her tidy little house, where Kolya was sitting in his shorts watching tennis, and this cheeky bastard started smiling and saying right at the door that he'd decided to give Kolya and Galina an apartment for their fine, devoted friendship.

Galina replied, holding her rolling pin: "That's your business. Leave me out. I'm not going to sign anything. I don't need anything from you."

Kolya, on the other hand, nearly started crying and tried to embrace his boss.

Galina went to the far corner of the garden and started weeding with a vengeance, streaming tears. She was shaken to the core.

Galina also thought, why was it Kolya'd become so indifferent? Had he hooked up with the boss lady? Or Rimma?

No, no, the boss lady was still going to her fitness trainer, Kolya drove her himself and said that, on the contrary, she was sleeping with the trainer.

The two sunbaked sticks had found each other.

This trainer of hers was a German woman.

But it made you wonder, Rimma wasn't visiting for no reason.

Such was the lay of the land in the driver Kolya's family when he brought the boys from Moscow to his boss's place. Two species of son.

What happened next the reader will find out at the end, in the story of Galina Kustodiev, who was now busy fixing lunch in the kitchen, and the kitchen and living room were one big room.

And so, on to Sergei Sertsov the businessman, citizen of Montegasco.

6

The Story of Masha and Sergei Sertsov

JUST HOW WAS it that he, this Sergei Sertsov, had ended up here in Moscow at all, inquiring minds wanted to know, let alone how he'd got into an institute like MGIMO, which only takes big shots' kids and everyone's from inside the profession, diplomats' families, as a rule. But this question will have to remain a question because Sergei—this short, unprepossessing kid from Krasnodar, from a district he kept quiet about—got in after the army. That's it. He'd also worked in the Young Communists' district committee for two years, preparing.

He got in and learned English plus Handi and Irdu well enough that afterward he could go straight to the embassy in Handia, but there was a hitch, because first he had to work a little after graduating.

But he had no residency permit, no nothing, and after MGIMO they would even ask him to leave the dorm. And people like that don't get jobs in Moscow.

Right then a certain Masha, who studied with Seryozha, intervened, and told her parents on an international phone call that she was marrying her classmate Seryozha to help him out.

She told them this all openly, honest Masha, that they only respected each other, nothing more, but Sergei needed help and she was prepared to give it. And that afterward he might be going to some country, Handia or Pakistan.

First was a conversation with her father.

"So where's he from?" her father, currently an ambassador, asked with a common touch.

"What's the difference?" Masha objected, offended. "Well, there's this town outside Krasnodar."

"Aha. Flyshitsville. An urban village is it? Have you been looking for a man like that for long?"

"What does his village have to do with this?" his daughter persisted.

"You're going to have to go with him to that country! With that bumpkin!" her father, Valery Ivanovich, shouted. "And live with him!"

"So what?" Masha replied. "And why 'bumpkin'? He—"

"Three years! A lifetime!"

"So what? He's a good person."

"Quiet! And there'll be children!"

"Correct," adamant Masha conceded.

"Do what you want, but I'm not registering him!"

"Yes, you are," Masha objected. "If you don't, I'll sue you for my room, and that'll be that. It's my right."

"Fool!" her father yelled. "You realize you're betraying me and your mother, who've done everything just for you! Everything! We're getting you an apartment! The co-op dues are paid! An expensive apartment, by the way, one everyone's dying to get into, and I arranged it for you! For you, you fool!"

Her mother, Tamara Gennadievna, had not been admitted to the negotiations. But she listened to everything on the extension.

Later, in the bedroom, she said, "Masha's no fool. She's in love with him, Valera. And he has to work in Moscow for a while if he's going to go to another country. But without a permit, he'll never get a job."

"As if I cared!"

"But the fact is that she wants to marry him. And she's taking advantage of the situation. She'll register him."

"Fool. And you're twice the fool she is. He's the one taking advantage!"

"Maybe. You would know better. You especially. Who if not you should understand?"

Silence, indignant huffing.

The mother went on.

"This is Masha's business. We have to meet her halfway."

"We're going to have some hick living with us?"

"We'll come for a month, that's all, Valera. In six months."

"And go back in two years?"

"And go back after they leave. He has a good future. His mother's cousin works in the Medimport system."

"Who's that?"

"Masha says Viktor Ivanovich. Chermukhin."

"Chermukhin himself?"

"His mother's cousin."

"Well."

"He wants to send him to Handia. For three years. A year from now."

"How do you know all this?"

"I know. Masha told me. I called her."

"You women . . . It's a conspiracy, you realize. Going behind my back."

"As you recall, my father was also against me marrying you," Tamara Gennadievna said.

"He was right," her husband answered angrily. "He must have had second sight. If I weren't such a fool . . ."

"My papa died over this," Tamara Gennadievna said.

"Stubborn," Valery Ivanovich objected. "He drank a lot, that's all. He was an alcoholic."

Clearly, this wasn't the first time they'd had this conversation.

7

The Story of Tamara and Valera

THESE TWO TALKING—Valery Ivanovich and Tamara Gennadie-vna, Masha's parents—were in fact from that very same Soviet stratum referred to in their own circles as the "contingent"—refined, university-educated diplomats, he of the handsome combed-back gray hair, Valery Ivanovich, also from the South, by the way, near Stavropol, from a Cossack village, a former soccer player and later a figure in Young Communist athletics. He was working as an instructor for the district committee when he was noticed.

Times then were such that the leadership generally chose diplomats from among trusted people of worker background, and rightly so.

It was on them, on their tastes and cultural level, that everything in the country was founded—theater, film, television, literature, and scholarly aspirations. Only the secret defense and space facilities (known as "mailboxes") were generously funded.

One scientific research institute even had a biochemical department where the director, a woman with an advanced degree in biology, broached a scientific topic for her colleagues: she wanted to create something that only affected a specific race. Later, when she retired, she happened upon the brochure of an enthusiast of raising the dead who filled enormous halls and sold his little books, which were powerful.

Back to Valera, though.

He sought out a wife for himself specifically at the embassy. She was the ambassador's daughter, a beauty, her mother descended from a cluster of Muscovite Georgian princes. Her father (the ambassador) was from the countryside, too, but she took entirely after her mother.

Tamara, a university student, had gone to that foreign country for vacation. All her people were there, behind the handsome stone wall; the entire embassy lived under the same roof and steered clear of foreigners and learning the local language. They were good at prices, though, knew where, at what wholesale warehouse, the food and wine were cheaper. The embassy wives trained the chef, a local they nick-named the Miner (because he was swarthy), to pickle mushrooms and cabbage, and he even made a Georgian-style cabbage, lobio, and ajapsandali, this the result of efforts by Madame Nina Georgievna, the ambassador's wife.

Caviar was shipped in from the homeland. They rolled out Russian dinners for the indigenous Communists.

They would sit in the garden, where the staff's children romped. They played word-snake.

Cards were banned. They had chess and checkers.

And local television, of course, which everyone watched in the evening.

To learn the language, they explained.

But all that was aired were singing and dancing shows and musicals filmed in the studio of the neighboring state, called Bollywood.

Those curly lines ran across the subtitles in the local language.

They didn't understand a damn thing.

Tamara, the ambassador's daughter, caught the eye of a young employee, Valera (disdainfully called "the soccer player" by her ambassador-father), caught his eye when he actually was playing soccer with the embassy children, training them like a team, even though there were only four little boys and a fifth who tripped over his own feet, a reserve preschooler.

Abroad, you could only keep your children with you until age eleven or twelve; after that they had to be sent home, there being no school for them at the embassy.

So he was playing with little kids. The things you'll do to avoid paperwork!

Tamara, sitting on the balcony, was their one and only fan. She would wave broadly there, from the second floor, while the children chased the ball below.

The first evening after Tamara's arrival, Valera the soccer player, tired of sitting at a desk, joined his team in the yard, cast a glance at the balcony, and poured his heart and soul into demonstrating what exactly he was capable of.

Tamara the ambassador's daughter seemed downcast, sat at dinner with a lackluster expression, and didn't eat.

The next day—at the request of the ambassador's clever wife, who that same evening had taken a timely glance at the balcony and, after going back to her room, immediately looked out the window at the yard, where the young soccer players were hollering—Valera was called in to see the ambassador's wife.

And this Valera set out to show the young woman the local capital.

He showed her his other talents—gave her his arm as he helped his lovely passenger out of the car, let the lady go first. He joked, too—though rather crudely.

It was wicked hot. The young woman was languishing.

Tamara, a Georgian on her mother's side, a very thin young woman with thin, tweezered eyebrows, vibrated like a string at his every touch. He picked up on that immediately.

A couple of times he didn't release her arm after the car but pulled her along.

Tamara's face remained aristocratically stony, though, inspiring his respect and simultaneously rather goading Valera's male pride.

True, Valera himself wouldn't have had the nerve to make a move until, out of nowhere, the ambassador summoned him and gloomily ordered him to squire his Tamara around town again.

"You see, she's expressed a desire to get to know the country and its customs. The market, the movies."

At the market, Valera bought her an enormous grapefruit, which he misnamed, of course, "grayfruit," cut it open himself and showed her how to eat it, removing the peel from each section.

Then he bought movie tickets with his own money, local currency.

The movie house at least had American-style AC. It was pricey for ordinary people. The hall was only half full. Children were running down the rows. Adults were calling to each other. The audience responded noisily to every plot turn (the film was taken from local life, with killings and singing and dancing).

Valera did his best at translating, leaning toward the ambassador's daughter's dainty ear (and the tiny diamond in the lobe).

His breath sent shivers down the young woman's neck, evidently. Sometimes Valera blew lightly on purpose.

The tension reached such a crescendo that eventually Valera's lips touched that velvety ear, and Tamara immediately turned toward him, questioningly, eyebrows raised, beautiful eyes half shut.

Valera had not erred. They made out until the film ended, and then they sat on a park bench, after which they crawled into the prickly local bushes and Valera turned his jacket inside out and spread it beneath them. They grappled like sambists. Stormily.

And went all the way. Valera hadn't even expected it to happen so soon.

They returned tattered, like from a trash heap, and at the gate examined each other, laughing. Like any man after copulation, Valera solicitously pulled a couple of straws from his future bride's hair.

Tamara wasn't a virgin: no wonder at twenty-seven. Although she couldn't be called terribly experienced either. Just a few times in her life.

A knowing Valera immediately understood the situation. She hadn't had anyone in a long time.

At first, Tamara sputtered in pain, but then she began whining delicately.

"Quiet," Valera warned her in a thunderous whisper.

It was good there was rousing local music playing nearby.

Tamara came good and properly, breathing hoarsely and roughly, but heaving silently. Valera was pleased with himself, although afterward he had to throw out his handkerchief.

Without which you couldn't last a minute here. The scorching heat and high humidity.

He'd been intending to keep the handkerchief, but then he realized his pocket would soak through. His trousers were cotton, locally made, thin.

You'd look a fool holding it.

Her skirt stayed clean because at the very start Valera had considerately folded it above her waist.

The former soccer player had considerable experience when it came to young women.

He'd already taken several to this park.

And, actually, everyone knew about it.

The embassy building was believed to be bugged, and the ambassador's wife liked to let the employees know just how much she knew. It was no accident it was Valera who'd been chosen as an escort. A twenty-seven-year-old single Georgian girl—who'd ever heard of such a thing!

The newlyweds finally barged in on the embassy building.

For a long time Valera stood in the dark hall with the young woman, mumbling something before letting her go.

He was whispering all kinds of nonsense, like "you have amazing eyes" and "you're my wife."

They kissed.

The light was on upstairs. Her mother and father weren't asleep, they were sitting there anxious, fully clothed.

Anything might happen with young people, there were even defectors.

One ambassador's daughter ran away with an employee and stayed abroad!

The civil punishment for a defector's parents was exile to the homeland!

"So. Where were you?" her father asked, approaching swiftly with a slap in the face. "We were about to call the police."

"Papa! I'm getting married!" Tamara exclaimed, dodging.

"Married? I'll say if you're getting married!" her father started yelling, on autopilot, but at that moment her mother, Nina Georgievna, stepped in.

She led Tamara away, questioned her thoroughly, and returned to her husband to reassure him.

"He's a snotnose kid! Who does he think he is? The fellows who were circling around Tamara—Tumanyan's son! Viktor Petrovich Dubbin's grandson!" Her father was livid. "And what does she do? Look their way? No! Not at all! And then! Can you imagine the problems we're going to have? They could recall me! You realize this is nepotism! Valera they'll definitely recall! Husband my ass! Where's he going to go, a grifter with no house or home? To Krasnodar as a kids' team coach? Fool. Fool! He doesn't have an apartment, he's going to drag Tamara to a dorm, is that it? Bare-assed on principle, is that it?"

"Wait, wait," his wife remonstrated with him. "Tamara's not so young! It's time!"

"Not only that! Valera has an assignment he can't abandon. Work's been done already, you realize."

He meant that Valera was simultaneously engaged in espionage and had recruited some old émigré who hobnobbed in local anti-Soviet circles. The old man very much needed the money. As a result,

Valera had been sending the office sensible reports about charitable balls, fairs, and literary evenings with a White Guard tinge. This way the office was keeping a finger on the pulse of émigré high society. Old man Trotsky (too bad he was so decrepit) displayed uncanny ingenuity because he burned with hatred for all émigrés, across the board (and the feeling was mutual).

After all the years that had passed since the revolution, the small Russian community (now in its third and fourth generation) had ticked off each and every fellow countryman beyond all measure. They'd quarreled and remarried multiple times, including Madame Trotskaya, who'd left him for Prince Sharakhov immediately following the demise of Princess Uigur-Sharakhova, taking all the treasured family pearls of the Trotsky house and now adding to them the celebrated Uigur-Sharakhov jewel case.

Evil tongues instantly informed Trotsky that those two had just been waiting to tie the knot. Supposedly they'd been cohabitating quite openly for a long time. And hadn't they poisoned the unfortunate old woman?

Five letters went to the police. To no avail. Now Trotsky (every bit of seventy-five years old) made a point of dragging himself around to all the events he'd previously despised, rudely invited himself to tea, even to children's birthday parties, and wrote denunciations against the Sharakhovs (violent anti-Soviets, a secret society), along with all the rest.

Making no effort to hide, he started dressing well (previously he'd gone around in the same shiny jacket) and started a platonic affair with a lawyer's widow who still had a car in working order.

Now he and his lady drove around to all the free events, like the municipal fireworks, about which Valera wrote (i.e., to the KGB) spiteful denunciations against local municipal officials wasting taxpayers' money.

He also mentioned all instances of bribe-taking by the authorities and police.

And although these letters were not quite to the point, provident Valera bought everything and sent it on, in the context of studying the moods of the local population and the growing corruption by name. That is, which officials were accepting bribes quite openly and which could be relied upon should anything happen.

Recently Trotsky had really distinguished himself by counting the number of indigenous tanks in a parade—six, though one stayed there on the square.

And now that Valera was getting married and was going to be sent away, this embassy activity would also be in jeopardy.

Not only that, who was going to let this proliferating family stay under the embassy roof (he himself and his wife, his son-in-law and daughter, plus possible children!)?

On top of everything else, the ambassador loved his daughter like any father does and could not stand the thought of some ham-handed hick using his smart, beautiful girl in bed like a floozy. She had to keep her virginity forever as a sign of faithfulness to her father—or so he understood the situation.

Although he did understand that his daughter had been left on the shelf, at the same time he believed that no one was good enough for her (Tamara had been working as a bibliographer in the ministry for three years, sitting at the back of the book repository in a purely female collective, where her loving father had found her a job)—but this way his mind was more at ease.

The next day Gennady Ivanovich, the ambassador, called Valera in, shouted, "What the hell are you up to?"—and dashingly punched his subordinate in the ear.

Not being an aristocrat and diplomat, streetwise Valera popped Uncle Genya one (good and hard), the ambassador fell, and Valera himself ran out and upstairs to Tamara, saying, "We have to talk," pulled her behind him, and took her somewhere by commuter train, a rather gauzy palm grove in front of a high wall, as it turned out, and there, in that very grove, ignoring the soldiers in the tower, Valera immediately impregnated Tamara, something he hadn't done the night before, protecting the ambassador's daughter's honor.

It turned out they'd lain down in an easement along the wall of the local garrison. Under other circumstances they'd have been arrested as spies, but this was all dispensed with (evidently the soldiers ran for their binoculars, up there, in the tower; something glinted as Valera and Tamara were walking away).

It had been important to Valera to knock up Tamara. His ear was burning and demanded payback.

Payback against her father, not Tamara.

So, in an atmosphere of spiteful vengefulness, their future daughter Masha was conceived.

When Valera and Tamara got back again it was nearly night; the ambassador was lying silently in the conjugal bed and didn't get up to greet his wayward daughter properly.

He'd decided not to escalate the situation and put the brakes on it instead.

That is, first get Tamara far away and then somehow ensnare and destroy Valera.

Catch him out in some unsavory business, shall we say.

The ambassador lay there letting himself get carried away (his blood was boiling) picturing various scenes.

There was one intrigue already spinning around in his mind, which was like an experienced playwright's.

But the next morning, Valera submitted his resignation.

Moscow sounded the alarm. The Lubyanka wouldn't stand for it. Moscow couldn't make any sense of it. The young man had written good reports. What had happened?

The ambassador had his answer ready, he'd put the night to good use, and on an international call he described Valera getting mixed up with a local prostitute and contracting syphilis, that is, Valera had lost and the housekeeper had found by her door a document bearing his name with the test results (he already had a physician's note, fabricated by the embassy doctor, everything at the ready).

In addition, there was an empty antibiotics ampoule. Supposedly from Valera's wastebasket.

The year before there'd been a similar incident with a driver, who the doctor had sent off for a test, after which the maid stated that something was wrong with her and she'd only slept with the driver. He and the maid were sent to the lab for swabbing and then were recalled, before the results were even in. By the way, the result came in positive only for the maid.

So this was a well-beaten path. On the ambassador's instruction, the doctor fabricated a similar note for Valera.

Tamara heard out her father's version, too, cried in her room for a long time, and was shown the ampoule and the test in the outcast's name.

The ambassadorial home was aboil. Everyone shunned Valera.

When he went into the yard to train the boys, no one was there. He popped into the apartment of Mila the maid, mother of one of the soccer players, but Mila came out, blocking the door, and said, "You can't come in here because you've got an STD"—moreover, with an expression of particular hatred on her broad face, since Valera had been sleeping with Mila the whole time.

And she added, "Stay the hell away, you SOB."

"Who's the SOB here?" Valera was about to object. But Mila had already slammed the door.

Valera had no idea what was going on. It was an awful situation. However, the ambassador had failed to consider the fact that Valera had taken a short course in being a young spy. Little contrivances came in handy.

In short, from internal embassy phone calls, which he'd bugged, Valera, stunned and sweating, knew all by dinnertime.

After which he composed an encrypted message to the home office describing the situation as follows. The ambassador had appropriated money allocated for Trotsky for an especially important assignment to walk along the walls of the garrison, possibly missile units, they needed specifics, at the NN station (Valera had taken the precaution of hiding said sum of dollars in the false bottom of a suitcase), and when he, Valera, had asked the ambassador about the money for Trotsky for this top-secret mission, the ambassador, Gennady Ivanovich, told him the money hadn't come in, i.e., the fact that he had appropriated money came out.

After the ambassador was caught, he spread the slander about the forged syphilis test (if they checked the place where the document was issued, they'd find no record of him visiting the lab!), which had been especially provoked by the fact that the ambassador objected to his daughter Tamara's marriage to him, Valera.

Valera also cited the garrison's address, the same garrison, in a wood half an hour's drive from the capital, where Trotsky was supposed to be sent to walk along the walls.

That is, Valera's denunciation arrived shortly after Gennady Ivanovich's message.

Then Valera went to the embassy doctor and demanded this alleged syphilis test of his so that he could find the lab and expose the forgery.

"What test? What do you mean?" the frightened embassy doctor objected. "Where did you see syphilis? Are you out of your mind? Or did you dream it drunk?

"You're the SOB," the reprimanded Valera replied again. He had nothing left to lose.

8

The Story of Masha's Birth

AS A RESULT, both the ambassador and Valera (and the doctor) were recalled. Tamara's summer vacation ended with bitter regrets.

Valera flew to Moscow without saying goodbye, the ambassador was laid up with a heart attack, and his wife feverishly packed what possessions they'd acquired, crying nonstop.

The furniture had to go by sea, by ship. The cost, the cost! Instead of a new Volga and a co-op for Tamara (which they'd already made the first payment on), diddly squat!

It was her own fault.

The ambassador's wife was deeply offended. Up until now she'd felt she was, if not the ruler of the world, then at least the lead actor in her universe.

She'd had everything at her beck and call: her husband, his colleagues, the local staff, even foreign rulers and their wives.

To say nothing of her relatives in faraway Poti! She still had a widowed sister there whose only daughter had married a newsstand clerk!

Need it be added that Nina Georgievna had cut all ties with her family for good and never opened the door to a stranger's knock when she was in Moscow on vacation?

Ne-ver.

There'd been one time when she'd had to let in pushy visitors with suitcases who'd shown up straight from the train station, supposedly her niece with her husband and young son! "I don't know you," Nina Georgievna had said, and she abruptly slammed the door.

Otherwise they'd make a habit of it.

And now this outrageous, irredeemable story!

An unemployed breadwinner and a disgraced daughter most likely pregnant by an outcast.

They traveled in mourning. Nina Georgievna didn't cry. She'd come to the brink of life.

When they got back, in anticipation of official sanctions, the former ambassador's family immediately left for their dacha. Tamara, who was still on leave, began experiencing symptoms of toxicosis right before her parents' eyes. She threw up in the mornings. Her mother demanded she have an abortion.

"What do you think, a baby who has syphilis, hey, are you listening? Tabes dorsalis! Paralysis! Darling, read the medical encyclopedia! Listen, your father's unemployed now! How are we going to support him, your syphilitic baby!" (Then came curses, to judge by the expression on the young mama's face.)

At difficult moments she switched to her father's language.

Most important, Tamara didn't know where to look for Valera.

And Valera didn't have the dacha address.

She'd underestimated her future husband, though. One night there was a scratching at her window. She opened the latch immediately and ripped the mosquito netting. Valera crept in like a thief. For a long time they kissed silently and Tamara wept.

"Get your things, we're going," Valera said.

"What are you saying? I'm pregnant," Tamara replied.

"Getting outside is good for you," the dashing Valera replied.

He climbed out and lifted Tamara under the arms. They went somewhere at random and spent the night literally by someone's fence. Tamara kept crying for no reason and saying, "You're mine. I love you. Do you?" And he would say through his teeth, "Yes, I do."

By morning they had it all worked out. Valera was waiting for an assignment to another country, under the TASS wing.

"They only take married men there," he said. "Where's your passport? Go get it. Otherwise they'll hide it, I know their kind."

Six months later former ambassador Grandpa Gennady had been sent to a godforsaken, still-neutral country in the very Far East as a trade representative, to purchase low-quality goods from the locals but in fact to oversee arms exports to support local pro-Communist rebels. And influence politics.

Nina Georgievna was again the mistress, but now of a trade office, an institution on a considerably smaller scale.

While Valera and Tamara were sent even before that to a country in Latin America.

Their daughter Masha, however, was born in Moscow for economy's sake, Tamara went back to give birth a month before her due date so as not to waste hard currency in the local clinics.

Subsequently, grown-up Tamara, later Tamara Gennadievna, followed Valery Ivanovich like a shadow her whole life. The classic wife of a spy—restrained, patient, taciturn, and exact. No more questions or tears.

He bristled and made fun of her, used vulgar expressions on purpose, and obscenities, to shake her sense of her own worth.

Evidently the words his father-in-law repeated on every occasion—"You've made a good career for yourself through Tamara and me. By drowning me"—gave him no rest.

At the same time, Tamara Gennadievna, that crass papa's daughter, was an aristocrat to the very marrow of her bones. She knew how to dress like a duchess and bought fabric abroad but had an inexpensive Moscow seamstress sew dresses for her from foreign patterns.

It should be noted that Tamara Gennadievna had just one model: Jackie Kennedy.

The same little coats, pillbox hats, and little open-collar suits.

Actually, she even resembled Jackie in the face—not that anyone ever noticed.

She raised her daughter in the typical clothing of English princesses: plaid skirts, patent leather shoes, blouses with big collars, and short jackets.

True, her daughter was not growing up very pretty (where have you ever seen pretty English princesses? Princess Anne? Margaret?), but she was a very striking little girl.

Meanwhile home was ruled by an intemperate Valery Ivanovich, who vented on his wife and daughter about all his failures and intoned time and again: "You're asking for the belt."

Tamara was crazy about her daughter, but when she was twelve she had to be sent to Moscow, to school, so she was raised by her grandmother, Nina Georgievna.

Who, in turn, accepted the upbringing of Valera's daughter as a life sentence.

As for her grandfather, the ambassador, Gennady Ivanovich exited the scene fairly quickly after his disgrace. A man-bear can't abide another bear in his lair, and the vanquished was forced to give up the ghost.

9

Masha's Love

AS A RESULT, Masha grew up to be quite a lonely and not very attractive young woman. She didn't know how to flirt or use makeup.

Oh well, princesses the world over are, to a woman, lonely, incapable of finding a partner, and ultimately falling for staff, unfortunately.

Secretly, Masha was good, ardent, and sensual, but she wouldn't dare let that show.

Her mama, Tamara Gennadievna, knew all this and clearly saw in her a confirmed loner.

They loved each other very much and called each other often. Her mama was Masha's sole friend.

White-blonde after her father, an unremarkable star student, a girl from a good family, polite, quiet, withdrawn.

Her first year at university, she secretly fell in love with Sergei because once in the coatroom he'd said to her, "Your purse is open, you should close it. You never know. Let me."

And he zipped up her purse. But her purse was hanging at her side.

His solicitous, capable hands ran over Masha's hip.

And after that he always said hello to her.

By the spring of her third year, a month before her birthday, Masha thought she would lose her mind and realized it was time to act, that is, she had fully matured, so she scrubbed her entire apartment and made sure it was spanking clean (her grandmother was often ill, and her mama, as always, was living abroad with her ambassador husband), and then during an international phone call she asked her mama to send by diplomatic pouch the trendiest records and fabric for new curtains, and also jeans, a thin sweater, lace panties and bras, too, and invited lots of people to her birthday party, went up to each person individually, and handed them a card with the address and date, including that very same Sergei, who was in a different group.

He said, "Thanks, I'll definitely come. What should I bring?"

"Just white wine, if it's no trouble."

Her grandmother didn't approve of a noisy crowd invading her apartment, so when everyone arrived (lots were total strangers, supposedly friends of the guests, pretty wild-looking), she lay down in her bedroom and locked herself in, and Masha took everything on herself.

People danced. Sergei sat off to the side.

Masha stepped on his foot by accident as she was running past with a cake. He nodded and in response to her apology said, "I forgive you." So solidly.

Then he left before everyone else. Before they threw up all over the bathroom and the living room rug.

But a few days later he went up to her in the hallway and asked whether she had notes on the First World War, the Balkan unit.

Masha suggested he come by her place after lectures. They drank tea. Her grandmother protested with her entire appearance.

Sergei was rather poorly dressed, and his shoes, leatherette hiking boots, were beyond the pale.

When he left, her grandmother asked, "My dear, where is he from, who are his people?"

"He's here on his own, from the South. He was born by the sea." (Actually, three hundred kilometers from the sea, but to her Georgian grandmother she could fib.)

"As if your soccer-playing papa weren't bad enough. Especially since our great-grandfather was a prince. Is he a good student?"

"I don't know. All right, I guess."

"Well, and what do you see in him? Listen to me!" Masha said nothing.

Then came another long hiatus in her relations with Sergei.

They said hello and that was it.

And so this one-sided romance puttered along. Occasionally they'd see each other in the library or the cafeteria.

A year later, in April, Sergei approached her again in the coatroom and joked, "Is your purse closed now? Hi." He had his coat on.

Masha immediately asked, "Where are you going? I mean, what direction?"

"The direction of Khabarovsk but not all the way. I've had an offer from the provincial teachers institute to do grad studies and teach. I think I'm going to focus on China."

"So why did you study Handi?"

They walked toward the metro but went down side streets.

Their first time walking together. Masha was trembling and her temples ached, but you couldn't tell.

"Have a good birthday?" he asked. (He remembered!)

"Not really. My grandmother was sick. We sat in a café together, that was it."

(Good move! In truth, Masha had invited a girlfriend she took fencing with to a café.)

"Have fun?"

"Oh, tons. After that other birthday I spent a week mucking out. Everyone drank too much, with major consequences. That did it for me."

It was all fairly straightforward.

Dreams, when they come true, look like ordinary life. No happiness whatsoever.

They walked toward the Kropotinskaya metro. They weren't even on a walk, they were just walking in the same direction. His direction.

Sergei said that, naturally, with his languages he wasn't eager to be teaching history in Flyswat.

He talked with Masha as he would with a close friend and discussed his future.

"So here's the thing," he concluded, gazing vaguely to either side, past Masha. "We're going to have to say goodbye."

"What about Moscow? Are you staying in Moscow?" Masha replied drearily.

"I've had an offer in one office, and I went through the training, in medical imports, they have a job, even with a stretch in Handia, but they won't hire anyone without a Moscow residency permit. I'm a perfect fit. They're very sorry. I know Handi and Irdu. And English"—like at an interview, Seryozha was listing his accomplishments. "But they'll probably hire Shatskin, and he only knows English and French. But they say they'll train him up in a year . . . He'll pick it up . . . You know where his father works?"

"This isn't good," Masha replied.

"Yeah, I know," Sergei replied, discouraged. "And they only send people to Handia with a wife."

Then Masha plucked up her nerve and took the plunge. "If you want, I'll talk to my grandmother. We can have a fictitious marriage and she'll register you."

What did he say to her offer of hand, heart, and a residency permit? He said, "That's all pretty complicated."

"Yes," Masha said slowly, sorrowfully. "Yes . . . But good. Why not?"

They reached the Kropotinskaya metro, where Sergei said goodbye.

"I've got business nearby at this place."

In other words, he didn't want to see her home or stop in for a cup of coffee, as Masha had planned.

Or stay the night, as she'd pictured—and there would be no

problems with her grandmother, none of the scandal or tears she'd imagined.

"Well, bye," Masha said. "Or maybe we can go to my place? My grandmother's cooked a great meal! Stuffed cabbage! Then we can watch a video. My parents sent a great film!"

"I can't now," Sergei replied distractedly. "I can't for now."

"Write down my phone number and come over today and we'll discuss the whole thing."

"I have your phone number," Sergei said.

"Well, come over. Bye."

That night Masha cried. She'd been the one to proposition Seryozha!

And apparently he'd turned her down.

She started to suspect that Seryozha already had someone. Maybe he wanted to marry her.

But what was it he said? "Only with a wife." Which means, you get hitched, and then also go to Handia, he takes you along like a free perk.

Nevertheless, the next day, in the evening (she hadn't seen Sergei at the institute), Masha initiated a conversation with her grandmother.

"Tell me, what would you think if I decided to get married?"

"To whom?" Grandma Nina said in horror. She always predicted the worst. "That one?"

"*Which* that one?"

"The one who came to see you. Hello? Otherwise I don't understand! I get everything right away! Who had tea with us! Him?"

Masha shrugged.

"And where is he from?" her grandmother continued.

"Our class."

"No, what city?"

Masha answered reluctantly, as if she was saying something indecent out loud.

"Aah. Well, of course. Listen, do you know that at your birthday party he was poking all around the apartment, even looked into my room when I wasn't there? I'm coming in from the toilet and I find him in my doorway and I ask him jokingly, 'Who are you?' and he says, 'You'll be calling me Seryozha.' As gauche and calm as you please."

"You didn't tell me that."

"Masha! I never tell anyone anything unless I have to. He shook me, my dear, simply shook me with his arrogance. I'm telling you. I'll be calling him Seryozha! So what, has he finally proposed?"

"That isn't important."

"What isn't important? That's exactly what's important. I'll tell you, my dear, all he needs from you is a residency permit! That's obvious right off!"

"In fact, he doesn't need anything," Masha said bitterly.

"And don't you go getting any ideas," her grandmother began to yell, paying no attention to what Masha said. "I'm not registering him, and you're registered with your father and mother, not me. And they definitely won't agree. They'll raise such a stink! You'll see, they'll form a united front. For this, they'll call a truce. It's no accident they've locked their apartment and aren't letting you in there. They had a feeling."

"Grandmother, he has no intention of marrying me no matter which way the wind's blowing."

"So where are you going to live? Not with me. He's not welcome. I'm old and ill. To put up with his presence in the bathroom! To listen to him spitting! Or God knows what even viler sounds! And he's going to be using you literally in my presence? Thank you very much! I have a son-in-law like that. Your papa. The soccer player. Who sent your grandfather to his grave."

"Calm down, Grandma. You're constantly blaming my father!"

"Don't tell me to calm down. I'm doing the talking! Who are you to shut me up! And remember, your parents aren't going to let you into their apartment. Let alone me! Understand?"

And she got all ready to cry when Masha replied, "Grandmother, the question's off the table. Seryozha has no plans to stay in Moscow."

"So what, you're going to go with him?"

"Grandma! He won't ask me. I'm the last thing he needs."

"Oh, he needs you. I have a sense where this is going. It's awful, just awful. Better you'd plucked out my eyes first!" And so on.

10

Alina's Story

THIS STORY BEGINS with Alina, a young student at Moscow State University living in a dormitory called In the Hills, who'd hooked up with another student she'd met at a dance. Avtandil.

On Saturdays at the university in the Lenin Hills, the dark-skinned students played incredible music in the dorm, in the halls on two floors!

All of Moscow was dying to get in.

Alina didn't sit out a single dance; she was asked for every one.

Alina was an orphan with a living father. Her mother'd died of TB a long time ago and he'd skipped out the second the diagnosis was made, divorced her mother (as was his perfect right), and married a young piece of shit who, after Alina's mother's death, rode into the house on Alina's father's shoulders (Alina was already living in the dorm) and literally would not let the young woman through the front door, claiming she was "contagious."

Her family home outside Moscow, in a dacha community, was now off limits to Alina. Not only that, all her mama's things were out of reach, everything she'd owned.

Her stepmother acquired a ferocious dog that she let out in the yard.

Alina couldn't get the police to help her move in!

As long as she had the dormitory, though, Alina wasn't particularly upset.

She was pretty as a summer's day, very blonde and slender.

Avtandil himself was like a mountain deer: curly hair, a straight handsome nose, big brown eyes, and a handsome mouth—you couldn't ask for more.

Not only that, when Alina saw Avtandil, she felt as though she already knew him, and well.

Later, when they wound up in bed for the first time and morning came and they had to run off to lectures, Alina looked at him sleeping and suddenly remembered the art club where she'd done sculpture as a child and where Avtandil was already present in the form of the head of Antinoüs.

The only thing was—he had short legs.

But that wasn't so bad. Who knows, maybe Antinoüs had the exact same.

What they lived on: Avtandil was sent good money. His father sold newspapers in a kiosk in Poti, a little seaside town, and rented out two houses to tourists, and the rooms were partitioned off. For a total of twenty cots. In the summer season, he and his family (wife and children) lived in a stone outbuilding in the yard. Avtandil's mama managed a pharmacy.

Avtandil majored in geography for some unknown reason (even he didn't know why; apparently someone his mama knew worked in that department, she'd stayed with them a few times)—and he didn't exactly knock himself out over his studies.

The woman from the academic office looked after his affairs.

There weren't even any mediocre grades on his academic record.

Nonetheless, the moment came and Alina told her beloved she was pregnant and wanted her child to have a papa.

Avtandil had no idea what she meant.

"Who, my papa?"

"No. You. You're the papa."

"Wait, I don't understand. Hold on. I'm the papa?" (He smiled like a child.)

"We have to go to the registry office."

"Where?"

Alina spelled it all out for him.

And she flew into hysterics, saying there was someone who'd been wanting to marry her for a long time.

And even though she didn't love him, the child needed a papa. And she was probably going to marry him. But he was a foreigner.

"Who, that Mbvala?" Avtandil shouted, crazed. "I'll kill him!"

Mbvala was a good-looking brown man, the son of his tribe's leader, and a Muslim. He really did adore Alina and had proposed several times in jest that she be his junior wife. At home, Mbvala already had two wives and three children living in the family tent. Mbvala was seventeen. He often showed Alina photos of his children.

"So what am I supposed to do?" Alina went on. "Since you don't want to marry me!"

"I do, my darling!"

But there was an obstacle. He hadn't turned eighteen yet. Alina was nearly twenty-one.

To marry, as a minor, Avtandil needed his parents' permission. He immediately wrote his mama and papa.

But they didn't seem to be in any rush.

While Mbvala continued to hug Alina every time they met and show her photos of his adorable tots.

This drove Avtandil insane (all these encounters took place in front of him, naturally, that's just how it was).

Three months later, when he turned eighteen, without waiting for his parents' blessing, he and Alina went to the registry office, where they applied for a marriage license.

Avtandil formally wrote to his father announcing the happy event.

Alina added a few words in Russian. A little while later, that same woman from the academic office told Avtandil that his father was flying in and had asked him and his bride to meet him at the airport. She handed him a note with the date and flight number. At the appointed time, Avtandil and Alina (she already had a little belly, she was in her eighth month, though she'd barely gained any weight) were standing in the arrivals hall.

All of a sudden, Avtandil's whole body jerked and he rushed forward.

Walking in the crowd of passengers was a fat little man with a mustache, wearing an enormous cap and a tight black suit. He looked like Charlie Chaplin. Hobbling along behind him was a beautiful, very plump, low-slung, wide-bottomed woman wearing a white shawl.

Avtandil rushed toward them, nearly in tears. They embraced him.

Alina turned deathly pale while continuing to smile. What, these were his parents? Awful sullen faces, a mustached fatman, a dumpy woman also mustached, both with bulging red eyes. As if they'd been crying or hadn't slept in a long time.

The fatman heard out Avtandil, looked at Alina by his side, and said something very brief in his own language.

Then all three turned around and went through the exact same door they'd come out of.

Alina stood there for three hours waiting for Avtandil.

Then she started feeling poorly and fainted.

She was taken to the hospital for monitoring. From there she called her neighbor in the dorm, her friend Faina, and Faina looked into it all and said that Avtandil had been unenrolled from the university at his own request. He'd sent in the form.

That lady who worked in the academic office had removed all his things from his room.

Alina shed copious tears as she lay in the ward.

They gave her a shot. Her due date was close. Alina swelled up from lack of movement, and complications set in.

They wouldn't discharge her.

Then another pregnant woman, also there for monitoring, came into the ward: Masha.

She was the same age as Alina, twenty-one, but she'd already graduated from MGIMO and was planning to go to Handia with her husband, Seryozha, for a job, to a city with some very long name—Pamparamparampradesh, or something like that.

When she'd somehow learned Alina's story (everyone there knew everything), Masha tried to cheer her up, constantly treating her to fruits and vitamins and giving her books to read on raising newborns, but Alina didn't react.

She didn't want anything.

She didn't want to read books about raising infants.

Most of all, she didn't want a baby.

She called in a lawyer and told that dumpy lady she wanted to leave her future infant there.

The lawyer responded to her rhetoric by saying that first she had to give birth, and she promised to bring the forms.

The more invigorated Masha felt and called on her neighbor to prepare joyously for the birth, the more she pushed pamphlets on her, the worse Alina's attitude toward the whole thing got.

And the more she envied her neighbor.

Every day boxes of fruit were delivered to her, and magazines, and people wrote her notes.

Alina's nightstand was empty. A glass and a spoon.

In fact, Masha's situation was also far from brilliant, she was having complications, they'd found protein in her urine.

That could lead to a fatal outcome during labor. They even started talking about doing a pre-term Caesarian.

But Masha kept up her spirits. Every evening, she walked over to the first-floor window to talk to her husband, Seryozha, and her grandmother, but her mama and papa were abroad and couldn't come.

Masha'd already decided she'd call the baby Seryozha, too, that is, Sergei.

"What about you?" Masha would ask.

Alina would turn away.

What was she going to call the baby? Hitler, for all she cared.

There'd been no sign of Avtandil since that day.

They're rich people! They could at least send money!

In the old days Alina and Avtandil were forever going to restaurants and buying good food, and Avtandil had three suits. He even bought Alina a sweet pink suit, jeans, and a goat fur jacket, as well as boots and two pairs of shoes, to say nothing of lots of little stuff.

Now she had nowhere to take a baby. They wouldn't give her a room in the dorm with an infant.

And what about her things? Her friend Faina promised to find out what had become of it all.

But she was hard to reach on the phone, there being only one for the entire hallway.

You could call and whoever answered wouldn't go look. Too lazy or too busy. The receiver could lie there for ten minutes.

And for a place in a family dorm—where couples with children and single moms like Alina lived—you had to apply in advance, practically the first day of your pregnancy, as they joked at the trade union committee.

There were no places there, though, as they said. There was a long line. That's what they told Faina.

A year ago this friend, Faina, had been in a similar fix. She gave birth, Volkov grinned and said "It's not mine," a ballsy grin, actually, and moved out of the dorm to live with a Moscow girl, Konvitskaya. He'd had his doubts and hadn't wanted it and now he'd been spurred on.

As a result, Faina had left the kid at the infant home, so she could finish up the semester, and when she went back a month and a half or two later, they told her he'd died and they'd sent him to the crematorium: "We couldn't keep him on ice waiting for you to show up!"

Alina thought about all that after every phone call, but she didn't tell anyone, and now Masha was cheerful, she was studying Irdu and telling Alina about Handia. Before the hospital she'd watched a few documentaries about the country.

"Just imagine, they have sacred cows walking down the middle of the street there! And no one leads them away. No one milks them! And if a cow starts to eat from a fruit stand, they don't have the right to stop it!"

"I wish I could do that!"

The two women went into labor almost simultaneously and were led away to the labor room.

They walked down the endless corridor, which was lined in white tile, like a bathhouse. Masha took tiny steps, bent over, hugging her belly, as if she were afraid of losing the baby.

Alina walked as if to her execution, but not proudly. She too held her ponderous belly, not to protect the baby but because of the excruciating cramps. Her belly burned like red-hot steel, and the full hopelessness of what was happening was revealing itself in all its glory.

They gave birth on neighboring tables. Alina yelled, but Masha was silent.

"That girl's got guts," Alina thought between contractions, and out of pride also stopped shouting. And all of a sudden everyone abandoned Alina and crowded around Masha's table. People came running with an injection, dragging an IV. They heard a squeak.

"Masha!" the midwife kept repeating. "Masha! You have a baby boy! Masha! Open your eyes!"

While another walked over and felt Masha's neck:

"It's over, girls."

At that moment Alina screamed desperately, "That's it! I'm having this baby! You damn bitches! Come here! Anyone! Don't leave me here—aaah!"

A woman in glasses dashed over to her:

"Don't yell! What's the matter with you! We'll just have a look . . . So. Come on! Go to it! Push! Now stop! Or you'll rip yourself!"

"What are you doing!" Alina wailed.

"It's not us, it's your baby," the midwife said.

And at that moment the baby started pushing, then pouring out of Alina's womb with inhuman strength and insane pain, like a huge lump of dense hot clay.

"A boy," the midwife said. "Look."

"No," Alina said. "Take him away."

"Ooh, mama, so angry. This is all going to pass. You're going to love him more than life itself! Your friend over there died. She left an orphan. No one's going to hold him to her breast."

The babies were taken to the operating room next door, they did something with them there, and the babies whimpered.

They brought in a gurney, shifted poor Masha's body onto it, and took it away. That was it.

And for some reason everyone left.

Alina got up like a madwoman, grabbed her bloody diaper, covered herself, and got ready to flee so she'd never have to think about this horror again.

Her baby would end up in a children's home and live the life of an orphan. While dead Masha's baby would go to Handia and live like a tsar.

Why was it others had all the luck—family, foreign countries, food, money—but not her!

Bleeding profusely, Alina staggered to the next ward to see the babies lying under the ultraviolet lamp.

Each was wearing one of two prepared bracelets with the mother's first and last names.

Here—Alina Rechkina, boy. Here—Maria Sertsova, boy.

Without looking at the babies, Alina switched the bracelets.

They were making a racket in the corridor; the midwives were coming. Alina scrambled back onto her delivery table.

"What's this? Covered in blood!" they shouted. "The whole floor! What did you do, get up?"

"I got up to look," Alina answered, trembling from the cold.

"Ah!" the midwife said. "Touched to the quick! Mama decided to take a look at her beloved boy after all. Did you figure out where yours was? On the right!"

"Yes," Alina answered, her teeth chattering.

"Well," the bespectacled midwife said, "now you're going to nurse him and love him. A mama who's looked at her baby can't give him up. And once you breastfeed—that's it, you're his slave for life. So we're off and running."

The nurse went to the nursery, maybe to check their bracelets with their mother's name. Bracelets that would determine their whole life, indeed.

They wheeled Alina away and left her in a dark place under the stairs.

"Lie there," the midwife said. "They'll come for you."

Alina spent several hours in this corner under a sheet, quivering from cold. Only one time a nurse came by and lifted the sheet: "If you have a lot of bleeding, keep an eye out!"

It was already very dark when they took Alina upstairs in the elevator and unloaded her in the ward.

Brought a plate of hot soup.

Alina ravenously consumed it all. A small happiness.

11

The Continuing Story of Sergei Sertsov

SERGEI SERTSOV WAS all set for Masha and the baby's return from the maternity hospital.

He'd scrubbed the apartment he and Masha had been renting for a year, and his co-workers had given them a stroller as soon as he took Masha to the maternity hospital. Maybe they were a little too quick. Maybe they shouldn't have.

But Sergei, when they told him they'd taken Masha in to deliver, he couldn't stand the tension and threw a small party for the whole department, at which point they rolled in the stroller they'd been hiding in the utility room.

That evening, after everyone was gone, he had his usual quickie with Lariska, the boss's secretary, and then walked her out, giving her money for a taxi, and then collected the stroller from the utility room and took it on the metro folded up.

The next morning a sleepy Sergei again ran to the maternity hospital with a jar of bouillon, sent in the food and a note, and stood at the window waiting for an answer.

Ten minutes later he ran outside and started vomiting right outside the front door.

After that he found himself at work. The females knew right away that something was wrong with Sergei.

"Did something happen?"

"Complications after the delivery," Sergei answered.

"She gave birth? What is it?"

Everyone rushed to congratulate him, they ran out for wine and cake again.

The females started telling each other about how it had gone in their own case.

Then they took a closer look at Sergei and wanted to send him home, but he said he'd do some work.

He pretended to go over documents. He was over his head in problems and he had to deal with everything himself. But his mind was a blank.

He had to clear a large shipment of medicines from Handia through customs, but there were problems with the expiration date.

As always with that firm, Ortena.

Viktor Nikolaevich, his boss, stepped into his room.

"So what's happened? I can tell from your face."

He'd already been informed.

"Come in."

He did.

"What's wrong with you?"

"Here's the thing . . . Masha died," Sergei said, sobbing.

"When?"

"Last night. In childbirth."

"Oh, my Lord. I am so sorry, Sergei. And the baby?"

"The baby . . . my son's alive."

"Well, congratulations nevertheless. Go on home."

"No," Sergei objected. "There are issues with Ortena again."

"No, there aren't. Shchukin just called. It'll be resolved the same way as before. Off you go."

"But what about the expired catheters? All those claims from hospitals? That they split right in their hands?"

"I'm telling you. Shchukin called. That's it. We'll accept them with these dates. Otherwise we'll have to pay a forfeit, you know yourself."

"Yes. Masha and I wanted to go to Handia and redo all the contracts there. Yes. Masha knew all about it. She'd nearly learned Irdu."

"Mmm . . . I wanted to fix the situation, too. I was training you especially for that . . . The Kama firm is waiting for you. Mr. Pradesh just called."

"I won't be going now," Sergei said. "It's too bad. Now that . . . what's his name . . . Motev will be going as Shchukin's representative."

"Yes . . . On his last stint Motev put together enough for a co-op. Ortena pays well. Shchukin turned out to be right to train him in parallel with you. As if he'd had a presentiment. If the idea weren't totally absurd, I might think your wife didn't just pass away . . . But that's foolishness. And don't think it. I have to call Pradesh. Here, have some brandy."

They drank.

Sergei couldn't hold it in, there was a kindred soul by his side.

"The worst part is that Masha never gave herself a moment's thought. Always thinking about others. What I'm eating, how I'm sleeping. You see, she knew she was ill. No! She was always busy with some nonsense, worrying about other people. She wrote me long letters about someone in her ward who everyone had abandoned, a university student or something, no money, no roof, going hungry, she was at her wits' end, she didn't know what to do with her child, told me to bring more food. And this young woman, she'd already asked for a lawyer so she could give up her baby. She hadn't even given birth yet and was already . . . Masha wrote me, couldn't we take a second baby, right away, and she wrote we'd solve all the problems. I'm probably not going to be able to give birth again, she said . . . And here we'd have two . . . And so I was bringing packages for them two . . . for four . . ."

"Yes, we've seen . . . Loads . . ."

"And now I'm sure that other one's perfectly fine. But Masha's gone."

They drank. Sergei suddenly felt feverish.

"Excuse me"—and he dashed out of the room.

When he returned, Viktor Nikolaevich looked at him with concern.

"What's wrong with you?"

"I don't know. Something with my stomach. I'm running every five minutes."

"Fear gives you the runs. That happens with men. Listen. I've been figuring . . . I should find out, that woman . . . you know, the one Masha was there with. Where is she? Who is she?"

"Relating to what?" a pale Sergei asked, exhausted.

"Relating to this. Don't tell anyone your wife died. Got it? Did you pay in for a cooperative, by the way?"

"Yes. Masha and I borrowed from her parents, my father-in-law, they paid the first installment . . . Oh no. I still have to tell them. I can't. I just can't."

"Sergei, if you don't go to Handia right now, all is lost. Motev will go and he'll have the contracts signed and sealed for the next three years. Kama was already ready to transfer a prepayment. I can't believe this all happened at once. Everything's falling apart. Including your co-op. But here's what. You have to find out what kind of lady this is. Whether she gave birth, who she is, where she's from."

A pause—and suddenly Sergei Sertsov got it.

"We won't have time to get her papers, what's wrong with you, Uncle Vitya."

"True, we won't. But we can send other photos for the application and the foreign passport."

"No, I can't, Uncle Vitya."

"Let's think."

"I'm done for. There's no life for me without Masha. I can't even imagine such a thing happening . . . Masha . . . Oh, what's the point in talking now! She was such a friend." He swallowed the lump in his throat. "I was all she thought about. There was love and passion, I appreciated that. It's like an adornment on the path to human procreation. And the goodness . . . When you can rely on that person in every way. When she won't let you down. The two years she and I lived together were like one day. Like a dream."

Sergei didn't know how to cry.

"Oh! I don't really care what happens to me. Work's all I have left."

"Don't say that! There's your son."

"Yes . . . my baby boy. How can I raise him now? I don't want to give him up. Oh, my God."

"She, that woman, if she gave birth and gave up her baby . . . couldn't she nurse your son?"

"I don't know. I'd have to think about that. Yes. Talk to her! Yes. It's a thought."

"A thought definitely worth considering."

"Huh?"

"I'm saying, definitely worth considering."

"Gotcha." He roused. "It's not a bad idea . . . I'm sorry, I have to . . ."

He came back. There were dark circles under his eyes. He was white as a sheet.

"Yes. Why not? I get your drift."

"Really, Sergei . . . this young woman . . . whoever she turns out to be . . . a thief, a prostitute . . ."

"Exactly. Whatever. Whatever it takes, just so I get out of here."

"Three years with her! She may end up making you scream."

"All the better. I'm screaming as is. My other option is to hang myself."

"And she might come to hate your child. She gave up her own, so what does she care about someone else's?"

"She might. But what can I do? I'm rescuing her, too, to some extent. I'm taking her abroad."

"Life there's not all that sweet, Sergei. I know. And in Handia . . .

they scrimp on everything. When she figures that out she's going to run away and leave you with the baby. You know that the children from our office sometimes faint from hunger in the Handian school. The parents begrudge them even the cheap bananas. They gave me a whole report on it."

"That's still better for her than ending up on the street. We're both washed up, I think."

"Just take care. You're betting on a dark horse."

"There's nothing for me to take care about."

"Don't say anything. Let's go to the maternity hospital. Do you have money? It's going to take a lot. I'll loan you some. You can pay me back when you get back from Handia."

12

Alina's Story, Continued

THE FIRST INFANTS were brought to the ward early the next morning.

The ward filled up with babies crying and young mamas cooing, their squealing and hissing: breastfeeding turned out to hurt a lot. They brought Alina the other little boy.

"I won't," she said. "Take him away."

"Just look how handsome," the old aide sang. "Poor hungry baby, he's all worked up!"

The infant was ugly-screaming.

"I won't."

"But if you don't nurse, you'll get sick. Look, your milk's already come in. You'll spike a fever. Nurse him for your own health, you little fool."

"Lay off."

But that night was really bad! Her breasts got all swollen and numb.

Again they brought the little ones. And once more they brought the deceased Masha's son. He was crying nonstop.

"Go on, nurse him, you're a healthy girl, give him some nice milk, you'll feel better yourself. Or else they'll chop off your nipples afterward, you'll get a tumor!" the aide insisted.

"Fine," Alina said. "But who's going to feed that baby?"

"Which one?"

"Well, Masha's. The girl who died."

"Bless you, who's going to nurse him! Well, they'll use a medicine dropper . . . mix the powder . . . He's not long for this world. He's in a bad way."

"Have them bring him, too. I'll feed just the two."

"Okay, I'll tell them. You're a piece of work, girl. First one, then another on top of that."

She nursed them both at once. The infants looked a little alike— both dark, big noses . . .

Her nipples burned, but she felt much better.

She fed the babies six times a day, with a six-hour break overnight. The ward barely slept.

Alina tried not to look at the babies so she wouldn't get attached, but still, without looking, out of her peripheral vision, she could tell them apart.

"Mine" tired quickly and dropped off, and they carried him away hungry.

"Masha's" sucked away like a little vacuum, and by the third day, without looking, just by body weight, she could tell he'd obviously put on weight.

Alina felt terribly sorry for "Mine." She kept tugging his little nose, trying to get him to wake up.

The nurse taught her that.

Alina tried not to look, squinted, her eyes nearly shut, but she would find his little nose and squeeze his nostrils, as delicate as lily of the valley petals.

But once set on his mama's breast, he'd rest against her gratefully, smack his lips a little, the poor abandoned child, and immediately drift off.

A pitiful, almost weightless, tiny baby boy.

He was probably going to be stunningly handsome.

Through half-lowered eyelids, she did notice—and it was imprinted on her brain forever—two coils of hair stuck to his poor little skull. Future curls.

A baby no one needed.

But a rich clan was going to take him. He was going to live like a tsar.

And justice would be restored . . . Farewell, my love, farewell, my little angel. They're going to take you away.

But then one day they didn't bring the babies.

"They're both sick," the aide said. "Pump milk for now. I set a jar aside for you. They'll feed them."

Angry and gloomy, Alina started pumping milk. She couldn't not. Otherwise her breasts would swell up and get marble-hard.

She felt sick to her stomach.

A lawyer came with the papers and suggested she familiarize herself.

She read for a long time, but there was a fog in her eyes.

None of the girls in the ward would speak to her.

Alina was constantly weeping over Masha, the one real friend she'd had.

If only she had her photograph, even a small one.

Masha had been so concerned for Alina, had tried to cheer her up. Fed her all the time.

The mamas had juices, milk cartons, vitamins, fruits, and flowers in jars on all their nightstands.

Alina had nothing.

Faina refused to visit her, acted like a stranger, as if they hadn't lived in the same dorm for two years, hadn't given each other their last cigarettes, as if Alina hadn't shared literally everything that came her way from Avtandil's parents—jam from young walnuts, from apricots and kernels, homemade sausage and cheese—all this brought in crates by people from home trading at the central market. As if Faina hadn't completely worn out all Alina's tops and pants and raided her cupboard for makeup.

Now, over the phone, Faina acted the indifferent and even malicious creature.

She kept saying she was living on just her stipend, was going hungry, and couldn't get out of bed.

When Alina called her, anxious that they might not find her (it was a dorm, after all, and a long way to go, the phone was in the hall), she spoke in a lifeless voice.

"Fai, did you find out? Are there any letters for me in the box?"

"No. And don't expect any. They're like that. They've probably married him off already."

"He loves me."

"Yeah, and he loves his mother and father more. He's totally dependent on them."

"Fai, come see me, okay? At least bring me some milk.".

"There's no point in you lying around there. Leave. Give up the kid right away. Or else it'll be like it was for me. They probably sold him, my Vanya, anyway."

"Most likely."

"There you go, Alina! Sell your little guy! For ten thousand! You can buy an apartment in the suburbs. Or a semi-detached house. Honest!"

"How do you . . ."

"You advertise."

"How can I do that from here? And where?"

"What do you think? That I'm going to help you? For fifty percent, sure."

"But where am I going to live in the meantime? With a baby? I don't have the family dorm. The lines for that are incredible."

"You'll go to your father's. You have the right. You'll go there with the police and move in. It's close, after all, just outside Moscow. Not like for me, cripes, three days' travel."

"No, I can't. How can I bring my little guy to my father's? All the neighbors would laugh. That wife of his would make my life a misery, and she'd feed the baby to the dog."

"What's that you said?"

"What."

"My little guy?"

"Well."

"Have you gotten attached to him or something?"

"Not really."

"Are you nursing, or something?"

"Yes."

"I told you! Don't get attached, don't get used to him! Oh, you're going to know grief just like me. Fine, then, but there's already a line here. You know, Alina, don't call me. Just don't. Life's sickening enough as is. There's nothing to eat."

"What about your mama? Didn't she send anything?"

Once a month, Faina's mother sent her daughter a package by train—mostly salt pork with streaks of meat, canned stew, and dried fish. True, Faina never shared any with Alina, repeating, "It's too greasy for you. You'll make yourself sick."

Now Faina had this to say:

"Mama! My mama's got two of her own there. She's always writing me to get a job, saying there's no point studying. So I can help her. Parasite, she writes, you've got it easy. While she's slaving away at two jobs . . . Catch my drift? I should leave right now. I've stopped going to lectures. Apathy through the roof. I'm so so blue. Ready for the noose."

"Don't even say that! We have a year and a half left! After all we've been through!"

"I don't know. I could transfer to correspondence courses . . ."

"And never finish at all."

"I'm faint from hunger. Gotta run."

"What about your Volkov?"

"Right, Volkov, he's married to that other one now. Their whole physics department had a party. He's living with her parents, walking the dog. They have this little dwarf dog with yellow moles like eyebrows."

"How do you know?"

"I know everything. Address and entryway. I sat on a bench a whole evening. Volkov came out, put down that Puss of his . . . He cares less about his child than he does that bitch."

("His child?" Alina thought, horrified. "He doesn't have one.")

"I'll show him a thing or two!"

"Oh, Fai . . ."

"Yeah! I'll buy rat poison and put it out. I'll get back at him for my little Vanya!"

They fell silent.

"All right already, I don't have the time," Faina said, yawning.

"You know, that last day, I was with Avtandil and I saw Volkov go off with Inga. But I decided not to tell you."

"What's there to tell? When it's as plain as the nose on your face. Alina! Forget about it."

"Volkov's a snake."

"Inga knows my little Vanya is Volkov's. Ivan Erikovich. So she's just as much a snake as he is."

"Fai! I mean . . . does Volkov know? Does he? That his son died?"

"No, he doesn't. He thinks he's in the infant house. No one knows. Don't you go saying anything, all right?"

"I won't. Fai, bring me a little milk."

"I don't have any money."

"Fai, no one knows where I am, right?"

"No. I said you broke your arm."

"Please go tell the department my father's sick."

"It's too late now. Who needs you in the department! I told the senior advisor, that Nadka."

"Semyonova?"

"She turned out to be a real piece of work. The only thing she responds to is money. That's it. She's not marking you down, but I slipped her a little something. By the way, you owe me. A half stipend for every reporting month. As if you were going to lectures. For two months now. That means you owe me a whole stipend."

"Thanks for the good word. But Semyonova's scum. And she was such a great student!"

"And what do you think you are? You milked that Georgian sniveler."

"Listen, Fai. Tell me, what about my things? Did you find out? Especially that yellow suitcase."

"Oh, I was a fool not to write to his father, too, I forgot what a beast you are. What do you mean your things? Those are Avtandil's things. I was more friends with him than you were! He was sleeping with me that whole time. I don't think so! You're out the door and he shows up, yeah! He called me his sweetie. I never told you."

"So does that mean you were sleeping with two guys?"

"Ten! You know, don't call me anymore. I've listened to you, but I can't anymore, that's it, don't call. Did you help me when I gave up little Vanya? No. We're done."

Dial tone.

13

The Story of Kirkoryan

MEANWHILE, A WOMAN well over thirty, pale, blue-eyed, full-bodied, with a big belly, well dressed in a fur coat and blue fox hat, entered the maternity hospital from the clinic side and immediately proceeded to the head doctor's office without so much as a glance at the secretary.

"Tatiana Petrovna? I . . . you had a call from Babayan about me."

"I'm sorry, what is your last name?"

"Kirkoryan."

"Kirkoryan? Hello, hello, Kirkoryan, you're our . . . Sit down. Well then. You're doing the right thing, the right thing, slipping a pillow over your belly. Ha ha. In the meantime, the neighbors know your status."

The lady did not pick up on this thread. She was pretty disgruntled in general. She said without further introduction, "I'd like a look at him. Well, in the sense . . . He should look like my husband, after all. I'm going to different maternity hospitals. Choosing."

"He will look like him, he will. I assure you. I have a sharp eye."

"No. But still."

"Fine. Here's a white coat. Did you bring shoes?"

"I took slippers."

"What should I call you?"

"Elena Ksenofontovna."

"So. Elena Ksenofontovna, take off your coat and put on the slippers for now."

The woman hung her coat on a hook, put her hat in her purse, removed her boots, put on the slippers, white coat, and cap, and let the head doctor tie a gauze mask over her face.

"We're going to the nursery, Elena . . . mmm?"

"Ksenofontovna," the other replied, put out.

"Yes, yes . . . Ksenofontovna. So, a mask, that's better for you. No one will be able to identify you later. Just in case."

The lady was stonily silent. A strong woman. Accustomed to getting her way.

They went into the nursery.

The infants were crying in their cribs.

Ksenofontovna and the director leaned over a baby.

The director started in: "Oh, he sleeps so soundly! Never cries! Oh, what a fine young man you'll have! Solid, look. They're all screaming and he's quiet. A leader, you can tell right away."

All of a sudden it was like a demon had poked Elena Ksenofontovna in the rib. She pointed to the next crib, where the infant was squealing.

"And whose is this little baby next to him?"

"What does that have to do with anything? This one's yours. His mama's already given him up. She's called in a lawyer and we're just about to sign the papers."

"No, just think! What baby is this? I'm absolutely in shock."

"It's . . . Let me see."

She ran through the chart.

"Ah. Maria Sertsova. A boy. The mama died. We're holding him, checking on him for now. A very difficult birth. Another mama is nursing him."

"He's the spitting image of Grant! It's him!" the lady under the mask began to wail. "Lord! The spitting image! Like all of them! Their whole family!"

She held out her large hands with large rings to the stranger's child, wanting to take him immediately.

"This is absolutely my Grant!"

"No, what are you saying! Elena Ksenofontovna, no. And don't get any ideas."

"I'm telling you, this kind of thing doesn't happen. For him to look so much like him . . ."

The woman was losing it. Beads of sweat appeared on her forehead. She looked like a woman madly in love.

"No, what's the matter with you? This child has a father . . . grand-mothers and grandfathers. They're waiting for his discharge."

"Let's go," Elena Ksenofontovna said imperiously.

They went out.

The head doctor dragged behind as if to her execution, gray in the face.

A little while later she went into the nursery, alone now, put a small suitcase on the floor, and hastily, abruptly unswaddled one, then the other, and switched the bracelets on their hands and feet. The babies screamed bloody murder. Then the woman in the white coat coldly switched the babies, put each of them in the other's crib.

On her way out, she couldn't help but cross herself but then nod-ded privately. In her purse lay a valuable burden worth all the bracelets and all the babies in the maternity hospital put together. It was a plat-inum ring with a full-weight rock. A co-op for her son. Or a Zhiguli.

14

ALINA:
Continued

A RATHER SMUG but also very busy lawyer came to see Alina.

"Well then, mama, have you looked at the papers? Quickly! We'll write up a formal application."

Alina said, "No, we have to go out in the hall."

"What's so hush-hush?"

Alina said nothing, stood up, and shuffled out.

The lawyer caught up to her in the hallway.

"Well, then, come to my office. What do you care about those girls in there with you! They won't hear! What do they care about you and these sordid affairs of yours anyway! Give up your baby. Keep your baby. They don't care. They're consumed with their own babies. They'll leave the maternity hospital and forget your face by tomorrow! What's there to be shy about? Why are you running me back and forth? Up the stairs even."

The lawyer was quite fat and short of breath. Hobbling.

They went up a floor and into her office.

The woman took her seat with a different expression on her face: contempt and a desire to finish up as quickly as possible.

"So what's the big deal? What are these secrets?"

Alina sat down next to her desk. "Make all the faces you want. I'm going to fight. I'm not going to agree just like that. I need money."

"In what sense?"

"This sense. There are people who can pay . . ."

"Rechkina. That's a crime! Do you understand? For me, too!"

"Okay. Then I'm not giving up my baby."

"Go think it over. If that's true, why call me? Why drag me in? I have diabetes, my feet are trashed! I'm working flat out. Understand? I have people sitting at home, all unemployed. Go to the exchange! The job exchange!"

Everything inside her was seething. She looked like a deeply deceived honest person.

"And you, what was the point in this practical joke?"

"I didn't do anything. What do you mean. What kind of practical joke?"

"An artist. Having a baby to sell it, right?"

"No. This baby was my husband's and mine. His parents took him back home with them, they're rich."

"What a performance. I know you women! Women who have babies to sell them. And one sat down in my office." The lawyer slammed her white hand on the desk. She was wearing two rings—a wedding ring and a massive ruby ring.

"Is that so!" Alina said proudly.

"She got a nice seven years."

Alina stood up and dragged herself out of the office.

15

KIRKORYAN:

Conversation with Her Husband

MEANWHILE, ELENA KSENOFONTOVNA got to work, hung her coat on a hanger in the closet, put her fox cap on the table lamp, sat down at her desk, pressed a button, and asked her secretary to bring her tea with lemon.

Then she made a phone call: "Grant, darling, here I am at work already! I'm here. I barely made it from the hospital."

"And what did they say?"

"What did they say. Tomorrow they'll hand him over. I was with the doctor. And the midwife. She's worried."

"What's wrong?"

"No, nothing in particular."

"No, why is she worried? What else happened? Tell me, I'm in a hurry."

"She says I'm a criminal! Yes, that's what she said."

"What did she say? Why a criminal? What did you do? Is it starting in again?"

"No! She said I'm a criminal meaning, well, how can you treat yourself this way! You aren't taking care of yourself and you're working up until the last day!"

"And why is that? Who asked you to work? Isn't there bread in the house?"

"I'm a specialist. I couldn't just leave. How would the department get along without me? I had to make plans."

"Plans for what? You work in statistics. Data collection."

"You don't know our specific issues!"

"Yes, I do. I know your sort of figures. It's a total mess. Every year the sowing starts earlier than the last."

"Those are the data they give us, and that's what we work with. Listen. It's not about that. Giving birth at my age . . ."

"My grandmother gave birth at fifty. And you're forty."

"That's your grandmother! She lives in the mountains! Fresh air, good food!"

"And she still has five cows and makes chanakh! Her son's sixty! Doesn't work a lick. Just plays his duduk. Gets invited to all the weddings. Can't be bothered. Lazy bum."

"She's got the cows, see. Fresh milk straight from grass. But our situation is different, the doctor says I should be on the safe side."

"What now?"

"Oh, nothing terrible. My due date's coming up. Well . . ."

"I'll get my mama to come. All of Dilijan likes her, they bring her their children to show her."

"But what for?"

"I think I should. I already did."

"I'm telling you, why did you go and bother your mama? She's so old."

"We don't have old people in our family."

"You don't have to yet, don't call her."

"She's already on her way."

"Oh, no! What have you done? Why does she have to come, Grant darling? Do you think I can't manage? My mama's at the ready, she's already hemming baby jackets. Even though I said she shouldn't before the birth. It's bad luck."

"I'm sorry, someone's calling."

"Don't worry. No need to call your mama. We have a whole regiment of nannies. Ha ha ha!"

16

ALINA:
Death of an Infant

IN THE MORNING, Alina drank a glass of water while she waited for them to bring the babies.

The other mamas were nursing, silently, concentrating, their eyes focused on their babies.

The aide brought the last one.

Alina asked, "What about me?"

The aide came right up to her. She reeked of liquor.

"Your boy died," she said quietly. "It's over."

"What's that?" Alina shuddered. The glass fell to the floor but didn't break. "They brought them to me at six! At nine they said they were doing some procedures on them ..."

"Yeah. I came on at nine and his crib was empty. The nurses said he'd taken a bad turn."

"I just don't understand." Alina shook her head. "He was alive and well. I just don't understand."

"Oh well"—and the aide waved her hand. She moved close to Alina and leaned over her. "Stranger things than that go on in this maternity hospital. The place is infected. Staph. They should really burn it down and build a new one. Get out of here, girl, before you catch an infection that lasts your whole life. I feel sorry for you. I had a baby without a husband myself. Now I bring packages to my son in prison, twenty kilos each, I stand in line at the window. And I have a mother at home, paralyzed. Yeah. But you . . . your suffering's over. You're free now."

Groaning, she leaned over, picked up the glass, and mechanically dropped it into her pocket.

"What about the son of . . . of Masha Sertsova? Is he alive?"

"Yes. Thank God. But they're not letting him be brought for feeding."

At that moment Alina started to quake, her face pressed into her pillow.

The aide moved closer: "Quiet! You'd think you didn't know anything. The things I've seen. They took your son away. End of story. His crib's empty. Just don't shout."

Alina turned her tear-drenched, smiling face toward her:

"I'm fine, hear me? I'm perfectly fine!"

And she howled at the top of her lungs.

"All right, all right, you're unwell. Calm down. I'll go now and have the nurse give you a shot. Just watch you don't shout, don't scare the mamas. Tomorrow you'll be on your way home and Godspeed."

The aide left.

The young mamas in their beds goggled at Alina, doing what they could to shield their infants from her weeping. Their babies suckled peacefully.

One mama, nearby, suddenly burst into tears, too.

Alina pounded her head with her fists, her face screwed up, and sobbing, not knowing why herself, wept tears of victory.

She already loved her child more than life.

17

Maternity Hospital Viewings

TWO PEOPLE WERE sitting in the head doctor's office: a respectable man, a boss by the look of him, and a sickly-looking younger man.

"Here's the thing," the older man said. "We know there's a young woman here who gave birth and wants to relinquish her child."

The head doctor promptly objected.

"You're too late. Her baby died."

"Died? When?"

"Only just. This morning."

"That's sad."

They fell silent.

"But this drastically alters the overall situation," the older man said suddenly, turning to the younger. "So . . . couldn't you talk to her and ask her to come here?"

"Here? What do you mean here?"

"Didn't they call you?"

"But not to that extent. It's prohibited."

"Right. Please, ask her to come."

"I can't. What do you need?"

"We'd like to take a look at her."

"Why so?"

"There's a certain necessity."

"Then go stand in the corridor and her nurse will walk her past you."

"Okay."

"Only wait a little. My head's spinning. First one, then another . . ."

The nurse went into the ward.

"Rechkina, let's go."

"Where? I don't need your valerian drops or any shot."

"To see the head doctor two floors up."

Alina got up, wiped her face with a towel, tied a kerchief over her hair, belted her flannelette hospital robe, and slipped her feet into the stiff hospital slides.

The pretty nurse walked ahead in her high heels, tall cap, and snow-white coat, while Alina dragged behind, blubbering, her nose swollen and her cheeks burning.

They took the elevator to the fourth floor and started down the corridor.

Two men were standing by a window.

They stood stock-still, meeting and following the odd pair with their eyes, the pretty escort and the newly delivered mother, who looked like a prisoner in her pathetic hospital garb.

As she dragged past them, Alina huddled even more. Men in a maternity hospital? Who were they?

The men exchanged looks.

"She'll do," the older man said.

"Hmm, yes, though not a patch on the one in front."

"Okay," the older man said, like a lion tamer. "You think you have so many choices right now, but that's not true. And then, she really does look like your Masha. Both very blonde."

"The one in front's still better. This one looks like a street person."

"Her baby just died. What's the matter with you?"

"Ah, right."

"I understand you'd prefer to take our Lariska?"

"Lariska?" the younger man got flustered. "Why bring up Lariska?"

"You think no one knows you lock yourself in with her every day after work? In the utility room, on the sly. That wouldn't work, though. She's married. Whereas here the cover story falls easily in place. Understand? The same maternity hospital, and they look alike."

Their conversation proceeded in hushed tones.

A minute later the nurse walked past, stepping with especial elegance. Men rarely visited the maternity hospital.

The young man glanced imperceptibly in her direction.

"A fine Masha, but not our Masha," the older man summed up.

A few minutes later, Alina proceeded down the corridor, sliding quickly on her soles, not looking to either side. She was smiling strangely, like a psych patient.

The younger man looked down and didn't watch her.

"She'll do," the older man said after a pause.

A heavy silence. Very heavy.

Suddenly the younger man sort of grinned.

"What about Lariska? Maybe for real? She'd divorce her husband for Handia . . . Because this one's pretty damn ugly."

A wild hope ignited in his small eyes. He even turned red.

"Your Lariska? Why, she has two children. And she loves her husband. She's a shameless hussy, that's for sure, she whores around, but not to that degree," the older man replied. "That's for one. For two, we wouldn't have time to draw up the papers. For three, we need Lariska here, she's a national treasure. Ha ha. I couldn't get along without her, she's pure heroin."

Sergei listened, his head lowered, as if he'd been insulted on purpose.

"Can you imagine the mayhem she'd cause in Handia? She holds nothing sacred. Even all our females say the collective's got itself a hussy. You'd get recalled . . . and our Lariska'd get driven out."

They went back to the head doctor's office.

"Maybe you can talk to her and get her to marry him? And right away."

"What?"

"You see, we have this idea. His wife died, and she and this . . ."

"Alina," Sergei specified.

"Were friends. His wife even wrote that she wanted him to adopt Alina's child, so they'd be twins. She felt so so sorry for her."

"Masha was a very fine person," Sergei said suddenly.

An awkward silence.

Then Viktor Nikolaevich started back in: "Especially since he has to go abroad with the baby."

"Ah . . . I see. This puts the kibosh on travel, right? They won't let him go without a wife, right?"

"That's the general drift."

"So . . . she'd become Maria Sertsova. But what are we going to do with the patient herself? Rechkina?"

"By all accounts, she doesn't have anyone. So you could issue a death certificate."

"Wow. That's a lot at once. Could mean a hefty prison term, ha ha."

"Well, we will show you our gratitude."

"This means reaching agreements with all kinds of people. We have to bring in the pathologist . . . And slip something to the nurses . . . That, too. You know, I wouldn't want the information to leak out."

"But all the money would be handed over to you."

"I need a car," the head doctor said bluntly. "A Zhiguli. Money's money, and there's a lot you can't buy with it." She laughed. "Given our shortages." (This was her little joke.)

Unconsciously, she looked at her fingers. She still hadn't put on the ring, though she really wanted to. That would be dangerous at work. But where else could she wear it? Where do we ever go? Balls, for God's sake? Work—home—parent organizations, that's it. You can't wear it to someone's wedding or birthday party, letters would start flying into the office. And there was nowhere to stash that million rubles, it would be too obvious.

"A business discussion, food for thought," Viktor Nikolaevich replied. "A car is where they've drawn the line for us."

"After all, I'll have to rewrite the medical history. And you know what? Organize a nice gift for her. You men have no imagination. Fruits, candies, cookies—that sort of thing. Two liters of milk every day. She's going to have to feed your little baby! What's she going to feed it with? Our soups and kasha don't count. No one's bringing her anything. I know all about it. While your wife was . . . well, alive, she gave Rechkina food. You can add a note, 'from an anonymous friend.'"

18

ALINA:
Remote Matchmaking

THE NEXT MORNING, Alina walked into the head doctor's office again.

"So, Rechkina. You're being offered a fictitious marriage. Very serious people and they'll pay well. Don't turn them down."

Alina looked at the head doctor frazzled, haunted even.

"What? Are you joking?"

"Oh no, I'm quite serious. They have no other choice. They need a nursing mama to nurse the baby. You'll wean him, you'll go your separate ways, and they may even pay you. And there's one more condition. You won't be living in Moscow. He's being sent somewhere. It's the husband of Masha Sertsova, who died. Agree."

A pause hung in the head doctor's office. Alina stood there, looking out the window with crazed eyes. Then she woke up and suddenly asked, "But . . . how much will they pay?"

"For crying out loud! Not a scrap to your name, and all you have to do is wash your feet and drink water for them to take you. You'll take what they give you. Understand? You're going to haggle? You lose your baby and you're all teary-eyed, and now you're ready to haggle. You sure wise up fast."

"I didn't lose anyone. Remember that! No baby at all!"

"Now now, I just meant . . . it slipped out . . . I realize it's hard for you. Here, have a sip."

She took her bottle of good brandy from her lock box and an ordinary faceted glass from the water carafe. And splashed a good third full. "Drink, drink. You're starting a new life. And remember me. That I advised you to take life as it is and not to fight it. I'm worried about you, too. About all of you, like a mother. Agree. Look, something always turns up. There aren't any honest people. There are only people who haven't been offered enough."

Clear as day, the head doctor had already applied herself to the bottle more than once.

"Here I am, an ordinary woman. I've got them all on my back: my daughter and her husband and child, my son, my mother, my husband and his mother. She's already peeing herself. But she has a tight grip on us all. And then there's my husband's brother, that so-and-so. An alcoholic. I've already raised two, better fed than taught, a daughter and a son, Oleg and Marinochka, and I'm supporting them, too. And their families. Finished? Have a candy. Ask your new family, they're bigshots, ask them to help me get an apartment for my daughter. As it is, they're all three living in one room. Or maybe not. Then there'll be an extra room and he'll start getting ideas and decide to divorce her and do an apartment exchange. But I do need a Zhiguli, my God I need it, maybe you'll put in a word with them?" the head doctor concluded abruptly.

"No, I'm not going to ask them for anything. I'm not. Period."

"Ah. Well well. Look out or I'll offer them another candidate and quick. I've got a girl here, seventeen, no comparison to you, a real bombshell. Wants to get rid of her baby, too. In the sense of leaving him with us. A prostitute, just like you. Wants money for her daughter, too. And her milk's come in."

"Who's a prostitute? Who's doing the haggling here?"

"Oh!"

"Offer anyone you like. I'm a student at Moscow State University. In my fourth year. A top student, by the way. A year from now, I'll be in grad school. I'll forget all about you. And your hellhole. Babies are going to die here, with you."

"You're not yourself. Any maternity hospital—in our situation it's a nasty business. When there's no equipment, no qualified doctors, I'm the only one here for all our patients. Yes! Some don't survive. It's nobody's fault. Difficult pregnancies. Your baby, he wasn't long for this world. He'll be better off with them there, believe me, than he would with you."

"Where is 'with them'?"

"What did I say? Better off in heaven. With the angels." She stank of alcohol. "With the angels . . . you know, the angels in heaven."

"Ah."

"If these . . . well, they . . . agree to your candidacy, which was my idea, then they'll talk it over with you tomorrow. Tell the head nurse, Lidia Semyonovna, tell her to let you into the shower. You can wash your hair. Otherwise you're like a vagrant. You're a beauty. Look at that, your eyes opened up. Blue eyes, you're in fine shape. Come, come. I do wish you well. And all that."

"You wish me well!"

"So you see . . . you'll be Maria Sertsova. You look like her, by the way. She's with the pathologist right now. I went down there. A marble beauty. There's misery for you. Understand? Don't be so upset. It's not such a disaster."

"What about my passport?"

"Oh that. Your passport will be destroyed. They'll write you up as deceased."

"Give it back."

"Don't get any ideas!"

"And what if they reject me, how am I supposed to live? She has a completely different biography, and she probably has a mother, and a father. A different field, three languages. When I come back with this name they'll figure out I'm not her in no time. If I have my own passport I can get reinstated at the university. And start my life where I left off somehow."

"I don't know. It's up to them."

"Whatever, but that's my condition. Money in advance . . . and my passport."

"Oh, so that's what you're like? I don't know. Go and get washed. Ask them for shampoo. Lidia has it. She lives out of town, in the country, she commutes two hours each way and bathes at work. Yes! You have to keep pumping. Your job is to keep your milk."

"Maybe they'll give me all my stuff? My underwear, skirt, and sweater? My boots?"

"They'll give you your underwear right away. Wash it out. But the rest of your things look like they were pulled out of your ass. We don't have irons here. Ask the senior nurse for another robe, a better one. Tell her I said so. But the boots—you're right."

19

Sertsov's Marriage Proposal

AT THE EVENING feeding Alina sat pumping into a jar.

And all of a sudden an orderly came in with a big package.

Milk, fruits, cookies, and foreign vitamins. Expensive soap. Wipes. But not a word, not a note with a name.

"But who's this for? Me? Really?"

The orderly nodded and left.

Her neighbors exchanged looks.

The next morning a nurse came for Alina, a different one, but also in heels.

Alina's hair was washed, they'd given her a nicer robe, and her washed things had dried on the radiator. Alina pulled on her pretty high-heeled boots. A very different matter.

She went into the office.

The two men, one old, one young, looked at her. The older man nodded. The young man sat indifferently. Red eyes.

"All right then," the older man said. "Tomorrow, you'll be discharged, Maria Valerievna Sertsova. Right? You have the basics. The rest will be in proper order."

"The baby will stay here for now," the head doctor interjected. "We have to keep an eye on him. More than likely, we'll transfer him to a specialized hospital. You never know what surprises there might be. His blood isn't quite right. His deceased mother did have a health problem, after all."

Alina wanted to interrupt and say there wasn't any problem, here she is, me, his mother, sitting here—but she bit her tongue.

"Yes, we have to build him up," the older man said.

"You'll bring expressed milk twice a day," the head doctor continued. "First here, and then, possibly, to the hospital. Never mind, you'll do fine. Go on, girl."

Alina didn't look at Seryozha, and he didn't so much as glance at her. Why should he? Neither of one of them had had any part in the decision.

She turned and walked out.

"Therefore two death certificates: for Sertsova and for Rechkina," said the older man.

"For sure, for sure," the head doctor responded.

"And for Rechkina's baby."

"I'll see to everything."

20

The Story of Tamara Gennadievna

AT THAT MOMENT the plane was landing. Grandma Nina Georgievna was meeting Valery Ivanovich and her daughter, Tamara Gennadievna.

They wept bitterly, embracing. Valery Ivanovich was stoic. No emotions whatsoever on his pale, haggard face.

"When is the funeral?" Tamara asked.

"We were just waiting for you." And Grandma Nina burst into tears.

They walked to the exit and got into a Foreign Ministry car. The ambassador in front.

They unlocked the apartment, where the furniture was covered with sheets, the chandeliers in gauze, the windows bare.

The far from young Tamara and her mother went to get rags, brushes, and buckets.

General housecleaning ensued.

"After the funeral we'll have to have a wake ... Get people together ... We'll have to call everyone, her friends will come. Seryozha, Masha's friend from the library ... Schoolmates," the grandmother said.

"I don't know. Whatever Valery decides," Tamara responded.

"What's that supposed to mean?" Nina Georgievna gave a start.

"Well, he doesn't like that sort of thing ... Strangers ... He doesn't see the point. A mob. We'll sit with our family. Drink a toast. Drink a toast."

"What's with this drink a toast, drink a toast! You keep going on about drinking a toast. Fine. Then I'll have a wake at my house." The grandmother shook her head. "Listen to me. This just isn't decent."

"True, it's not. You're right."

"How she cooked! The pleasure she took!" the grandmother started crying. "And instead of that a funeral. I wish I'd died first, oh Lord!"

Nina Georgievna, a Muscovite Georgian, started tearing her hair out. Tamara didn't try to stop her and did nothing to console her. Silently she wiped the dust off the windowsills and radiators with a rag. Pulled the sheets off the furniture. Nina Georgievna dropped to her knees and started scrubbing the floor with her hands.

"Use a mop, Mama," her daughter said sternly.

"My legs won't hold me, daughter dear." And she lay down on the dusty floor.

The ambulance came presently. Nina Georgievna was taken to the Kremlin hospital. As the wife of a former and mother-in-law of a current ambassador, she was "contingent." But the contingent suffers even in Kremlyovka conditions. Four people to a room, snoring all night long. They might serve dinner on covered trays, but what good is that?

By the time of the funeral, the grandmother was in a very bad way. They wouldn't discharge her.

But they still hadn't given them the infant. They were studying him for something, or maybe treating him. Tamara Gennadievna had a serious talk with the head doctor. She spread her arms:

"There are still concerns. The baby is very, very, very weak."

"You'll answer for everything, I assure you," Tamara Gennadievna said in parting.

"Stone, not a woman," the head doctor said to her secretary as she left her office. "Granite."

At that moment, a large, pregnant lady entered the waiting room.

A minute before, they'd bumped into each other in the corridor—Tamara and this lady. Exchanged looks. Recognized each other as equals. Karakul coats, the moiré pattern of the finest silky pelt, an unborn lamb pulled out of a live pregnant sheep's split-open womb. Both had coats like that, a coincidence. The creation of the special atelier for certain government departments. Only Tamara was wearing a black silk scarf, a sign of mourning, while the lady wore a polar fox cap, the elegant headwear of Central Committee wives.

21

Kirkoryan's Delivery Prep

"AH, ELENA KSENOFONTOVNA," the head doctor exclaimed with unfeigned pleasure. "We have everything ready for you. A room on the second floor."

"Is there a telephone?"

"Yes. It's the staff room number, of course. So it'll be busy at times. Let's go, I'll take you there. Only you'll have to remove all your clothing and give it to us. Did you bring a robe, nightgown, socks, and slippers?"

"What do you think."

"Who brought you?"

"My driver, Ivan."

"What kind of car?"

"A black Volga, that's what kind."

"They'll give him your things."

"A black Volga."

"Yes, yes."

"Don't get it mixed up," the lady said. "First ask him his name. Ivan Petrovich. Here's the license plate." She wrote it down. "Except the coat."

"No, give him the coat, too. Security here isn't all that . . . you know, there's a little mustiness . . . a sort of mold. Everyone complains about people being admitted unaccompanied, and there are single mothers and no one to give their things to . . . Fur coats stiffen up."

"But what if I have to go out?"

"Oh, they'll discharge you tomorrow! Why should you have to go out?"

"No. I have to be here five days. That's what people expect."

"Hmm. You know. We only have one room like that. For very complicated cases, when we have to urgently . . . It's actually a small OR."

"I don't understand. Didn't they call you?"

"Fine, yes, fine. Well, we're agreed. Five days it is."

"When will they bring the baby?"

"Today, Elena Ksenofontovna, so . . . you'll give birth tonight. At five in the morning."

"Better seven."

"No, it's already written down."

"Change it."

"I see. All right, then, fine. Rewrite everything. We've already got the seals and signatures here. They'll bring you the baby tomorrow in the late afternoon to see him at the first feeding."

"I won't have milk."

"They'll still bring him. They'll feed him later. We have mamas expressing milk. He'll get a full portion."

"I want to . . . with a bottle . . . I need to practice."

"Fine then, under guidance."

"Let's go. Oh my God."

"It's all right. Don't worry." They went out into the long corridor.

"Me? I'm not worried. Rest assured. I always get what I want. Even my little Grant knows nothing. That's how far it goes. I grew my belly specially. Ha ha ha."

"Really? Ooh. Very funny."

"He praised me. Said I was his rare treasure. He liked my belly. Turns out, men need cows like that."

"It's like the old joke, a real man just pretends to like dry wine and skinny women."

"You and I know that men have pretty young secretaries at that age."

"We do know and how. From personal experience."

"A baby's the one thing that binds. I come from a town where there was a nuclear explosion. They didn't write about it anywhere. Chelyabinsk . . . Lots of people can't give birth. But I was determined. I took yeast and beer on purpose and ate my fill of pastries and cakes. Rolls, anything starchy basically. Fifteen kilos! You're a beauty now, he said."

"You look very good."

"And now I'm going to diet for five days."

"What for? Lots of mamas don't lose weight after giving birth. They drop ten kilos in the birth. It's barely noticeable. Ninety-five kilos, eighty-five, who can tell."

"Ten kilos in five days. I'll try. I tell myself nothing's impossible."

"That's dangerous for the heart."

"I'll use the Bragg system. Have you heard of it? You can fast for five days without damage. So. You'll call my husband at seven in the morning and say I had a boy."

"Yes. Three point nine kilos, fifty-two centimeters."

"His name is Grisha. Tell him, 'Congratulations, you have a boy, Grigory Grantovich.' Oof! I got the shivers. I have a son!"

"He's not born yet."

"Right. Right. How is he doing, putting on weight?"

"A real hero! He's gained back the weight to what he was at birth."

"Meaning what? You mean he lost?"

"They all lose weight during the first few days. It's hard work being born. Now he'll add it back."

They stood there waiting for the elevator.

"And how much weight has he added?"

"Well . . . a hundred grams in three days."

"Not enough. We need more. I want for me to lose weight over these five days and him to gain it."

"Oh, you'll have everything you want."

"I've got the shivers. I have a son! Do you understand?"

"Hey, what's holding up the elevator?"

She banged on it.

"You see the way things run around here . . . And who would want to work here? Believe me, we have probationers in the kitchen, the cleaning woman, too, we keep them, but what can we do, the pay is embarrassing."

"Convicts?" (The lady pronounced it "convicts," like they do in prison.) "That's all I need. I have to keep my things safe."

"Oy, that's not the only way out of a situation." (Laughter). "You'll be coming to see us in a couple of years and we'll find a little blonde girl for you."

"Oy, don't say that! Now, don't forget to give my things to the driver in the black Volga. Especially my fur coat."

They went into the elevator and disappeared.

22

Tamara Gennadievna
Goes on the Warpath

TAMARA GENNADIEVNA WARILY came out from behind the bathroom door, black as a thundercloud.

She'd heard it all.

She took the stairs down and found the janitor shaking out a rag over her bucket.

"Good evening!" Tamara Gennadievna said.

"Same to you, unless you're pulling my leg," the slightly tipsy janitor replied.

"What's your name?"

"Whatsa."

"Whatsa, I need a cleaning woman for two days. To do my floors. You'll make good money. How much do you make?"

"Oy, comrade, don't ask."

"You'll get two days' pay, cash in hand."

"In advance, comrade."

"I don't know you from Adam. You could drink it all and skip on me."

"Me? Who, me? I don't drink. Today's my birthday."

"What did you turn?"

"Whatever you say, sweetheart."

"Okay, shall we go?"

"Right now?"

"When else? My mother's been taken to the hospital and I can't manage myself. We're getting ready for a wake."

"Who died?"

"My daughter . . ."

Whatsa gave a low whistle.

"With us, you mean?"

"Why else would I be here? I came for the certificate."

"Well, sweetheart . . . I'm on the job 'til morning . . . So no dice."

"Fine. I'll send a car to the front door for you tomorrow. I'll even come myself."

"Oh! I'm going for a ride. My name's Auntie Sonya. Though I'm younger than you."

"And your full name?"

"Sofia Stanislavovna Dorsh."

"Tomorrow then?"

"Unless you're pulling my leg. You need something?" The janitor suddenly looked keenly at the woman, who was standing there charred, shriveled, in her fine coat. Exactly like a member of government at a funeral. Oh, right! Her daughter died. She wants to clarify the details.

"You know, lady," Sonya said. "I'm the very bottom here, right? But I'm not for sale. I don't forget a good deed. I won't squeal. I'm not like that. I wait for the streetcar, ha ha ha."

And an alcohol reek burst from her open maw.

"Tomorrow then."

Five minutes later, Sofia Stanislavovna was struggling out of the bathroom with a bag of garbage. A nurse was lying in wait:

"Auntie Sonya, leave the garbage for now. These things have to be taken down to the front door. There's a black Volga waiting. Is that clear? The driver's name is . . . I forget. Well, it's a common name . . . Ugh. Here's a slip of paper with the license plate. Basically, there's a black Volga and you have to take these things to it."

It was snowing. One black Volga drove right up to the front steps. Another stayed where it was.

Sonya, wearing two robes and rubber boots over bare feet, a waffle-weave towel wrapped around her head, chilled, shuffling her scrawny little legs, leapt out onto the front steps. She was carrying the bundle in both arms in front of her belly. The slip of paper with the license plate was fluttering in her hand.

The black Volga by the front steps honked and flashed its headlights. The back door opened. The driver said, "The daughter's things? In here."

"Just a minute," Sonya bleated. She wanted to check the license plate but couldn't finesse it.

When Sonya stuck the bundle on the seat, something happened to the piece of paper, carried off by the wind, so to hell with it.

Sonya darted back through the maternity hospital door.

The black Volga stayed where it was, waiting for someone.

And right then its passenger, a black scarf on her head, came out of the maternity hospital and got into the car—which whisked around the turn and vanished.

In the other car, parked a little farther away, also a black Volga, the driver was sleeping a driver's honest sleep.

23

The Story of Kirkoryan's Coat

WHEN THAT DRIVER woke up, his watch said midnight. No instructions had come in. Wait? Leave? The driver thought and thought and went back to sleep.

In the morning, at the appointed time, eight thirty, he drove the car up to the front door.

His festive, albeit rumpled, boss came out. The car started to smell of brandy.

"My son was born!" his boss said. "Last night! All of a sudden!"

(Sometimes his boss had a wonderful way of putting things.)

"Oh! Big news," the driver replied. "Congratulations."

"All of a sudden, understand? Three point nine kilos, fifty-two centimeters."

"Big news."

"Here, take this." His boss put a nice big bill on the front seat.

"Really, you shouldn't have," the driver said slowly—and pocketed the money.

"Drink to his health. His name's Grisha."

"I don't drink," the driver replied, as usual.

"You should start," his employer exclaimed, as usual.

"Ulcers," the driver explained.

"All the more so. Brandy's the best medicine, you know."

And they were off. The car arrived at his place of work at five to nine. The boss was never late.

At five after nine, though, the secretary went down to see the driver. His boss was summoning him upstairs.

He had a strange look on his face.

"Did they give you her things? Her fur coat?"

"Her fur coat? What things? When?"

"Yesterday, at the maternity hospital."

"No."

"What, did you sneak out?"

"I was parked there all night," the driver said slowly, turning red. "By the front door."

"Right."

His boss dialed.

"Get me Kirkoryan. Hello! Lena! No, he wasn't given anything . . . Hello! Say something! Lena! Well . . . okay. I'll call back."

He hung up and without looking at the driver said, "Ivan! It turns out someone stole all my wife's things."

"I was parked there, she told me to wait, and I waited. No one came."

"Did you fall sleep?"

"No! I was up all night! There were no instructions!"

The phone rang.

"Yes!" The boss listened for a long time, nodded silently, doodling acute angles on a slip of paper. Then he said, "Right away"—and, gripping the receiver, said to the driver, "The hospital cleaner says she gave the things to a black Volga. That was parked by the information desk."

"How am I supposed to know!" the driver implored him. "No one gave me anything!"

"Hello!" the boss barked into the receiver. "You there? Don't cry! Your mama called and says you shouldn't get worked up or else your milk . . . I mean . . . it'll stop. But I don't think you have any anyway,

I forget. Lena, darling, here's how things stand. It turns out Ivan was parked by the maternity hospital door all night. You didn't give him any instructions. How did you send the note?"

The driver shook his head, pursed his lips, looked up at the ceiling, and spread his arms palm up, like a Muslim in prayer.

"No, he says no one brought him anything. Your things and a note? Did you see the things?"

The driver thought and shrugged.

"And he didn't see anything. No, he says he wasn't sleeping. Why would he lie?"

The driver looked sharply to the side, out the window, and twisted his mouth sideways. All his thoughts could be read clearly on his face. They were obscene.

"Don't be getting upset. So it's missing . . . I'll buy you a new coat, you know that . . . But of course! Mink. I'll do what I can. Naturally, we'll clear this up. The janitor delivered the things? Well. Well. We'll take the janitor to court. Have her put on probation at her job. There's no point firing her. Yes, and they'll take it out of her pay. Compensate . . . how's that . . . Whatever you want as far as the driver goes. He'll compensate us, yes. Fine."

He hung up wearily and said, without looking at the driver, "You're going to resign. Unless you want to go to prison."

24

Tamara Gennadievna and the Janitor

AT NINE IN the morning, Tamara Gennadievna was sitting in someone else's Moskvich near the maternity hospital, by the door marked "Maternity Admissions."

She had to wait nearly an hour for a tear-stained, puffy-faced Sonya to finally skip out into the freezing cold. She was wearing a dark blue satin robe over her coat, cheap patched felt boots, and a green woolen scarf. Her small nose, red. Her eyes behind glasses, red.

Tamara opened the door:

"Sofia Stanislavovna!"

"Go to hell!" Sonya swore. "I'm in no mood for you!"

But she got in the car, in the back seat.

And immediately told her they were taking her to court for stealing.

"How am I supposed to know? They said there was a car there, a black Volga, and I gave it to him! They've been yelling at me since nine o'clock! The head doctor and that . . . that one from Ward Twenty-Six. In stereo! They brought her in yesterday to give birth. I'll tell you one thing, though, she sure as hell didn't . . . but she yelled as if she did! Like I stole her fur coat! Yesterday Lida gave me a bundle in a white sheet. I didn't even look to see what was in there! And I swear I took it to the black Volga right away! And she's taking me to court. Again! Black Madonna of Częstochowa . . . From Ward Twenty-Six! Just think! I'm

124

already on probation as it is! I'm working it off here! Who else is going to wash their shit for that kind of pay! Now, it turns out, I'm a repeat offender! Two years in a penal colony! And what am I supposed to do with my housebound mother? And who's going to visit my son?"

"Who was that yelling? That chubby one? With the rings on her fingers?"

"Who the hell knows. They're all chubby! No flat bellies here!"

"In Ward Twenty-Six," Tamara Gennadievna repeated. "She gave birth did she?"

"The hell she gave birth! She did not! She's standing by her bed and yelling! She rang for me! Went straight at me with her claws! And the head doctor was right there, too! Galina Petrovna!"

"Wait here a minute," Tamara Gennadievna said, and she got out of the car. She opened the door marked "Information Desk." Inside, on a small window, there was a list of last names and ward numbers. The new mothers' names were accompanied by a standard "Congratulations." Listed in Ward 26 was E. K. Kirkoryan, boy, 3.9 kilos, 52 centimeters. Date of birth today, seven in the morning.

"Sure," Tamara Gennadievna, the wife and daughter of professional spies, told herself.

She returned to the car, walked around the back, rummaged in the trunk, got back in, and continued her conversation with the sober and vile-tempered Sonya.

"Here's what, Sofia Stanislavovna. I can see we won't be getting any work done today. You didn't sleep all night, am I right?"

"Let's face it. There are no nights in a maternity hospital. Actually . . . my mother's at home with Parkinson's and I'm the only one to give her her shots. And they pinned a shortage in the store on me. But I'm no thief! I'm no thief!"

"Fine," Tamara Gennadievna said brusquely. "Then let's do this. Do you have a telephone at home? Let me write down the number. My brother's a lawyer. He'll help you."

"All against one! All against me!"

"I'm writing. Okay. That's that, go on."

Sonya got out of the car and nearly fell down. Lying in the road was a bundle wrapped in a sheet.

"Fuck a duck!" Sofia Stanislavovna shouted, bewildered. "What the hell? This is it!"

And the poor janitor picked up the bundle and dashed back into the maternity hospital.

25

Sergei Collects Alina and the Baby

SERGEI ARRIVED AT the maternity hospital to pick up Alina bringing Masha's things, her small suitcase, which Masha herself had packed before she left. He handed it all over. Plus a bottle of good Hungarian Tokay and a cake for the nurses.

Though they didn't give them the baby, who'd been transferred to the children's hospital, to the neonatal unit.

An hour later this young woman walked out the front door. A total stranger. Carrying just Masha's small suitcase, which she immediately handed to Sergei. But it looked as though she hadn't touched any of it. She was wearing a badly wrinkled gray fur coat and a fur cap that poked up like a stake. She had no suitcase. Just a purse. No things of her own?

Sergei sat next to the driver. Alina took a seat in back. A foul, musty smell came up in the car, like some kind of medicine. Well well.

Ah. That's what mold smells like. That's what it smells like in warehouses.

They didn't talk.

They got to the apartment.

"Don't be opening up to the neighbors now," Sergei said in an immediately overfamiliar tone and without even saying hello. "Otherwise they're really going to wonder. Basically don't answer the door. Or pick up the phone. I've found another apartment for the time being, my friend's—he's gone abroad. Masha's mama is coming tomorrow, she'll take her things. You know, her photos, letters, and papers. Try not to show your face here in the afternoon, understand? Up until around four."

"I'm going to the dorm early. To find out about my things. But by five o'clock I have to bring the milk. I'll go to the hospital and express it there. You don't have to worry."

"You know best," he said expressionlessly.

They fell silent. She made no effort to keep the conversation going.

Sergei realized something and said, "I'll try to get my mother-in-law to come a little earlier. Here's my phone number. At work."

"Fine. I need to buy a few things . . . Food . . ." Alina mumbled.

A pause hung in the air.

"There are good pirozhki at the university cafeteria," Alina finished up uncertainly.

"I can eat pirozhki," Sergei replied, surprising himself. "I like them with jam and with meat."

This was their first family conversation.

"They also have them with liver and with cabbage."

"Whatever. Buy them. I'll come from work on the late side."

"Fine."

"Around eight thirty. And the day after tomorrow we'll move to the new place. We'll have to hang out there for two months until departure."

Alina didn't reply. What was there to say? She had no part in the decision.

They got out of the car. And proceeded to the apartment. Sergei took off his coat, put on slippers, and went in. Alina removed her stiff, pathetic coat, cap, and heeled boots, spent a long time putting it all away in the foyer, and then, unable to bring herself to put on Masha's house slippers, walked into the main rooms, where she stood stock-still in just her socks, surveying her new housing. For some reason, she couldn't bring herself to sit down.

Sergei went casually into the kitchen and put on the kettle. Took cheese and sausage out of the refrigerator. Sliced the bread. Took cups out of the cupboard. Poured the tea.

Shouted to Alina, "Soup's on!"

Alina went in, took a seat, and sat there like a dolt.

They had their tea. Alina had to restrain herself from scarfing down mouthful after mouthful.

"I need a jar," Alina said.

"A jar?" Sergei perked up. "What kind?"

"To pump milk. I'm supposed to deliver it this evening, and I'm still not ready. The baby has to be fed breast milk."

"Ah. You know, look around. Masha should have had something here. I have no idea."

"And I need a pot to sterilize the jar."

"You'll find it all here. It's time for me to go to work."

"How am I going to come in and out?"

"Ah! That's true. I'll show you now. It's pretty easy. Two locks. Here's the key to the top one."

"And the address?"

"Here, I'm drawing how to get here from the metro. And writing the address. Make sense? I'll be back at eight thirty."

"Yes. What should I call you?"

"They've been calling me Sergei since first thing this morning. And you'll be Masha."

"My name's Alina. Right. Give me some money."

Another pause.

"What am I supposed to buy pirozhki with tomorrow?"

"I don't have it now. Tonight."

26

Sergei and Lariska

SERGEI WAS AT WORK, talking on the telephone, typing up documents. Larisa, his secretary, an unremarkable young woman with glasses, stuck her head in:

"Will you be soon? I've got to run."

"Where to?"

"An appointment."

"Who with?"

"Oh, you don't know him."

Sergei followed Lariska to the utility room, they secured the door with a chair, and as usual, had sex. It was their daily ritual. Lariska was an easy lay. She made no claims on him, didn't ask for presents except maybe for International Women's Day, New Year's, and her birthday. True, she did take small sums, allegedly for a taxi home. And occasionally asked for a loan. For that reason Sergei suspected Lariska had someone else besides him, otherwise where did she get those nice, expensive things you could only get at a foreign-currency store? Not only that, she had a husband and two children waiting at home. It was a mystery why Lariska gave in right away, from the first day he grabbed her ass in the hallway. He took her straight to the utility room, with all the mops and buckets, securing the door with a chair leg, and quickly got down to business. Lariska herself solicitously opened her mouth. Good girl.

Maybe Lariska was convinced that if she didn't put out for her bosses they'd fire her. She was an average worker not noted for her literacy.

She'd been hired by the previous chief, hired for specific needs. Lariska was young and fresh, she wore miniskirts and high heels.

Even then Viktor Nikolaevich would sometimes invite her to join him on his couch.

"The most beautiful female body I've ever seen," he said to Sergei once after Lariska went out. Said it so lustfully.

True, Sergei didn't notice anything special, just another female, good specifically because she never turned him down.

When Masha got pregnant, she was terrified of a miscarriage and excused herself from sex. They kissed sedately, like relatives, and slept in the same bed like children, sharing a blanket. Masha loved to sleep with her head on Seryozha's shoulder. Seryozha loved putting his arms around Masha and inhaling the scent of her hair. He cut her toenails for her when Masha couldn't bend over anymore. He scrubbed her back in the tub. He listened to the baby kicking in her belly. Every night, she gave Seryozha's weary back a massage, drummed with her puny fists. She waited for him to come home from work like a god. He would come home after Lariska pacified, happy, guilty, and always brought something tasty from some store downtown.

Lariska did everything efficiently, properly.

"Lariska," he said to her, closing up, "do you get anything out of this?"

"Of course," she replied. "What's up with you?"

Liar.

"What do you get?"

"Health. It's good to eat sperm. What's got into you?"

"But why do you do it for me?"

"I love you, silly. Listen. I have to pay for childcare. Lend me some?"

This was a thing with them, lending. He counted out thirds. One for you, one for me. And one for her.

They parted coolly. On the way home, Sergei thought long and hard about what kind of person Lariska was. She sucked up to the bosses, but what did she really feel? What did she think of him?

Only Masha loved him alone. She'd loved him for years without any kind of hope. And it wasn't about bed. Masha, Masha.

He shed a few quick tears in the metro, standing right by the door.

27

SERGEI AND ALINA:
Family life

NOW SHE'S HOME. A dummy with two big sacks in front. And a fat belly. Gushing blood. A drop on the bathroom floor that morning. Earth mother. Would Masha have looked like this, too? A milk machine. A cow. No. Masha was always comforting, with her warmth, goodness, and concern. Masha was a soul, not a body. How selflessly she'd fought to make her parents register him! She didn't get anywhere, though, and couldn't bring herself to sue them to divvy up the apartment, so their relations were spoiled and her father never talked to her at all. But Seryozha started grad school and registered at his dorm. And they got married anyway. By then they'd latched on tight to each other, like two halves of a single being.

But what about this girl, what did she feel? After all, her baby died. And now she was collecting milk for someone else's son. That is, she was thinking about him, worrying about him. Clearly she knew the lay of the land, knew that everything, her whole future, depended on it. At least for the next three years.

He came home. Alina was sitting in front of the television. There were clean, empty bottles in the kitchen.

"What happened? Didn't you take the milk?"

He grinned.

"I did. They gave me these clean ones for tomorrow."

She fell silent.

"You know . . . You didn't even leave me money to get there . . . I rode without paying."

"Ah. Here you go."

He put the money on the nightstand.

"You know, the head doctor told me you were going to pay her."

"What for?"

"Well, this whole business."

"We did. I gave her the money."

"What about me?"

"She didn't give you anything?"

"How could she do that?"

"Hmm. Well, don't go expecting the money from her."

"Right."

"Spilled milk, as the English say."

"Really?"

"I don't have any more. I'm flat out. I've borrowed a lot as is."

"Well, that's that," Alina said. "I guess they tricked me."

"Yeah, I guess they did. Me, too."

He sighed with relief.

Went to the kitchen, where he shouted, "Are we going to eat?"

"Yes, thanks."

"You mean you ate?"

The television was muttering something.

"Okay. I guess we're each going to eat separately?"

Sergei rallied.

All he could cook was fried eggs and jacket potatoes. He washed the potatoes and clattered the pot on the fire. Took out a skillet. Poured oil into it. Cracked four eggs. Gave them a quick stir. Tossed in some old dried-up sausage. Let it cook. Carried the skillet to the table.

"Want eggs?" he shouted into the room.

She heard him, turned off the television.

"Sure."

She definitely hadn't eaten. There was just as much cheese and that piece of sausage in the fridge as he'd left. The bread hadn't gone down either.

"You need to get your strength back. Bear that in mind." He said that and laughed. "Seeing as how you have to give milk, like a cow."

"Right."

Sergei divided the eggs in half. Sliced the bread. The potatoes were cooking. He added two frankfurters to the potatoes.

She ate quietly, delicately. Unhurriedly. In small bites. Sergei shoveled it in like he'd worked all day at a factory.

Masha had always greeted him with dinner. She'd come up with something . . . There were always snow-white starched napkins, a candle in an antique holder, a little flower in a crystal glass.

"We need to buy some groceries. Without Masha I didn't really eat."

"I can go tomorrow after I pump and drop it off, I'll stop by a store. I'll leave at seven in the morning. And probably be back by nine."

"Meaning leave you more money?"

"Right. I'll bring you the receipts later."

"Receipts? Oh, okay."

"And where's the store here?"

She was going to cheat him, of course. But what choice did he have? His son would be showing up soon. One way or another, she was going to have to keep house. God forbid she ran away. Not that she had anywhere to go.

"The better store's right here, on Nizhegorodskaya. Turn left at the front door and it's on the corner."

"What should I buy?"

"Whatever they have."

"Milk, kefir."

"I'm not great on dairy. I shouldn't have it."

A pause. Alina looked aside. She was the one who needed milk.

"I'd like frankfurters," he continued automatically. "Sausage . . . canned fish."

"Do they have that?"

"Well, yeah. Sometimes they do. True, the lines are long. I can't do lines. This they gave me at work, we have a standing weekly order."

"And I always ate in the cafeteria."

(She wasn't going to mention the restaurants.)

"Where did you live?"

"In a dorm. But I've already requested academic leave. They've probably moved me out. My things are lost, most likely. My girl-friends say other people are living in my room. They don't know any-thing about my things. They took me to the hospital straight from the airport."

These thoughts brought tears to her eyes.

Sergei jumped in: "I still have Masha's things . . . You look about the same size."

"You know, my heart's not in it."

She was being honest.

"It's up to you. Where are you from anyway?"

"I had a house. Near the Zagoryanka train station. My mama died."

"What of?"

"Tuberculosis. She was in the hospital the last year, and she died in a sanatorium in Crimea. They wouldn't let me see her. She's buried there."

"Gotcha."

"She commuted to Moscow for work as long as she could. She traded at the market to the very end."

"Gotcha."

"Flower seeds. But it can get very cold there. She was trained as a plant breeder, she graduated from agricultural school. But then I was born. She would get up at four in the morning, even in the freezing cold, every day but Monday, and go to the market. You have to pay for your spot there, too. At first she had to set up on the street. On vacations we would help out."

"A working education."

"But she was already very weak. Constant pleuritis."

"What about your father?"

"My father abandoned us. It was only when my mother died, he came and moved into our house with his wife. I'd started university by then and was living in a dorm. My brother enlisted in the army. I come home on the weekend, and there's this dog running around loose and some woman starts telling me I'd better not be coming around. My father comes out on the porch and waves me off, 'Go away.' And after the army my brother got married, he stuck his nose in there, too, and that same woman told him, 'I'm not letting you in,' and he went to live with his wife in Dedovsk. And my father turns out to have two more kids."

"Heavy stuff," Sergei said, bored.

"But I had the prospect of grad school. And a room in the grad dorm. My academic advisor offered it to me."

With the emphasis on "offered." He got the message. She was implying she was an honest student.

"Which department were you in?""

"Russian, in the School of Philology. The ancient classics. I guess it's not very trendy."

"To say the least. You know Old Church Slavonic?"

"Well, so to speak. It's a dead language. There's lots that's unclear about it. I went on archeological digs twice. Novgorod the Great, have you heard of it? It makes a scholar of you. But I was too busy with my personal life, naturally. So it ended up a total disaster. The baby died, and I had nowhere to go. Oh, the utter misery."

"What languages do you know?"

"The Slavic ones, mainly, Bulgarian, Polish, Czech . . . I can't speak them yet, but I read them. And my English is so-so. I translate pretty well with a dictionary. I also had to read a little literature in French."

"Good. You should go to bed, you have to get up at six."

"Five. I have to be there at seven with the bottles. Excuse me, I'll move over there."

She sat down in the corner of the room and took all her belongings out of her bag: two wrapped cloth sanitary napkins from the maternity hospital, a mayonnaise jar . . .

She thought, "Where am I going to get enough money for at least some underwear and a second pair of socks? I have to wash my sweater, too, and dry it on the radiator."

Sergei went into the bathroom, splashed around, and then disappeared somewhere. She slipped into the bathroom.

Sergei turned out to have gone to bed on the kitchen sofa. She washed all her underwear, the blood-soaked napkin, her sweater, her socks, and her undershirt.

She took it all with her and spread it out on the radiator.

She searched the closet and found a man's shirt and went to bed in it. What could she do?

She couldn't wear anything of Masha's.

She spread old newspapers under her so she wouldn't get blood on the bed.

She found a whole bag of absorbent cotton, Masha had stocked up. It takes so much money to acquire things!

She didn't have anything at all.

Anyway, tomorrow she had to go to the dorm to see Faina. To rescue what she could.

Oof. She'd never known this kind of poverty in the full sense of the word.

If Sergei knew the baby wasn't his, he'd drive her out in a flash.

She prayed in her own way, "Lord, forgive me. Lord, have mercy on me and my little boy. We have nothing, we're alone in the wide world.

Me and my little son. The only way I can save us is through cunning, by concocting something."

There was a little money on the nightstand. A miser, though, that Seryozha.

28

Tamara Gennadievna and Zokha

"HERE YOU GO," Sofia Stanislavovna, the maternity hospital janitor, said. "Can I pour you some? I'm a guest but I brought my own. We can't expect kindness from strangers! Here you go. Have some? No? Fine then. I"—glug-glug-glug—"was walking by and overheard. This lady was shouting right in Nursery Forty-Eight: 'He looks so much like my husband, I want this little boy.' Well . . . to your health! So. Galina the head doctor offers her the one that girl from Ward Forty-Eight, Rechkina, wanted to leave at the maternity hospital. But this lady dug her heels in. 'I want the other! The Maria Sertsova boy.' We register the babies under their mama's name. The nurses said they'd already drawn up a death certificate for that Rechkina baby, we have a pathologist, you know, a doctor for autopsies. In pathology in the basement." (She said it very distinctly: path-o-lo-gy). "She'll sign anything for money, Dr. Kanaeva. Any diagnosis you want. But if a mother abandons her baby at a maternity hospital, according to the rules there's all kinds of red tape, documents to draw up, and then he has to stay with us for a month. Then he gets sent to an orphanage for infants. But there's a line for children, too. And it's big money. So all they do is they just declare them dead. We have the highest mortality rate. I'm standing outside Ward Forty-Eight, the nursery, on the fourth floor. The thing is"—she took a healthy swig—"great port, Kavkaz port, I bought it specially, try it. I know a thing or two about that. I'm a specialist but I got fired. A production engineer in the liquor industry. Here's the thing. I'm mopping the floors in the hall near Nursery Forty-Eight and I can hear everything. We have the adult wards numbered the same as the nursery. They're coming out, the head doctor and this definitely not young woman, so I make myself scarce fast in the ward across the way. Forty-Seven. Pretend I'm wiping down the door from the other side. No one's wiped it down for ages. The window's all cloudy. But I can hear everything. They left. I went back to finish mopping the floor in the corridor. I've finished up and just started for the nursery when I see Galina Petrovna, the head doctor, at the end of the corridor again. I go back into the ward across the way. Galina, the head doctor, she slips into that Nursery Forty-Eight so fast! And I say, 'Girls, I'm back, I didn't finish wiping down your door.' Our nurseries are numbered the same as the mothers' wards. I don't have anything against her, against Galina the head doctor, but what did she want to go taking me to court for? You saved me, though, slipping me that bundle. You sure as hell didn't have to. They would have put me in prison. But I have a mama who'd be left alone and paralyzed. To croak." She polished off the half-full glass. "And no packages for my son. He's been in prison for over a year. But I didn't take their fur coat!" (Which brought her back to a detailed recounting of the previous day's incident.)

Tamara Gennadievna interrupted her.

"And what happened then?"

"So I creep out into the corridor. But the door to the nursery is right across the way and not shut tight. I see them unswaddling both babies, switching their bracelets . . . and switching their cribs. We have each crib in the same position as where the mother has her bed. So they don't get mixed up. The nannies aren't always so sober. You know, the fathers bring them stuff, at discharge. That's what I'd tell you, dear lady. Then I mop the floor there in the nursery. I look especially to see who she's switched. There are four cribs on the right, and two beds by the door, Alina Rechkina's son and Maria Sertsova's son. I tell you this has to do with the baby that died. Ah! I guessed right! Your daughter's. That's it! But they told the other one that her baby died. And they put him where the other one had been. Is that clear?"

"Not yet."

"Just a sec"—she chugs some. "What I mean is that Alina Rechkina's baby . . . right? Is now Maria Sertsova's. And Maria Sertsova's boy . . . pour you one last? No. Good. Hic! So Maria Sertsova's baby is going to this woman. Oy! Where are you going? Don't cry! Ah! So thank you for the money. This is a big deal. I . . . I've been wanting to buy my mama a wheelchair. To take her for walks. I can't carry her. She hasn't seen the light of day in a long time. She lies there yelling at me, I never see the light of day! As an invalid, she's entitled to a wheelchair, and they offered me a wheelchair after one invalid, they died, yes. But it cost too much for us. They take twenty percent from my pay. They wrote off a big shortfall in the wine department to me. Thank you, dear woman. I'm a trained production engineer. My mama calls me Zokha. You can call me that, too. You're like a mother to me. I respect you so much, just like family. Let's hug."

"The babies have to be switched back somehow," Tamara said, cutting her off.

"A production engineer in the liquor industry," Auntie Sonya kept hammering away at that. She plunged into her past, lamented, shed a tear. "Then I worked as an ordinary salesclerk . . ."

"I'm saying, the babies have to be put back," Tamara stood her ground. "Hey! Sonya!"

Sonya blinked.

"Oh, no, she's taken your baby back to her ward. That lady. Even though it's prohibited. Even though he's been declared dead."

"Well, think of something! What?"

"I'm all mixed up . . ."

"So . . . Sertsova's baby is with that woman?"

"You said it. Not only that . . . her husband's in the prosecutor's office. I'll sing you a song you haven't heard." She started caterwauling, "Oh, my maple, my fallen maple!"

"Ah! Now I see. While we ordinary Soviet diplomats . . ."

"Did the maple ice over . . . or something?"

"Fine then. Thank you, Zokha."

"Thanks for nothing."

"Fine. Will you have some brandy?"

"Yeah. Sure! You said brandy? You have some? Why didn't you say so? Fuck a duck!"

They drank.

"Here's some more money for you. You'll call me and tell me all about it. You'll be my informant. I work for the KGB, understand?"

"Why are you spinning . . ."

"Fine then. Godspeed."

"Who do you think I am? I'm a pro-pro-production engi-engineer . . . Mama! My dearest darling mama! She's waiting unwashed! And they won't let me onto the metro." Tears gushed from her eyes. "M'drunk! What now? Walk? Trolleybus? All the way across Moscow?"

"Ah. My driver will take you home. Let's go. I'll get you in the car."

"You're v-v-very nice, my beauty. Before, after prison, I lived with this woman, Teodoraki, she looked like you, respectable. From Sukhumi. She had this . . . s-s-say . . . s-s-say . . . s-s-saying: 'Zosya, make me a baby.' Sometimes they call me that Zosya, or Zokha. Zokha Dorsh, fuck a duck . . . But who I really am . . . mum's the word. A pro-pro . . . duc . . . tion engi . . . neer."

"Go, go on."

"Let's get married!"

"Good Lord. There's the door! Not that way!"

"One for th' road . . . for th' road! . . . th' road! Where's your . . .? Call my granny . . . Powder my nose." She started wailing. "O-o-oh, my fallen maple . . . No, wait up." Coming from behind the door. "Tiny steps . . . in a blizzard oh . . . so . . . white! Or who's seen . . ."

"The elevator, the elevator. No, I'll push the button myself. Listen. I need that scum's address. Elena Ksenofontovna Kirkoryan."

"Easy as pie. Hic! Hic . . . ofontovna. No, it's . . . it's hard."

After she saw Zokha off, Tamara Gennadievna went back to the kitchen and polished off her brandy.

Not that there was much left.

29

Alina and Faina

ALINA SHOWED HER pass and took the elevator to her floor in the university dorm. Her room was locked. She set off to find the super.

The super wasn't in.

She went to the next floor to Faina's. Knocked, went in. Faina was lying there smoking. Wearing Alina's sweater. She turned red and rose up on one elbow.

"Hi, Fai."

"Discharged?"

"Faina. I have none of my things. None at all. The super's out and my room's locked."

"There's an Uzbek and a Latvian, second-year, living there. They probably have all your stuff."

"Faina, give me my things."

"Fuck if I have any of your things."

"I have nothing to wear."

"Sell your baby."

"Did you hear me? I have nothing to wear."

"What's that got to do with me?"

"You're wearing my sweater."

"Oh ... This? This was lying around in the hall ... Like a rag. I didn't know it was yours. I sleep in it."

"I need my socks and underwear."

"I haven't seen them."

"Faina. Be nice and give them back."

Alina nodded toward the cupboard.

Faina answered shrilly: "Just try rummaging around my cupboard! I'll tell everyone about you."

"And I'll tell Volkov about you!"

"Bitch. You are such a bitch."

Alina opened the cupboard and started methodically looking through the gross pile of clothes lying there, keeping the recumbent Faina, now red as a beet, in her field of vision. Everything was dirty and jumbled, like at a dump. That's Faina. Oh! She found one green sock, some dirty pants, and two stained T-shirts. She set them neatly on the chair.

Faina said, "The Uzbek girl Firyuza sold me that! You have no right to take it!"

She lay there fuming. She was reconciled to the reality, the scum.

Alina calmly turned back to the cupboard and found the most precious thing, her gray mohair top.

Right now, in the cold, this was just the ticket. She took the top and smoothed it out . . . A soiled collar. She started picking the hairs off the wool.

"You're a real pig, Fai. You live like one." At that Faina flew at her from behind, knocked her down, scratched her face, and threw her out the door. Her purse and documents flew out three minutes later. Without a kopek in it.

Alina said through the door crack, "Give me back my money!"

"You owe me."

"I'll go to the police."

"Nothing's going to happen to me! But go ahead and try," Faina shouted through the door, puffing away. "I'll tell them how you sold your baby! You gave birth but you don't have him! You don't!"

"He died."

"There you go! I know that hanky-panky! You sold him, sold him! They'll open an investigation! You'll be expelled for your absences! I'll tell them everything! They sold my son? Yes! Don't play the innocent. You're rolling in money! You're going to give me even more! Monthly support to keep me quiet! Get out of here! You Georgian ho! You tried to get that boy to marry you! He doesn't give a shit about you! I wrote his father all about it! When you dragged your Avtandil off to the registry! I'll go to the police! Selling your baby!"

Drained, Alina went to the cafeteria, stopped off in the bathroom, and looked at herself in the mirror. Her nice clean sweater, her admittedly enormous breasts. But still skinny. There was some kind of dirt on her face, a scratch under her eyebrow. Faina'd aimed her nails at her eyes.

Alina sat in the cafeteria aimlessly looking from side to side. Maybe someone she knew would turn up and feed her.

Oh! Looming up in the distance was Mbvala.

She waved to him with both hands. Happy to see him. They exchanged kisses.

"Alina! Wow, you've got quite a figure now! First-class boobs! What do you say we go up to my room? Where's Avtandil? Have you been crying? What a face! Listen, lend me some money! Just a little!"

"Mbvala! What are you talking about! I don't have a kopek! Faina cleaned me out."

"That can't be! Faina? Are you lying?"

"Honest! All the money in my purse! I actually wanted to ask you to buy me some soup and bread!"

"I'm broke! Not a kopek to my name! Where's Avtandil been? Where've you? I check and no one's in the dorm."

"Mbvala, I nearly died, and Avtandil's vanished somewhere. I don't know what happened to him."

"Oh, oh. Horrible. I feel so sorry for you. I know Avtandil left you. Dropped you."

"No, that's not how it was."

"Lend me some money. All of a sudden I'm broke."

"Where am I supposed to get it, Mbvala!"

"I know you sold your baby. No money? How can that be?"

"Not so! How could I sell my baby? What's the matter with you! Who told you that? I don't have enough to buy myself soup!"

"Faina. She said you sold your baby, but you're saying he died."

"Faina? Well that's just great. I don't have any money. Why would I be sitting in the cafeteria hungry if I had any money!"

"You mean you don't? You know, let's go pay a visit. They'll feed you there and give us something to drink. And some money. And you'll live well there. If you want, I have a friend. That's it! Let's go to his place. In the Lumumba dorm. He'll give you money. Three dollars. I've got another friend there. For two dollars. And we can find more at a dollar apiece. There's a lot there. You can spend the night. You'll put out for them."

"Are you an idiot, or something? Mbvala, you should be ashamed."

"A girl like you can make money. I can't."

"You can make money selling girls to your friends."

"Whatever. You'll find the price is different later."

Mbvala stood up and left.

Alina got up, took a glass, and poured herself hot water from the big samovar.

Drank two glasses.

Her breasts slowly started to swell up. "Oh Lord. I have to go pump. I don't have the energy. I didn't eat anything this morning, that Sergei sleeps in the kitchen. I have to take a glass of milk to my room for the morning and make a sandwich at least."

She could get her things back, of course. But what a scandal! And now, after that slut Faina had worn her things, she couldn't put them on.

That's it. I'm done with university. Maybe later . . . in a couple of years. When this leave runs out . . . I can get reinstated.

Nadka Semyonova, the senior advisor, walked by.

"Oh, Rechkina! You! Are you back? Hi!"

"Hi."

"Why do you look like that? Have you been crying?"

"As you see. Nadka, buy me soup and bread, okay? I'll pay you back. Faina robbed me, took all my money and things."

"Really? But you do know you're in trouble, don't you? Wait up. Just a sec."

Semyonova went to stand in line, dislodged something, and brought soup, a cutlet and mashed potatoes, and fruit compote on a tray.

"Eat."

"Semyonova, you're brilliant. I'll pay you back twice over!"

"Are you a fool, or something? You'll pay me back exactly this much." She held out the receipt. Alina put it in her purse and fell on the food.

"Here's the thing," Semyonova went on, "they're expelling you for your absences."

"But didn't you . . . Faina told me you didn't mark me down."

"Why? You were absent for nearly two months."

"But Faina told me . . . she'd spoken with you."

"Right. Rechkina. Who is it who could talk to me about things like that? I'm furious. Turn in your certificates, your certificate of illness, immediately, understand? You're supposed to get them for maternity leave, after all. Bookkeeping made an inquiry. Did your baby die?"

"How do you know?"

"Everyone's known for a long time."

"Great. He only died two days ago."

"So go to lecture. Go! They're very strict now!"

"I'm on maternity leave! I applied for academic leave!"

"Ah. Well that changes things. Who did you write to?"

"I put it in a letter addressed to Faina, she was supposed to take it in."

"You know, I don't think anyone ever saw that application. Write to me this minute. I'll take it in."

"I don't have anything . . ."

Semyonova rummaged in her briefcase:

"Here's a piece of paper. Write. To the Dean of the School of Philology . . ."

Alina decided to find out everything, though.

"Tell me, Nadka, Faina just said she even paid you half a stipend a month so you wouldn't mark me down as absent. And now I owe her a whole stipend."

"Where did she come up with that? You know, everyone judges this life by themselves. Faina is Faina. Write."

"You mean you know what Faina's like?"

"She's our certified crazy woman now. She doesn't sleep at night, drinks and all that, there's something going on with her, then she can't get up in the morning, can't attend lectures, and now the only person who could give her her freedom turns out to be a psychiatrist. She's been on leave over two months. She's quitting academia."

"Lord . . . I'm looking and wondering why she's lying there smoking during lectures. What does she live on?"

"I think she hooked up with Mbvala. He's always got visitors. She's gone to pot. Drinks. The auxiliary police check in on her but she's a certified psycho. She can do anything."

"Yes. She had a breakdown after her baby died."

"That's quite possible . . . Right! But did he really die? She tells everyone he's living with her mother and is sick and she has to send money. That takes the cake."

"You mean you didn't know? She kept not going to see her baby after the semester, kept putting it off, and when she finally did go to the infant home, they told her he'd died six weeks before and they weren't going to keep him on ice so they'd sent him to the crematorium."

"Meanwhile Volkov is paying her child support. Okay then, write the application. This is a waxworks, not a university. A terrarium."

"And she just beat me up and cleaned out my purse. Didn't leave me a kopek."

"Bring your medical certificates and you'll get two stipends. But within the month, bear in mind. You absolutely must bring them! The documents, those are the basis for your stipend. So you don't get expelled. You're an excellent student, Rechkina! What's wrong with you! They're proposing you for grad school. You and me. And all of a sudden you vanish. Maybe you gave birth, maybe you sold your baby… What's wrong with you?"

"It's all envy, Nadka. Ordinary human envy."

"Write. To the Dean of the School of Philology. Good. From Alina Rechkina. What's your patronymic? Vasilievna. Alina Vasilievna Rechkina. Fourth-year student. Good. Application. Then you'll take it to the dean's office yourself, understand? With your own hands. Don't shift it off on anyone. Scholarship and long-suffering Old Slavonic await us."

With the clear eyes of a top student, Semyonova, blinking quickly through her thick lashes, looked at Alina the way she would look at her own shining future—matter-of-factly, relentlessly, and apprehensively.

30

Alina the Thief

ALINA WALKED INTO the grocery. Stood in line for frankfurters. Waited her turn. Asked for a kilo and a half. They weighed them out for her and slapped a price on the package. She fought her way back through the line. And stood at the end of the line again. Waited through this new line. Weighed out three more franks. Went behind a door, slipped the kilo and a half under her coat, under her sweater. Got super cold, the frankfurters being frozen. Looked around and found an old newspaper. Which she slipped under the frankfurters. Otherwise she'd lose her milk. They'd had an experienced mama in the ward, and she'd said that if your breast swelled up, the only remedy was ice. Then the milk would stop.

She spread the frankfurters out evenly on the newspaper. Stood in the long line for the cash register at the exit.

Waited her turn. The cashier looked utterly frazzled, her gaze beleaguered and her cheeks crimson, inasmuch as people had come running to buy the frankfurters on sale as if there were a fire.

And there'd just been a dustup. Someone had skipped the line.

"Oh no . . ." Alina intoned at checkout when she looked into her purse. "Oh . . . no, people . . . oh no, what on earth . . ."

She started looking around from side to side, about to start wailing.

"My wallet! Oh, people!"

"Are we going to pay?" the cashier asked in a neutral voice.

"I'm a student! I just gave birth! What on earth's happening?"

"Pay, citizen," the cashier said in the same tone of voice. "You're holding up the line!"

Alina swiveled her head.

"Oh no!" she sighed. "Oh no."

She grabbed herself over the frankfurters hidden on her chest.

The people behind her grumbled: "What's going on! Don't hold up the line!"

"She was robbed," someone spoke up.

"So, what now? Are we supposed to stand here . . ."

"Okay," the cashier said. "Give me the frankfurters."

She picked up the packet of three pathetic frankfurters with an iron grip and set it aside.

"Find your wallet and skip the line!"

"In your pockets, check your pockets!"

"Did it fall?"

They spread out as best they could. Everyone started looking under their feet.

"Next," the cashier announced. "Don't just stand there like a scarecrow."

Alina shifted haplessly to the other side of the checkout and ran her hands through her pockets. The people who'd been behind her were already gone.

Biting her lip, eyes cast down, she went out with eyes half shut.

All of a sudden, at the entrance, the cashier ran her down and handed her the package of three frankfurters.

Alina was scared out of her wits, turned red, and tried to refuse.

"Take it. They won't be any the poorer," the cashier said sullenly. "They walk off with bag loads of them. And you're a nursing mother."

She nodded at Alina's hilly breasts.

Alina took the frankfurters, wandered off, and immediately hopped on the first bus that came by . . . in completely the wrong direction, blushing from shame.

She transferred and made it in time to the maternity hospital, where they took her into a room, gave her a napkin and a jar. She poured a glass of water from a pitcher and drank it all.

She started stuffing the frankfurters into her empty purse and couldn't help herself, she ate two.

And sat down to pump.

When she was finished, she ate another frozen frankfurter.

31

Tamara Gennadievna and Sergei

AT THAT SAME time, Tamara Gennadievna was having a talk with her son-in-law.

Tamara Gennadievna, mother of the deceased Masha, had shown up for her daughter's things.

They were sitting in the living room. On the table lay a packet of photographs and some documents.

"Where's Masha's passport, Sergei?"

"It must be at the maternity hospital."

"They said they gave it back to you."

"It wasn't there. What's the matter with you! I went to the window, they told me . . . about her death . . . and that was it, I left. Who gave me anything?"

"But how are we going to draw everything up?"

"I don't know."

"So . . . Are you going to give us the baby?"

"No. Why should I? The baby has a father."

"But you're going abroad, aren't you?"

"No. I'm not."

"But who's going to look after the infant?"

(That's what she said, "infant.")

"I'll find a nanny."

"Give him to me."

"No."

"Sergei! You know this is going to be a burden for years! Your whole life! And whoever you go on to marry, a stepmother is always worse than a grandma!"

"My mind's made up."

"Something's off . . . there's too much that's odd. I want to tell you something, Sergei."

"Really," he responded stonily. "I have no time, I'm sorry. I still have to run by work."

"You'll have time to *run by* and *run off*," his former mother-in-law said in a significant tone.

What was this? Did she suspect something?

There wasn't a trace of Alina's presence in the apartment. No toothbrush, no nothing. The sum total of her things consisted of two bottles, two hospital pads, and a mayo jar. One pad, dried, on the radiator. He'd hidden all of it in the fridge. His former mother-in-law wouldn't stick her nose in there.

"Will you at least come to the funeral?"

"Don't worry. I'll be there, Tamara Gennadievna." She'd already collected her daughter's photos and books, her notebooks. She didn't touch her clothes.

"Yes, Masha's there. And we're here. It's unfair, my dear." There was fervent Georgian sadness in her blue eyes. "I should have gone first."

"Don't say that."

"Listen," she began with terrible intensity. "They switched our boy. I know this for a fact."

A fevered look, a piping voice. She'd lost her mind.

"Yesterday I was in my car near the maternity hospital and a black Volga drove up, I have the license plate written down, a man went in with a bouquet and an hour later left with his wife and baby. They took your child, Seryozha. I followed them. I know where they live. I know the building. Does that interest you, Seryozha?"

"Of course. Naturally. How could it not?"

"There!"

" . . . except that it's impossible."

"Fine. We'll each believe what we believe. I'm going to steal that little boy. He's our little boy. You can raise whoever you want."

"Stealing children—that's not good," Seryozha said in Masha's voice.

"She stole our baby. She was supposed to take the one that single mother delivered. You know, the one who gave hers up. They declared him dead, that suits them better, they don't have to draw up all those papers. And, I assume"—here she pursed her lips for a second—"they don't have to pay the mother for the sold baby. Understand?"

"Not quite."

"In plain words, the supposedly dead child was intended for this Kirkoryan. But! She saw our little Seryozha and started shouting about how he looked exactly like her husband and she was taking him. My mama's a Georgian. And your child has dark hair! Even though both you and Masha are fair."

"My father was a Kuban Cossack, he had dark hair, too, and a dark mustache. He ran a stud farm. My mama's fair."

"Your mama's alive?"

"They died in a car crash."

"May they rest in peace." She crossed herself. "Here's the thing. This Kirkoryan, her husband's a big shot in the prosecutor's office. She has the head doctor on the hook, I don't know why, but that's for certain. They've been stealing children from that maternity hospital for a long time. Understand?"

"Yes. You have to calm down, Tamara Gennadievna."

Like all lunatics, she had it all arranged in a harmonious system. A chain of logically connected consequences.

The finale had to be a crime.

"Can I give you some tea?"

"No! And don't check me into a psych hospital! I have a witness. Sofia Stanislavovna Dorsh. Remember that!"

"Who's she?"

"The janitor, she's working off her probation, an alcoholic."

There it was.

"No one's going to believe her testimony."

"It's not like I'm hiding who she is. I believe it, that's enough."

"There are too many crimes. This one declared dead. That one switched. And a crime committed by a prosecutor's wife. And the witness is in prison, right?"

"Not in prison. She's working off her probation in the maternity hospital."

"It's just all these miracles," Sergei replied mechanically, and it occurred to him that arguing was pointless. He had to agree with her across the board. Otherwise she'd pile things on in a fit of temper.

"I'm only getting back our child."

"They'll put you in prison, you know that, right?"

"Seryozha, they won't dare call the police. Even if her husband is a hotshot prosecutor. They won't dare. I described it all, the whole story, and I'm giving it to you for safekeeping. If anything of that sort happens to me, give this notebook to someone at Radio Liberty."

"I can't be in contact with them."

"Well, you'll find someone. If only that lover of yours."

"Excuse me?"

"You know who I mean."

"You may know more than I do."

"When I steal the baby, I'm going to call you over to look at him, so you understand. All right?"

"I hope you aren't going to do anything illegal."

"But I need your help. I need a car with you at the wheel."

"And where am I supposed to get a car?"

"Ask your Viktor Nikolaevich for his, for a few hours tops. And put on a KGB license plate."

"What does that have to do—"

"I'm the daughter and wife of counterintelligence. And a lieutenant myself. But that's not for public knowledge."

"You can tell this to anyone you want. Just not me."

"You're refusing?"

"I don't have the capabilities."

"My husband is in danger of a heart attack. You have to help me. I need a car without a driver and a switched license plate. They'll take him out for a stroll, and I'll swoop down like a whirlwind. They can't not take him out for a walk!"

"Tamara Gennadievna, it's not like we're in the Caucasus! These aren't the wild mountains! There are people everywhere! This is kidnapping! Abduction!"

"I'm going to do it, I assure you. This is our Masha's son, to say nothing of the fact that it's your own child. I'll do it even on foot, if I have to. I have an entire layette ready, I brought it back. All my neighbors know Masha died but they still haven't given us the baby. *Us!* Understand? I'm rescuing him."

"Don't."

"What do you mean 'don't'? Don't rescue your own child?"

"Tamara Gennadievna, don't pile all this on me."

"I haven't slept in seven days."

"That's obvious."

"Well, you've never been known for your manners."

"This can't be our Seryozha."

"Seryozha, yes, it's Seryozha, I assure you. I met a deeply unhappy woman who gave birth in this maternity hospital and who was told her baby died. Now she's gotten a job there as an aide under a fake name so she can clear things up, get at all the documents, check all the options. They sold her baby!"

"Right . . ."

"No, I haven't lost my mind the way you think. I'll call you later and invite you over to look at the baby. And very soon! Masha's baby was stolen!"

"I repeat. Don't do this! Under no circumstance will I support you!"

"Fine then. My mind's made up. After Masha nothing scares me. You know she visited me yesterday."

"Right."

Bingo. His mother-in-law was bonkers. Horrors.

"She visited me in my dream and said, 'He's not my son, he's not my son.'"

"Okay, all right. I'm sorry, I'm in a rush."

"I understand, you're in a rush to see your lover. She's always in a rush."

"What a load of gibberish."

"Masha told me about her."

"In a dream?"

"No, she complained over the phone. Shortly before she gave birth. Every day, she says, he's with her every day. What torture. He and that Lariska. He'll never get along without her. They've got themselves a Jezebel at work."

"What? Who said that? More gibberish."

"Maybe that's why Masha died. She didn't want to live anymore. She gave birth and left her baby to live but died herself. Masha had a very strong will."

Sergei started yelling with tears that surprised him.

"No! No! What's wrong with you! Are you trying to crush me completely? It's all my fault? What kind of . . . damn it . . . What do you take me for?"

"Lariska, Lariska. Lariska the devil, who blows everyone so she won't get fired."

"You spy. Fucking hell!"

"Goodbye, Seryozha. Look at yourself in the mirror."

Looking out from the mirror was a totally red face, twisted and ridiculous.

32

Baby Seryozha-Vasya

SERGEI AND ALINA took a car to the maternity hospital.

"Right. Grab the suitcase. That suitcase of Masha's. The layette's in it now."

"I can't. You take it."

"I'm carrying the cake and wine."

"I won't take it."

He had to lug it all.

They sat in the waiting room and waited for them to bring out the dressed baby.

They didn't talk.

Finally, the swaddled treasure emerged in the arms of the tipsy aide, Sofia Stanislavovna.

She mumbled, looking at the bottle in Sergei's hand.

"He looks so much like his father, the spitting image!"

Sergei stuck the money in her pocket and the cake in her hands.

She grabbed the main thing from him, the bottle, and read the label:

"May your life be a success, as sweet and strong as this beverage!"

They went out the front door, Sergei carrying the baby. A smooth-tongued voice wafted after them: "I hope it's a three-star!"

Alina lingered in the doorway, let Sergei go ahead, and heard something else:

"Doesn't take after the mother or father."

And the nurse's reply:

"That happens."

Riding in the car. Sergei holding his treasure on his half-bent knees. Alina could barely see the baby. He was already two weeks old. He must have grown.

Sergei put the baby in his crib and dashed off to work.

In the fridge, though, there was milk, two boxes, and kefir, and there were apples in a bowl on the table.

When did Sergei have time to buy all this?

Since that time Alina brought home that kilo and a half of frankfurters and nothing else (but she didn't bring the receipt either, said a girlfriend bought them for her and hadn't taken the receipt, Alina hadn't warned her to so as not to raise suspicions), and she'd looked unhappy and sick, and gone straight to bed without eating anything, Sergei had suddenly started taking on the groceries himself. He'd picked up something somewhere. During his lunch break? He arrived home like clockwork, at eight thirty.

Alina unwrapped the baby and looked at him.

Lord! He'd grown so thin! She barely recognized the little man! Just his little nose poking out. He'd changed.

Or was this not he?

Skinny and translucent. A few curls plastered to his head.

Both of them had had that.

He'd grown.

She washed his chest and his little face, wiped everything carefully with cotton wool, everything.

Brought him to her breast.

He wasn't suckling. What was going on! He was smacking his lips but not making suckling movements. He'd forgotten how!

This was him. MINE.

Weak, no appetite.

She didn't know what to do.

"Eat, little one! You have to eat, Vasya!"

For some reason he was already Vasya. First he was "my own" and then he was "Vasya."

She rubbed her nipple against his lips and stuck it in deeper.

He didn't know how, he'd forgotten how.

How was he going to survive? How had they fed him there, at the maternity hospital? From a bottle. So it all flowed freely, and he didn't have to work for it.

She'd have to pump and bottle-feed him, too. Oh, the misery.

All that milk that had come in had nowhere to go, jostling, eager to get out.

"Well? Suck, Vasya!"

She sighed and started to pull her nipple out of his limp little mouth when suddenly, at the last second, the little one latched on to the treasure slipping away and sucked it in. And suddenly started sucking— and how! Hurriedly, greedily. Alina nearly screamed in pain. Her breast was being squeezed savagely, with terrible force.

Not my own.

Or my own?

But when he leaned back, sleepy, a drop of milk under his nose, suddenly, for the first time in a long time, Alina smiled:

"Good job, Vasya."

Why Vasya?

Lord, this was happiness! Happiness being the absence of unhappiness. The baby ate his fill. Her breast emptied out.

She turned him upright and rested his little chin on her shoulder, so the little one would burp, the way they'd taught her at the maternity hospital.

A few minutes later, Vasya made a "pff." Air escaping. She could put him down to sleep.

He had other ideas, though! He started screaming!

We're not going to spoil you, though, Vasya. Holler away, you'll get tired and fall asleep. Otherwise you'll quickly learn that if you start screaming, that means we'll pick you up.

No. We have to teach you starting now. That's what Dr. Spock's book says. The one Masha gave us. Oh, Masha, Masha . . . Easy now! Easy now, Vasya. They barely picked you up at the maternity hospital.

He was screaming like a stuck pig.

She realized the milk wasn't the same as what they usually gave him. They fed him formula. That's why he'd gotten so thin. They must've fed her milk to someone else.

Sergei came running in at eight thirty.

Vasya squirmed. Started wailing.

Alina sat down next to him and read a book by Professor Likhachev (borrowed from the university library).

"Why are we crying?" Sergei asked.

"You know, I have no idea."

"Did he eat?"

"Yes."

"We need a scale, those old women said. We can rent one. To see how much he eats. Make sure he's not hungry."

"Fine."

He ran to put something on to cook. An omelet again, most likely.

"Did you eat?" he shouted.

"No."

Thank goodness they were on polite terms now.

He banged around. And appeared again:

"What's he crying for?"

He awkwardly picked him up.

Vasya immediately quieted down, like a radio turned off.

"Eh?" He said delightedly. "Well? Papa's home? Eh? Did you see the Wolf? Did you see our Bunny? Did Papa see the Wolf? Did he see my little crybaby? My bouncing baby boy?"

And so on.

The smell of something burning came from the kitchen.

"Oh, you . . ."

He dashed to the kitchen with the baby in his arms.

Alina burst into tears.

This was what Alina should have had in her life.

A bedroom, a crib, Vasya, and his papa, Avtandil, holding Vasya in his arms. That's what she'd dreamed of, that she'd have Avtandil and Vasya.

Just like that, with a wave of a wand, their apartment, their bedroom, and crib with Vasya. And Avtandil holding him in his arms.

"So!"

He appeared with Vasya.

"Take him, please."

She took him. Vasya was quiet.

She couldn't put him in his crib or he'd start screaming.

Alina went on reading Likhachev with Vasya in her arms. She'd be writing her thesis soon.

Tomorrow she had to go to the maternity hospital for her medical certificate. Ah! She'd get her maternity leave. She'd have her own money! She could run from store to store . . .

Get underwear, that was the main thing. A rattle for Vasya. Little Vasya was breathing as softly as a kitten. A contented little face. Like a Buddha. A handsome mouth, classical. A little Antinoüs. Lord, how amazingly fine!

How could she go tomorrow? She couldn't with Vasya. He was too small for traipsing through the city like that.

So this was the last free day of her life, right? Vasya was going to be with her all the time now? Every single minute?

Right. She wouldn't leave him. That's it.

Fine, then.

33

The Kidnapping, Continued

THAT ONE, THE mother of the one who died, is standing in the waiting room of the head doctor's office again, standing for as long as it takes, right next to the secretary's desk.

The secretary: "She's out. She went to the health department."

"And when will she be in?"

"Come tomorrow. Who let you in anyway?"

In that instant a sealed perfume bottle, a foreign brand, appears near the secretary on her desk.

"Fiji, Fiji."

"Ooh! Is that for me?"

"Yes, you."

"Oo-o-oh . . ." (that's how she said it, all drawn out). "Oo-o-oh . . ." And she slipped it in her drawer.

"It's a little thing, but a headache. My son-in-law, the husband of my daughter who died . . . well, you know . . ."

"Oo-o-oh . . . Of courssse."

"We've come from abroad for the funeral."

"Oo-o-oh . . . I don't know what to say . . . Horrorsss."

"Yes. In his panic he lost the birth certificate . . . The funeral, the running around . . . Can you give me a duplicate?"

"Of courssse . . . Oo-o-oh, I just can't . . . Horrorsss . . ."

"If you'd be so kind. And we can agree not to tell the head doctor."

34

At the Kirkoryans' after the Birth

ELENA KSENOFONTOVNA, LENA to her family, was reclining on pillows, bottle-feeding the babe.

Standing by her side, leaning over her, were the two grandmothers: the Armenian one, Eranui Aslamazovna; and the Russian one, Lena's mama, Eleonora Anatolievna.

Eranui was murmuring, "Oof... pure gold! Precious! How he eats! Num num! Grisha-djan! The spitting image of his father! His father ate well, too!"

Eleonora yet again, "He's not eating well. He should be taking in fifty grams, and he's doing well if it's thirty."

The baby ate a little and fell asleep. The grandmothers took him to the scale.

"He threw up!"

General panic.

"He needs changing! His outfit's wet."

Lena said, "Oh, give him to me."

"Lie there!" ordered Eleonora. "You're exhausted from the birth! I had such hemorrhaging after giving birth! It came pouring out! I bled for six weeks like a slaughtered hog! But I breastfed! I breastfed you to one year! I barely weaned you! But I couldn't not breastfeed because everything was contaminated, that damn Chelyabinsk. And still you grew up nice and healthy! And you were able to give birth! Thanks to my milk!"

"Ma! I've heard that story a hundred times!"

"But now you're in the same position, and now you understand! Eranui! Grant has to protect Lena! He should sleep on the couch!"

"That's news!" Lena replied. "Do you want to wean him away from me? Is that your dream? For us to divorce? So you can move in?"

"Don't be silly! I just remember how we all lived in one room—Senya, his mama, and you and me, and Senya slept on the floor a whole six weeks and slept like a dead man even though you hollered. Your so-called father. He never came near you, and neither did his crazy mama, only me, I'm bleeding, my milk's flowing, I'm so young, and you're crying out . . . Chelyabinsk . . ."

"Enough."

"Lena. But you have to finish feeding him! He threw it up, look! See, his outfit is all wet in front! He needs changing!"

"I'll warm the milk . . ." said Eranui. She grabbed the bottle and was gone.

"MAMA! What are you up to? Tell me! Why did you come? Please go away!"

"This is my grandson!!!"

"I'm wiped out. Go, I'll call you when I need you."

"Number one: Grant has to sleep separately. Two: let me take the baby for a walk while you get some rest. You aren't sleeping! Look at yourself! You're old, you have circles under your eyes! Dark circles! Messy hair! You need to see a hairdresser at the least! A cosmetician! Did I teach you to make a mask from anything? Yes, I did. That's what I do. If I'm making borshch, I apply beets . . ."

Lena groaned. "Ma . . . Oy . . ."

"Yes! If I'm making a salad, I put cucumber slices around the whole perimeter of my face. Or I chew it up, spit it into my hand, and rub it all over. And yeast, yeast with egg yolk and lemon. I brought you an aloe, where is it? Did it die? I brought it a year ago! You have to use aloe juice! Look at me! I'm going to be fifty-six, and I have the skin of a young woman! I take care of myself! You have skin like mine! Very difficult, problematic! Oily around your nose and forehead, and also your chin, look, but your cheeks and temples and especially your neck are dry! You have to know that!"

The baby started grunting.

"Give him to me! Give him! You know very well . . . My poor baby! What a pity he came into their family! Poor little Armenian! Everyone's going to tease him. We had Shakhpenderyants in our class. How didn't they twist that name of hers around! Can you imagine? But she was Assyrian, not Armenian, it turned out. Bootblacks. She and I got to talking, the most ancient race on earth, she said. Here's a dry outfit, let me change him. Let me!"

"No. Go home."

"Lena, darling, you're exhausted! You're crying! And that's bad for you! Tears dry out your face! You'll have early wrinkles, though it's already time for you. Late births are a dangerous thing, and a late child is at risk, too. We still don't know, oh my God . . . There should have been a neurologist checking him out! His speech development! I've read the literature. Fine motor movement! The violin! Pottery making! That's how they make deaf-mutes into people."

"MA!"

"Have you checked that he's hearing?" She clapped loudly. "Look, Lena, darling, he startled! He can hear, my sweetie pie!"

"How could he not! Even I startled."

The idiot Eranui poked her head in:

"*Merope spasy!* Just a minute, just a minute! I hear you! The milk's boiled over!"

She nipped back.

"Naturally, there's a burning smell all through the apartment. She doesn't even know how to use this kind of stove. Does she have a wood stove at home or something? A hearth? Like in Papa Carlo? Lena! Garik misses you so! Oh how he misses you! And you went and chose this one. Of course, you have an instinct. You saw he had a future. But Garik! Curls, golden hair! A tiny little nose! Tall and so slim!"

"That Garik works as a moving man at a furniture store."

"Really? Where?"

"The furniture store on Leninsky. Grant and I went there for this bedroom suite. I look, and it's Garik. Bald now. Stubble. A blue work jacket! He looks at me proudly. No, he says, I don't know you. Who are you, lady? I don't remember you. And he walked away."

"Lena! You dropped him, so naturally he took a bad turn. It was too much for the boy! Especially a professor's son!"

"Sure, he's his son, but his father left them a long time ago."

"For them, for men, this is the end and a disgrace. When they're abandoned and not doing the abandoning. We women, we recover quickly because I, for example, had a purpose in life: YOU! And my mama helped me a lot! Not like you, driving away your own mother. Oh! Grisha pooped!"

"How do you know?"

"It's that little wince . . . and then the smell! You mean your nose is stopped up?"

"A little."

"I knew it. I'll make you a gauze mask immediately! Even two to switch out! Where is your bandaging? You'll infect little Grisha! Right now! This instant! Come now, it's basic, a mask! All the doctors wear one even! Where is your bandaging?"

"In the kitchen, the drawer on the left."

"Don't get up, I'll find it, I'll find it."

She bumped into Eranui in the doorway.

"Nice warm milk. Just the ticket. Come, Lena, let me feed him. I raised six of my own. *Ay, vay,* Grisha-djan . . . there . . . he took the nipple. Eat, my darling!"

Then Eleonora triumphantly brought two gauze masks but was herself now covered in white threads. She kept trying to get her daughter to put on the mask.

Lena was sick to death of her.

Then Grisha fell asleep.

All three went to drink tea with milk. The kitchen was a disaster. Scissors lying around, the entire first aid kit disemboweled.

They bickered for a long time over whether to go for a walk. They decided yes, the weather was decent.

"Lena, dear, I'll take him out. While you rest. Eranui will feed you while I'm gone. Eranui, make her those cabbage rolls . . . dolmas, or whatever they are. I'll eat, too, when I come back."

Eleonora spent a long time getting dressed, as if for a space flight.

Grisha was an unattractive little boy, swarthy, big-nosed, eyes like on a Chinese person. Lena felt nothing for him, no feelings whatsoever. As soon as she picked him up, as soon as her husband, Grant's, eyes got nicer—and he made sure it was his son—that would be it.

She had no interest it him whatsoever. A baby cries at night. You have to get up for him. Worse than prison.

Finally her mama went off with the stroller.

Lena went into the kitchen and sat down.

Eranui had unleashed a storm of activity there; she had everything ready. Two minutes later, there was a platter of Armenian cabbage rolls on the table, and they smelled so good, you couldn't tear yourself away.

Lena went to talk on the phone, to find out how things were at work.

Ten minutes later, the doorbell.

Oh Lord! Mama, see, she forgot the bottle of warm water! Scatterbrain.

"Downstairs a neighbor kindly agreed to watch the stroller. On the bench by the front door. So friendly. Elderly. Her grandson is in the sandbox. She's not doing anything anyway. Otherwise I'd have to lift the stroller up eight steps. What an inconvenient front entrance you have! One more misery for you when you start taking him out for walks yourself. What you have to do is take the baby out and drag the stroller behind you. That's my advice."

They found the bottle, and now they had to boil fresh water and let it cool. Eranui advised adding a little sugar to it.

"Under no circumstance!" Eleonora exclaimed. "He'll have wind!"

"*Vay,*" the frightened Eranui responded.

35

Meeting Mishulis

THE BENCH BY the front door. The sandbox close at hand. A couple of children in it shouting various sound effects as they push a steel truck, a dump truck filled with sand: "Zhzhzhzh! Dzhzhzh! Ti-di-di-di . . . Ddddzhzhzh . . . Bshchshchshch . . ."

An elderly woman sitting on the bench, smiling. Steel teeth, knit cap pulled down on her forehead, a scarf on top of that, a fine scarf, imported, lustrous.

Glasses on her nose. Marvelous in a way. Strange overall. Rocking a stroller.

There'd just been a crotchety old grandmother in a short jacket and pants here, with a stroller.

She'd carried out a heavy stroller and sat down.

"Granddaughter?" The elderly lady with the bizarre apparatus on her head nodded to her.

"Oh no, bless you! A blue stroller! A grandson! Grigory! Grigory Kirkoryan! Grigory Grantovich Kirkoryan! Eh?" She leaned over the stroller. "Eh? Who's our little Grisha? Eh? Who's our little Armenian? Eh?"

"How old is he?"

"Ten days! Just ten! But the weather's good, they have a doctor on call, he stops by daily, and he advised a walk. A walk. Specifically! Not just the glassed-in balcony."

The lady in the bizarre headgear glanced condescendingly at the stroller. Her glasses glittered sharply.

"Blue eyes, is it?"

The grandmother smiled patronizingly. "Well, all little ones have eyes like that . . . cloudy." She started to squeal. "Did he open his little eyes? Did he?"

"He looks like you, am I picking up on something?"

"We don't know who he looks like, can you imagine? Possibly like me, but possibly . . . Sometimes it's a cousin. My late husband came out looking just like his uncle. Everyone was simply amazed. Are you a widow?"

"Me? As good as." She laughed and straightened her hat. "Does he have hair?"

"He's our curly-head. Dark."

"And what's his name?"

"I told you. Grisha."

A pause.

"An unusual name."

"It's a name in their family. They had a great-grandfather . . ." She glanced into the stroller. "Eh? Who's our little Grisha here?"

She bellowed so from pure joy that the baby started chirping. Fool. She rocked the stroller. The baby whimpered.

"You know what," the strange lady sang sweetly. "He needs a little water. Nice and warm. He's got gas. Is he being bottle-fed?"

"Yes . . ."

"So here's the thing. I can tell. I was a pediatrician originally. A doctor. Now I'm a neuropsychiatrist."

That's obvious, Grisha's grandmother thought, but she said, "Is that so."

"Bottle-fed babies always have to be given a little warm water after a feeding," this neuropsychiatrist insisted. "About thirty minutes after."

"Oh! Yes! How is it I don't know that?"

"There, you see."

"Now there's the whole business of dragging the stroller back. How on earth! And the doctor didn't tell them!"

"The doctor is one thing, but my Denis was bottle-fed, too." She nodded toward the sandbox. "Go get it, I'll stand guard. I've got a healthy boy over there in the sandbox, we raised him. It's no big deal. I take him out, even though I have otitis, inflammation of the middle ear." She touched the right side of her heavily girded head. "You go. I'm sitting here anyway. Before we went out I wrapped up my ear good and tight. So I'll be sitting here."

"Well, thank you. This is the first time I've taken the baby out. His mother is a real slattern. Lying around. I didn't lie around! I didn't have the time! I had the whole family to take care of! I was quick! Nora the rocket! But this is a late birth for her, you see, and tough going, too ... An older first-time mother. Twelve hours' labor. And a surprise for us, too. She was due in two weeks, but they brought her in for safekeeping."

The baby was growing agitated. The poor thing was whimpering like a kitten.

The grandmother rocked the stroller.

The lady with the ear said, as if by the way, looking toward the sandbox, "Go on, go get the bottle. It's dangerous for him to cry, the air's not that good. The air's a little cold for crying. It's winter, after all."

"Yes, you're right."

"Go get the water. Or he might suffer consequences after his very first outing. But the water has to be perfectly fresh. Just boiled. You know that, right?"

"Oh yes, yes, we know. But how?"

"Boil it, pour the hot water into the bottle, it's like sterilization. Then cool it off under running water. You know? I'll be here another hour. So there's no rush. Someday maybe you can return the favor when I need to run to the store. Or you can go to the store sometime and I'll keep watch. I'm always sitting here with my grandson. But I think this is the first time I've seen you."

"We don't buy anything in the city," the grandmother replied casually, standing up, the stupid fool. "We order from Granovsky. The Kremlin dining facility."

"Yes, so do we, but sometimes you need bread."

"Well, I'll be right back. What's your name?"

"Polina Ignatievna Mishulis."

That is, a typical Jewish psychiatrist with a bad ear.

"Mine's Eleonora. No, we don't eat city bread."

She was very definite.

And at that she went off, in her expensive boots pulled over her thick ankles. Piano legs. Trousers tucked into her boots, cowboy-style. Silly boob. She went up to the front door. The door slammed.

Three minutes' pause. No, another minute. Right. A holler from the sandbox: "Dzhzhzh! Dzhzhzh! Turn around! What's your problem? Really? What are you doing with the truck? Idiot, you knocked mine over!"

"You're the idiot!"

An answering shout from a bench: "Denis! Get up off your knees! Your pants are filthy now!"

"Right! Antosha! Really! Get up off your knees!"

A mama duet sitting slightly off to one side.

It was time!

The mamas were sitting like birds on a telephone wire, chirping away.

"It's time we cleared out."

Her heart starts pounding so! Her mouth gets so dry!

Polina Ignatievna Mishulis stands up, as if stretching lazily, straightens her glasses and her head, horned like a cow's, and, glancing at her watch, then at the front door, cheerfully pushes the stroller toward the metro.

Right then there's shouting at the sandbox, nearly a brawl, the mothers get up and stand over their children, their backs to the building.

"Why'd he have to push!"

"But it's not his steam shovel!"

"Cut it out, Denis! You should be ashamed. He has exactly the same one at home!"

"We just thought this would be enough for the two of you! Apparently not! What kind of friends are you after this!"

"Why did I drag this heap around for you at all!"

The lady around the corner raises her arm and stops a car.

Then she takes the baby out of the stroller and picks him up, and the driver folds up the expensive stroller respectfully, saying, "I know how, we have the same kind."

They drive off.

The car stops at a building. The horned lady slips the driver money and asks him to help carry the stroller to the elevator. The driver willingly agrees.

Then he runs down the steps, young and good-looking.

He slams the door and the car drives away.

The lady pushes the stroller into the elevator, puts the baby in the stroller, takes the elevator to the mezzanine, removes her scarf and hat, takes off the aluminum foil on her teeth and the big glasses, and it's Tamara Gennadievna.

She gets something white and lacy out of her purse. Stuffs everything she's taken off into that purse.

Picks up the baby and wraps him nice and snug in the white receiving blanket.

Then she takes the elevator down and gets out, leaving the stroller in the elevator.

She quickly goes down the stairs and pokes her head out the front door.

No one. She raises her arm.

Catches a car, a Zhiguli compact. Gets in back.

"See where that flower stand is? Stop there, please."

36

The Stroller

A DRUNK STEALS into the lobby like a shadow, his head full of air. Unzipping his fly, he dashes into the elevator—and look! A stroller, new and disemboweled. As if someone had just snatched a baby from it. And left.

Without even doing the necessary, the drunk looks around, listens closely . . . Not a soul. Lightning quick, he pounces on the stroller and carries it outside.

Pushes it on the double around the corner, farther and farther.

Enters a poor, rag-bestrewn room.

"Ma! Look! I found a stroller in an elevator! Somebody threw it out! Just look. Imported and new! And they left it!" An old woman is lying on the bed, under a pile of blankets. She smiles brightly. Seems to be looking at the ceiling.

Only after a little while, from the movement of her pupils, can you tell she's blind.

She has one arm lying on top of it all, bandaged at the elbow, a black stain running all the way around the bandage. The ambulance hit the wrong vein.

The one with the stroller: "I'll run it over to Tolik's sister, okay? We'll buy everything, okay?"

The old woman, softly: "Okay, Kolya . . . Okay. Go on, then. Get

going, then. To Lida's . . . Go over to Lida's . . . Kolya . . . The jar of sau-
erkraut . . . Take it to them."

Loudly: "Mom! Your Lida died a long time ago! I'm not your
Kolya!"

37

Tamara Gennadievna's Baby

NEXT, TAMARA GENNADIEVNA, flowers and baby in her arms, dials from a payphone:

"Valery! Here's the thing! The car we took from the maternity hospital broke down . . . Yes. The baby and I are on the street . . . Well, don't shout . . . Yes, I collected him after all . . . We can talk later . . . I'm on Leninsky Prospect, on the sidewalk by the House of Shoes."

Half an hour later a black Volga pulls up to a fine, light-brick building.

Standing by the front door are two women with bags.

One keeps talking, "So he says, 'Sue me. But I'm not giving you a thing.'"

"And he wouldn't let you into the apartment?"

"He totally blocked me! Oh! Hello!"

Both look wide-eyed as Tamara Gennadievna gets out of the car with the baby, a big bouquet of flowers, and her bag.

The driver takes her bag and bouquet and escorts her to the front door.

And then dashingly walks away.

"That's her daughter's baby. The one who died in childbirth," one of the women says, shaking her head.

"She has the baby, and that's a happiness."

"Oh yes . . ."

Both are practically in tears.

* * *

In her apartment, Tamara Gennadievna unwraps the baby with quick movements.

"You're all wet. I knew it. Valera! Can you come here for a minute?"

The television is rumbling.

The baby has started crying softly, plaintively.

Tamara Gennadievna dashes around, opens the cupboard, gets out a sheet, tries to rip it. It won't rip. She tears it with her teeth and it splits with a crack.

Rips it again. Wraps up the baby.

He's very agitated.

"VALERY!"

The television gets turned off. Heavy, disgruntled steps.

Two gazes cross like searchlight beams.

"What are you doing, cooking up this show? What kind of mother are you going to make? You're old, you're an old woman, understand?"

"Valery, it's too late for talk now. It's done. I'll explain later."

"Take the baby back. He has a father."

"That father . . . he let him go without blinking. Right in the maternity hospital, in front of the nurses and aides, in front of everyone. There's information that he has a new woman, that is, the one he had before. Lariska."

"So what are you cooking up? Lariska. We're leaving in three days!"

"You have to take care of everything. We'll hire a wet nurse there. We just have to get through these three days and draw up papers for him. We have to adopt him."

"What?"

"Valery. Don't make a scene. You don't want me to stay here, after all."

"What do you mean stay here. What does that mean, stay here?"

"And what use am I there? Why should I go there? An old wife?"

"The rot you talk. What old wife!"

"Everyone's just waiting for us to be recalled . . . over this sexual hanky-panky. I won't name names. Enough."

Turning red, he spoke his piece perfectly calmly. Called her an old alcoholic.

She just nodded.

"Valery. I'll stay here and file for divorce. I have no choice."

The baby she was rocking in her arms was silent.

"Masha's gone, and I have nothing else to live for. It's only for her sake. I sent her what I could. All I have left now is one thing—divorce and dividing up our apartment. Our property. And the money at the Royal Incorporated Bank."

"That's what you think, bitch," he replied quietly, obviously spooked. "This is your drunken ravings, that's all. You cooked this up, you cunt, you dipso."

"You're the dipso, and everyone knows it. They'll be recalling you for good soon."

"In your dreams, bitch."

They fell silent. He was panting.

She spoke very confidently and firmly:

"Two years ago you refused to register Sergei, and now he's showed us he doesn't need Masha. He's taken a junior wife. Masha knew about this Lariska. Masha didn't want to live anymore."

"One more thing you say is my fault."

"Everything in the world depends on everything else. My father hated you, and you never forgave me that. You did the same exact thing to Sergei. You didn't accept him. Sergei went down the same road. He responded to Masha the same way you did me. And the result? A baby is an orphan."

Her red cheeks and flashing eyes and this baby at her breast suddenly made her look fifteen years younger. Her usually smooth hair was disheveled, a mass of curls. Basically, the usually taciturn and restrained Tamara Gennadievna had now suddenly come out of hiding, grown a spine, and was celebrating this victory of hers. Her hour had come. With this baby in her arms, she was fearless.

"Take care of everything. Little Seryozha and I are leaving. We'll adopt him and give him your name and patronymic. He'll be your son."

"Why?" He said this sincerely, testily. "Why didn't you say sometime beforehand? Why didn't you warn me? How can I do anything in this amount of time?"

"You can. Now go."

"But . . . I'm not up on this. What will this take?"

"I have the baby's birth certificate and Masha's death certificate. If Sergei's consent is needed, you'll have to make do without. Understand?"

"How?"

"We had a fight. He gave me the baby but said he'd have his revenge and would do nothing for us. Because I gave him a fright in front of everyone, saying I knew about his hanky-panky and he'd see Handia the way he'd see his own ears."

"You did the right thing. I approve."

Oh, Valery was chickening out, starting to back down. She had to move on that. Tamara Gennadievna added fuel to the fire.

"Sergei promised to crush us. So do what needs doing without him. Call in all your connections."

"Who does he think he is! The pygmy!"

(Valery had taken this word from his contacts with the leadership of his country of residence, for whose representatives the very expression "pygmy" was an insult. The Pygmy tribe was the nation's disgrace, they hid them, sent troops into the jungles, although later it turned out that for the newly reviving young state the funds foreigners gave specifically to study this small, in every sense, people came in handy and most of those dollars landed in leaders' bank accounts.)

Valery Ivanovich even took a turn around the room, as if trying to wind himself up.

Tamara Gennadievna had studied his nature like an experienced animal trainer.

Sometimes he was a languid, inert cat too lazy to get up off the couch, sometimes a sophisticated and mighty boa constrictor.

And sometimes—like now—a has-been rooster.

"So you see, Valery, he won't make a peep about the baby. He'll never bring it up."

He nodded. He was used to the fact that his wife ("spouse," in military-diplomatic lingo) staked her life on what she said.

No idle promises, but if she said something, then that's what would happen.

"For now, call the driver and have him bring some Nestlé's powdered milk from the Kremlin pharmacy. I was planning to buy it if Masha's milk didn't come in." She tried not to cry. "Immediately."

The tears began to flow as she stood holding the baby and looked at Valery with big eyes.

Suddenly he actually started sweating and went outside, struggling to catch his breath. Masha was gone. That was the thing. Masha was gone.

He paced and swore, and his face looked like a small hurt baby's.

38

An Outing for Keeps

ELEONORA DID EXACTLY what that horned toad Mishulis had advised—boiled the water, carefully poured it into a bottle, and immediately ran it under cold water. Bam! A scream and the crash of glass shards against the sink. Eleonora jumped back, shaking her scalded hand.

Eranui, eyes wide, watched it all happen.

Lena came in and started screaming:

"Who did this!"

"You're lying there, so lie there!"

They spent five minutes blaming each other.

Now they cooled the water in three saucers. Eranui did everything. They cooled it. Poured it into a new bottle. Glory be! Eleonora made a quick pit stop before going, put on her coat, and smartly (new boots, trousers, gorgeous) slipped out of that madhouse into the fresh air. Oof.

No one by the building. Or in the sandbox or on the bench.

She swiveled her head. She ran all the way around the building.

Ran all the way around everything.

Her head light as foam, her mouth mute, her hands trembling, she ran and ran. Incoherently questioned passersby.

It started getting dark. Oh, how quickly it started getting dark.

She went into the building. And up to the twelfth floor, and started ringing doorbells at apartment after apartment.

They told her they didn't know any neuropsychiatrist Polina.

One old lady asked, "Who did you call her for?"

"No," the unfortunate woman replied, barely in control of her mouth, "I just need her."

"Where are you from?"

"I'm from apart . . . apartment twelve . . ."

And she started sinking, sinking, down down down, into the netherworld, into oblivion, into a heaven-sent heart attack.

And no one ever found out from her what happened to little Grisha.

And the investigation yielded no results.

The stroller in which Sveta, the proud janitor at House of Fabric, pushed her own son down Kosygin Street, did surface, though. She'd bought the stroller, imported, French, not at all her sort of thing, from some jittery drunk next to the pediatric clinic on Fifth Sovetskaya. The portrait the tear-stained Sveta drew was typical:

"Well, kind of a blue face . . . no teeth . . . about thirty, or maybe fifty . . . a dirty mouth. And a hat with earflaps. A . . . blue . . . nose. A mustache. Voice? Well, a drinker's voice. I don't remember the shoes . . . A very shabby coat . . . Hands? I think they were black. Sturdy as shovels. Oh yeah, wearing jogging pants, that's what. And rubber boots . . . What color? They were muddy."

"So was it a man or a woman?" the special investigator pushed her.

"Why a man? She was selling a stroller!" Sveta answered stupidly.

Sveta's baby, Maxim, was big and white as wheat bread, four months old. A giant. He was shown to the Kirkoryans.

Sveta's husband, a supply store worker, was a short man who didn't know anything about anything since he'd just come out of the DTs, specifically the Soloviev Hospital. Literally the night before.

"He's my spiritualist," Sveta delicately explained to the investigator.

"Why spiritualist?"

"Well, he likes spirits."

Kirkoryan was exasperated by the whole story.

His wife was acting like a crazy woman, sobbing nonstop, shouting.

Eranui wasn't crying, wasn't saying anything.

She didn't look up. Her son-the-boss didn't utter a word about his thoughts.

She went back to her Dilijan.

Eranui knew the boy wasn't an Armenian. More likely he had some Georgian in him.

Not only that, the bride didn't smell of a new mother's blood.

Eranui was a neonatologist.

Authorities all over the country pulled up and checked out all the Polina psychiatrists, and four of them were not given permission to go to Israel just in case.

A legend went around the neighborhood for a long time about the woman who lost her mind, lost her baby, and the mother who ran around afterward looking for a psychiatrist and died without ever finding her.

39

ALINA:
Three Years Abroad

ON DEPARTURE DAY, Sergei demonstratively set two suitcases in front of Alina, maliciously kind of, and said, "Masha's things. Take them. That's all you're getting out of me."

Once everything had been squared away and Handia had become a reality, he'd celebrated his victory by treating Alina like a lazy servant.

But that evening, when it was time to go to the airport, she silently went out the door wearing her own things, pushing the stroller.

In Moscow, it was late winter.

Alina had put on jeans and a cami and sweater and her fur coat over that and boots. Hanging from her shoulder was a small backpack, almost a child's: new clothes.

The thing was, thanks to course leader Semyonova she'd received two months' stipend, "maternity leave money" (thank God she hadn't lost her passport).

It wasn't much, but it was her own money.

With Vasya in her arms, Alina ran around to the cheap secondhand shops at the market, bought a couple of dresses, a robe, and house slippers with rubber soles, and was able to find used sandals.

Underpants, bras, and camisoles she was able to get at the maternity store by jostling in the lines. Masha's permission to use that store was still in her passport, she just had to add two lines to October.

That is, the paper had said X, and now it said XII.

All this fit in her child-size backpack.

In her other hand, Alina carried a huge briefcase with textbooks and dictionaries. She'd borrowed them from the library for the next three years. Her entire length of residence.

Alina had transferred to distance learning and planned to send her work in by mail.

When he saw this scene, Sergei cursed and refused to pick up Masha's two suitcases.

That was the moment he truly began to hate his life companion.

Who had her own opinions about everything, opinions that came totally out of the blue.

You're a servant, a wet nurse. Shut your mouth!

She, on the other hand, faced three years' hard labor with someone who'd been nasty from the get-go, nasty and callous, who despised his son's wet nurse and derived considerable satisfaction from that.

Sergei was angry. This was the continuation of the Moscow conflict between him and Alina, when she refused to wear Masha's clothes, but no opportunity to purchase anything had presented itself in Moscow, as official language phrased it then.

In the trade office you were supposed to make sure the wife of an upper-level employee was decently dressed.

"What are you going to buy here? I forbid you to stand in lines with the baby! And I can't babysit him myself. I'm working. What are you going to wear in Handia? It's forty in the shade there! Where are you going to buy anything? I won't allow you to drag my son around the markets! Fat chance of that! Now you're expecting money from me! Masha's father and mother sent you the very best things from their postings! And you go and turn your nose up! The only place you can buy anything like that in Moscow is at the foreign-currency store! But I don't have any foreign currency, and even if I did, I'll be damned if I'll let you rake it off me!"

He had a life plan: make enough money in Alaya for an apartment and a car.

He had no intention of spending anything on this stranger.

He enjoyed despising her.

In the morning, after they landed in their country of destination, they still had to transfer to their town, where the Soviet trade office was located. It was a three-hour wait.

The heat in the airport was hellish. Sleeping on the floor, wrapped up like mummies, were local inhabitants, a small child was crying, and Sergei vented all his frustration on Alina:

"You're dressed like an Eskimo on an iceberg! You're in the Tropics. Hello! Anybody home?"

Alina went to the restroom and, while holding the baby with one arm, used the other to remove her coat, hat, boots, and woolen socks, keeping on her trousers. She took her slippers out of her backpack and put them on her bare feet.

And what was she supposed to do with all this? She looked around.

The airport cleaner had evidently just emptied the garbage bin and changed the plastic bag for a clean one.

Alina looked around, and a Robinson by the name of Alina took the bag out of the bin, quickly put her belongings in it, and quietly returned to the waiting hall, holding a bag—a plastic bag the size of a pillow—in one hand, the baby in the other, and her backpack on her shoulder.

Sergei could only curse for all to hear when he got a look at that.

Fine, then, the locals didn't understand anyway.

Although the quiet, courteous locals did shudder and exchange glances at that thunderous outburst.

You weren't supposed to swear here, and even dogs and cats could tell this was swearing.

Intonation has a universal translation. Pent-up tears or laughter, kindness or threat—it all sounds identical in any language.

The only difference is in the gestures. The people of Handia and Bulgaria shake their heads negatively to indicate agreement, whereas in other countries it's the exact opposite. In Spain you pat yourself behind the cheek in reproach, in Western countries it's considered impolite to stare at a stranger, to say nothing of the disabled, whereas among us you're not supposed to smile in anticipation, though you can frankly stare at foreigners and mental cases dressed like who knows what.

In Alaya, the couple was given a one-room apartment with windows facing the sun in the trade office building, where all the employees lived in a hive.

The sole luxury? A pool on the building's roof with chaises under a plastic roof.

There Alina-aka-Masha spent all her days with little Seryozha-Vasya, and when the sun set, she went downstairs to her scorching hot apartment, took milk out of the fridge and rice out of the cupboard, and cooked porridge with banana.

For purposes of economizing, Sergei bought only milk, bananas, rice, and flatbread.

Soon after, winter set in, the rainy season. It was as hot as a steam room.

Nevertheless, Alina still went upstairs, sat under the plastic roof, read, and wrote.

She swam with little Vasya.

He learned quickly and at two months acquitted himself wonderfully in the water.

True, the other women were put out. A baby can't control himself, he might poop in the pool. And the water here was changed once a week if they were lucky. By then it had turned to bouillon.

Alina had brought a few used, well-washed diapers, a rare commodity in the Soviet Union.

The mamas here laundered, dried, and used them to the bitter end.

Now the infant was swimming, like a foreigner, in a diaper.

At night she awaited the usual torture. They slept in the same bed, and Sergei used Alina like an ordinary whore. Sometimes he contemptuously called her "Lariska."

A fight every night, she slept on the bare kitchen floor, and even there he came for her—and she dreaded every step—until finally it was too much to bear and her son would scream at the slightest noise. And she put up with it.

You never know, women ended up in brothels against their will, like slaves. Here you could either hang yourself or wait for your liberation.

This blockhead took satisfaction in telling her practically in a whisper, as he was getting up:

"You're a trash pit, a garbage pail. For getting dumped on! You came here! You thought, a foreign country, you'll make out like a bandit! You abandoned your own child. You're a milk cow, nothing more. Any girl off the street is worth more than you, at least people give her money, she knows how to do something, not like you, you lump."

One day he lost it:

"You think I don't know how to shake up the likes of you? A two-nipple board lying there. I know everything. Mike in our group, in the shower after basketball, nothing to look at, six centimeters, maybe, but he could stick it to them: 'She's got an itch she can't scratch, they're all of them satisfied when they leave me, they're lining up, they keep calling.' He kept saying over and over, 'I'm a lesbian man.' And now, you fucking whore, you'll get it from me, understand, you whore, and good. Even though I'm nine at rest. I couldn't to Masha, but you, you Lariskas, you don't care what you take, five or ten."

Alina—a delicate soul, gentle, the daughter of her unfortunate mother, but also the daughter of her despotic father—had to listen to all these unhinged speeches.

Unfortunately, she had a wonderful ear. Perfect pitch, as her piano teacher, Natalia Petrovna Petrova, told her mama at music school.

Only her baby, Seryozha-Vasya, brought her peace and joy during the day; that was all she had.

One couple with a baby was leaving for home, and they had a youth's foldout couch, and Alina exchanged her crib for it with them. They were sending their things by rail anyway.

So now she slept with Vasya on that foldout couch, next to the wall.

Her master couldn't let himself curse loudly, so he sputtered in his bed.

Panted demonstratively under the sheet, whacking off. The only thing that brought Alina joy was her baby, who she continued to nurse, her one nubbin of happiness amid her great misfortune and utter despair.

And her books in foreign languages. And the local holidays.

By the way, the locals' holidays were extravagant. These poor people, who had two handfuls of rice a day, had these incredible celebrations!

Some evenings, stretched out to the horizon along the empty pavement, not a single person or car to be seen (people crowded on the sidewalks or stood on balconies), passed magnificent columns of illuminated elephants and detachments of dancing soldiers in skirts and splendid uniforms, as well as the most important part—far off, visible hundreds of meters away, huge shining floats thundering music, with flat five-meter-tall figures of painted gods decorated with small burning, blinking lamps, hung with chains, giant jewelry, little flags, and panels of cloth. After them came carts with mobile power generators pulled by the shafts by men wearing national costumes, then came bands, and then little girls carrying pompoms, wearing identical short skirts, turtlenecks, and field caps, who swayed and jumped simultaneously. The beginning of such beauty!

It was a holiday, a delight in Alina's life, and she went downstairs and walked into the crowd with the baby, and they put a red dot on her forehead and joyfully surrounded the white foreigner at their celebration.

The trade office looked askance at such forays.

But she was already conversing readily with the locals, and they understood her, and responded delightedly, gave her candies and cautiously, gently touched the white infant, who was like a god to them, nothing less than a being of divine beauty.

Inasmuch as Alina—along with the whole collective, talentless and against their will—had assiduously studied Irdu with the Handian teacher who came to them, on holidays she started to get practice.

By the way, in this building of theirs, the trade office building, they had their own, Soviet holidays—May 1, May 9, November 7, and New Year's—which the employees' wives attended bestrewn in local jewelry with what they believed to be precious stones and wrapped up in the local shawls, silks, and batistes.

But Alina didn't go to those parties. You weren't supposed to with a baby.

These were official meetings with reports, and only afterward the feast began and you could congratulate each other, have a drink, chat and joke in your own language, even laugh.

Not that jokes were welcomed. The bosses, the Fozhkins, and their guest, Captain Beryozin, would lay into the booze, and there was nothing to laugh at.

After the women had a little to drink, they started singing, dissonantly, "Oh the birch, oh the tansy" and "Look who's coming down the hill." Upstairs, from the pool, Alina had to listen to all this because the parties were held in the courtyard.

The only exception was New Year's, but there were only two of them during the time Alina lived at the trade office.

Up top, though, she sat by the pool every day and couldn't help but meet a few wives, who were also sitting with small children.

And she made friends through this simple contact with similarly unhappy women economizing on every runee.

Although she had a less than stellar reputation, Sergei went up to the pool more than once and tried to lead her away, affectionately, as if she were crazy. ("Come, let's go, don't, don't show them all this, these things of yours, the doctor didn't give you pills because you don't take them.")

At least he didn't stoop to fighting in public. But Alina knew how this would end, and delicately but firmly shook her head, holding the baby close.

"I should take you to the doctors," he said every time, and made off.

A relationship like this between spouses was no rarity here. The chief trade representative himself went out in the morning wearing dark glasses often enough, as did his wife: they fought.

They were from outside Kishinev, tested cadres, regular people, but with degrees.

These were the kind of people who were bosses all over the Soviet Union.

The exception was the cadres from the Academy of Sciences, the Union of Architects and Artists, and the Union of Composers. They did have to have some kind of specialized education.

But, for example, the writers were led by people about whom the song went: "We all come from the people, a fraternal worker family." To be able to write, after all, you just had to finish first grade. Such were many leaders of the Union of Writers, and if they understood what Socialist Realism meant, it was praising the leadership in a form they could understand. People wrote parodies of the works of Writers Union Chairman Markov, for instance: The doorbell rings. The District Committee secretary comes in, hugs his wife, and says, "Klava, we're going to have a baby."

So the contact Alina had was simple human contact, the kind everyone needs.

You can't help it, whoever lives next door, whoever's your neighbor, that's your friend.

Who else was there to have contact with since mingling with the locals was discouraged (with "those blacks," as the wives called them, with the serving staff).

After all, among this swarthy population one came across both Trotskyites and supporters of Western teachings, and there were positively scads of Buddhists.

The Communists among them showed certain deviations, left-leaning ideas.

Therefore the leadership did not mix with the people there, only with representatives of trade organizations, who had no interest in ideology.

But these ordinary Soviet women shared their woes with Alina, how their mother was back home, and how their older children (who they weren't allowed to keep here) were, too, and they told her where she could buy things cheaper, although this good advice was useless to her because Alina didn't have a single kopek.

Ultimately, she was regarded with respect. Everyone saw her sitting over foreign books, they knew Alina was a university student, that she knew English and French since she was constantly sitting over translations of scholarly works on the etymology of Slavic languages, part of her thesis topic.

But she had no one even to talk to, no one to tell about the strange similarities there were between ancient Russian and all the Slavic languages and with Sanskrit in general.

And what the sources were of various words of ours.

Our *umora* was their *humor*. And our *umora* was the ancient Indian *moras*—death.

Our laughter was their smile, the ancient Indian *smayati*.

And what kind of language Old Church Slavonic—which no people, not even one single small tribe, had ever spoken—was.

Alina read the prayers quoted in her textbooks, and no one had to know she was praying.

One day, though, upstairs, during work hours, a trade office employee showed up at the pool, walked past all the wives, including his own, that is, past in general, like a stranger, demonstrating he was on the job, and addressed Alina specifically with a request to immediately translate some letter and compose this response in French.

Alina did as he asked.

A day later, Sergei raised a scandal because she hadn't taken money for her translation.

Saying that the trade office didn't have anyone with French, and there was work underway right now on a joint project, and she should demand payment.

And that he wasn't going to leave it at this.

A month later, on payday, Alina was surprised to receive a large sum from bookkeeping.

"How much did they give you?" Sergei asked.

"What interest is it of yours?"

"Because you're going to start paying me for your food now, see? However much you eat, that's how much you'll give me, understand?"

And he brought his massive fist up to Alina's face.

"If you start threatening me," Alina said, "I'll write a letter to the Foreign Ministry."

"Oh! Not so fast. I control all the mail. I haven't sent a single one of your tests to the university. I threw it all out. Is that clear? You thought you'd get an education at our expense? And I'm throwing out all your textbooks! You stole them all from the library! They're going to take you to court! The stamps are there."

That night, Alina locked herself in the bathroom and spread a blanket on the floor. Sergei was afraid to knock loudly. Vasya started crying, but Alina didn't come out. Sergei spent the whole night cursing and rocking his son. Tomorrow his co-workers who lived next door, as well as those above and below, were going to ream him out if he couldn't quiet his baby.

In the morning, Alina came out after her shower as if nothing happened, fed the baby, ate calmly, holding him in her arms (her sole defense against battering), and, paying no attention to Sergei's whispered curses, took her backpack, went to the top floor, where she put the stroller under a potted palm tree, filled a watering can in the pool, and apparently dug up the dirt in the planter and then generously watered it with chlorinated water and pushed the stroller out of the building.

You see, late the night before she'd hidden her wages by the pool, dug up the dry soil in the palm planter with a spoon, stuck her envelope with money there, and covered it with dirt.

She walked in the rain, having pulled an old slit plastic bag over the baby like a hood, quickly acquired a cheap umbrella for her and her son, stopped into a shop, bought fruits, vegetables, and cans with a buffalo on the label, went home—it was already deserted there—made soup with the meat, ate her fill, fed the baby, and slept with him, and in the late afternoon, after eating more of the same soup and finishing off every last bite, she made her way upstairs, under the plastic roof toward the pool, and there, in the rain, went for a swim with her son.

No one was up there, and an amazing feeling of freedom filled Alina's soul to the brim. For the first time in all these months. It was already getting dark, the smells of dinner, of cumin, pepper, curry, and sandalwood, wafted over the city, advertising signs lit up, and Alina still didn't leave. It was so good to be alone, to be her own master, without that constant feeling of enslavement.

He went upstairs at ten o'clock, pale, as if he had the plague, took the stroller and baby, and started for the exit. Alina stayed there, pensively watching him go.

He stopped at the door and looked around.

"Let's go. No one's going to touch you," he said like a human being. "Are you going to stay here like a vagrant?"

Alina didn't move a muscle.

Then he left the stroller and went away, dejected.

Alina fed the baby, stretched out on the chaise, and to her surprise fell asleep to the rustle of the rain.

It wasn't that hot, maybe twenty-five degrees, and the child slept peacefully in his stroller.

When dawn broke, Sergei showed up again. White as a sheet, with an imploring look, frightened.

"They'll send us back," he said. "Is that what you're after, you piece of shit? What are we going to do in Moscow?"

Alina said nothing.

"Okay, do you want me to sleep in the kitchen? I won't lay a hand on you again, is that what you want? Not a finger."

Then she got up and pushed the stroller to the elevator.

From that day on, Sergei really did start to sleep on the kitchen floor because purchasing a couch, first of all, would spark general interest and undesirable consequences and, secondly, it cost a lot of money.

Alina won the chance to live like a human being.

She and the baby slept on the foldout couch.

She had the occasion, more than once, to translate from French and even write in English when there was no one to do it.

So that she did come into a certain number of runees.

Workers were paid in runees. Rubles weren't accepted here. No one would take them at the currency exchanges.

Unlike all the building's stingy residents, Alina didn't save her money. She had no thought for the future, and given the very tough economy, she wasn't going to save up enough for a Moscow apartment. Even if she did, co-op fees were a pipe dream for her. Nonetheless, the lessons she'd learned since childhood, that you should buy as cheaply as you could, made her into a scout, analyst, and psychologist rolled into one and brought her tremendous joy when she did find something good for kopeks.

All the women in the building knew the addresses, frequented the cheapest stores and the sales, and Alina cheerfully tagged along, pushing her stroller.

She was even initiated into all the local gossip, who was sleeping with whom, who was beating whom, and that recently in Hilau they'd been building something there as a gift to the Handian people, and in the barracks there one evening a husband had killed his wife because she'd given a banana to their son's classmate, who had come over.

The Handian authorities sniffed around and opened a case, but our people in Hilau sent the body home in secret, by rail.

And sent the husband and child on the same train to accompany their boxes. Crime and punishment.

Let him sniff around.

Seryozha (Vasya) was growing up, and Masha (Alina) was gradually transforming from a beaten, impoverished, hunted creature into a pretty young woman with golden curls who wore beautiful locally sewn clothes and native-made high heels.

To say nothing of her bathing suit.

She had the breasts of a nursing mother (she hadn't stopped nursing), but her waist had returned to her former sixty centimeters.

Colleagues would eye her at the pool.

Locals on the street would send her smacking kisses, cars would honk and throw their doors open, and at the two New Year's parties at the trade office Alina had great success, with the men falling all over themselves asking her to dance, leaving her spouse to sit with the baby (New Year's Eve being the only time children were allowed at a party).

And from time to time she'd have a visit from KGB Captain Beryozin, who worked in Handia next door to the trade office, worked supposedly for the PNA, the Political News Agency, drank, was bored, rode around from village to village, and counted rifles.

A few times he and Alina walked around the city, as if meeting up by accident, and talked about the sights and customs, about the brothels behind nearly every locked gate—there were Soviet girls there, too—

and about how disagreeable wives were burned to death in Handian families. According to tradition they could be taken to a backyard, have gasoline poured on them from a lighter, and quickly be set on fire with that same lighter.

Fire was a sacred substance here, direct passage to their heaven.

Recently, judging from his stories, Beryozin had accompanied a doctor from a Moscow burn center, who had come to consult with doctors. Consulting here, that's part of local custom . . . The burn patients are silent, at most they say they want to kill themselves. Because they have nowhere to go, from the hospital they'd have to return to that same house, to their mother-in-law. A divorced woman's own family won't take her in, here the woman brings the husband a dowry, that is, her mother and father have already spent a lot on her and aren't about to spend any more.

After all, there are always lots of children growing up in a home here.

Some never do get to start a family if they don't have any money. Young women are rarely allowed out of the house. Finish school and sit there your whole life. Especially if you don't have a dowry.

There are plenty of bachelors, they walk through the streets in groups, some holding hands. Not that that means anything, it's just a sign of friendship. There aren't enough young women with dowries for everyone.

"Here they come," the captain said, not pointing, though. "Coupled up. There was this time when a young fellow of eighteen died soon after the wedding, and the family tried to talk the newlywed into climbing onto the funeral pyre and burning up with her husband. The good old ways. Well, they pumped the girl full of drugs, wrapped her in a greasy sheet, put her on the fire next to the deceased, and lit the fire. And she started screaming and rolled out of the fire, and people came running, saved her. The whole family on both sides was put in prison, and so were the observers, for complicity.

By the way, in good-humored moments the husband of alleged Masha alleged Sertsova himself would say, "I should sell you (bleep) to a brothel when my time here fucking ends. Beryozin agrees. He had everything taken from him here, so he visits Russian girls at the bordello out of fucking boredom. You think those girls agreed to be taken there, arms fucking behind them, fucking gagged? Shit, their husbands sold them. It's not much money, but a Soviet man's happy for any gift before he leaves. Especially getting rid of a woman he's fucking sick of. They're all ready to slit each others' fucking throats here. Shit, the wives threaten filing for divorce when they get back and rake off fucking half the apartment and car earned by the man's hard labor, dammit! Wives here are an unpaid appendix, they live off their husbands, all they fucking do is cook. And fucking spend! That builder in Hilau was right for offing his cunt wife over one banana. He would've offed her even without the banana. I'm not going to dirty my hands on you, you cunt. I'm going to take the baby away from you in Moscow anyway and you'll have no fucking place to go. Shit, here, Beryozin promised me, in a bordello in a nearby town, I won't say where, you'd have a roof over your head, and meals. Fucking straight in your mouth. He's had his eye on you for a long time, and they'll pay me well."

And he laughed, the scum.

Sergei continued to despise his slave, considered her a worthless creature who had abandoned her own child for the chance to travel to Handia.

This somehow reinforced his male self-esteem, made him an angry but fair judge to whom all was permitted.

For that reason he took Alina's money and only through small ruses did she manage to keep something back for herself and her child.

Someone sussed out the trick with the planter, and one day Alina didn't find her stash.

Now she hid her pay envelopes in supposedly sealed baby food (she could already read all those squiggles in Handi and Irdu) and bought super-glue at the supermarket. She would open the baby food, stick in the money rolled into a tube, cover it with the food, and neatly glue it closed.

Rather than hide this miracle glue, she kept it in the bathroom because one day they'd had a leak and the local handyman had tried to use it to seal the pipe. It didn't work, of course, but Alina took note of this popular tool, and she had glue on the shelf as a matter of course, just in case.

Everything comes to an end eventually, though, that's life's rule.

Perestroika was underway in Moscow.

Sergei kept going away on business trips and returning excited, boasting to Alina that lots of people were following him and that a barrel of liquid concrete wasn't the only way, and that hired divers work better in a pond.

Later, according to his co-workers' wives, Sergei left Odessa on a ship escorting strategic cargo, scrap copper. A second ship followed behind.

Our country's leadership had placed great political hopes in this trip: it was a gift to a friendly nation where our copper Christopher Columbus was being erected in its capital!

Meanwhile, customs resisted for a long time.

But copper is a precious metal, you never know, they thought, eventually it could be melted down.

No one ever heard a thing about the ships or Sergei again.

Especially since besides the copper our people had sent something else, which was why the authorities there had agreed to such a patently awful gift.

But the ships were lost. Both of them. Evidently sunk in a storm in the Bermuda Triangle.

Someone had taken out insurance with Lloyds and someone cashed in big-time.

No one knew who, and the ladies gossiped, glancing at Alina.

While she, who was still earning her keep through translations, was living independently and could finally breathe freely.

She wasn't afraid of anyone anymore, only she avoided Beryozin like the plague.

Her window faced the street, and Alina saw the drunken captain every time he returned home.

But everything in the world comes to an end, especially happiness. And Alina was called in by the higher-ups.

This was their famous Fozhkin, known to the reader already for drinking and fighting with his wife, but she drank, too, and sometimes both of them went around with black eyes and dark glasses, even at night. This Fozhkin said, "Your husband's gone missing. We don't know what happened to the ships. You have to go home. Buy tickets."

"I don't have the money," a distraught Alina replied.

"We'll take care of that."

Alina really didn't have the money.

Not only that, she didn't know where Sergei had stashed his savings.

Evidently, he'd had his own channels for diverting money to foreign accounts.

40

Russia Welcomes Alina

ONE NIGHT IN June, Alina and her child deplaned at Sheremetyevo, with no clue where to go.

She had luggage, two large suitcases, a folding stroller, and a toddler.

The trade office had exchanged her runees for rubles. Other cash for Russian cash.

She sat in the arrivals hall until morning, then took a bus to the city, where she took a taxi to the Belorussky train station.

She'd decided to go to her father's. Maybe he'd let her live there at least for a while.

By the time she managed to make her way to the right house, carrying the child in one arm and having piled the suitcases on the stroller, it was evening.

She started rattling the bolt on the gate.

The dog didn't bark, but a strange woman did approach. It turned out they'd bought the house the year before.

And she didn't know where the previous owners had gone.

They'd bought the house from a woman. Not a man? No. There was no man. A single woman with two children sold it.

"Could I possibly stay with you? I've just arrived from abroad. Until I find them?"

"We have nowhere to put you," was the answer.

"I'll pay you," Alina promised.

"No, no, you can't. My man doesn't like strangers."

"Won't someone rent a room? A terrace?"

"We don't know anyone here. Go. Go. I mean it."

Standing at this stranger's fence, Alina thought hard. She'd gone to school in this village, she had girlfriends living here.

Eventually she was able to find lodging on a former classmate's veranda. She was living at her husband's house, and the woman renting her flimsy little house let Alina spend the night.

The lady showed her a trestle bed and brought one bunched up quilt. She was not at all friendly. To a request for tea she said she didn't have any brewed, but she'd get hot water.

Alina couldn't bring herself to ask for bread.

After the hot climate it was tough getting through the night in the damp and bone-chilling cold.

Alina held her son in her arms, wrapped up in the quilt, and thought about where she could exchange dollars here.

In the morning she jumped up cheerfully, splashed water on her face at the washstand, and reached an agreement with the sullen lady that she would leave her things here for now, take the train to Moscow with the child, and be back by nightfall.

When she got back, tired but with a bag of groceries, the gate was locked.

No light in the house, no one there. Alina went to her girlfriend's.

She said that her mother had rented out the house and left—it was her mom's house and they were on bad terms, and who she'd been dealing with and when was a mystery, at first no one was living behind the gate, but smoke had been coming from the chimney for a few days, some people, not Russians, had started living there.

Either they were squatting or there was some kind of understanding. No one knew.

But she had no reason to deal with them. It was her mother's house.

Alina explained she'd left all her things with that woman.

People shrugged and looked at each other.

Her girlfriend blew her off completely, retreated behind her gate, and spent a long time on the other side locking the latch, shaking the chain-link.

Distraught, Alina decided to find a way into the yard of the house where she'd spent the night.

The fence was leaning in one place, creating a wide gap, and she was able to tear away two badly nailed boards.

Then Alina took the baby and dragged the stroller inside.

There was a lock on the front door.

Alina went around to the other side, pushed the stroller and baby farther, used a board to break a window, and brought over a crate to climb on, but right then she was struck on the head with something heavy. She came to lying in the street, her little boy sitting next to her crying. Her head was pounding. She touched the bruise—there was blood on her hand. The stroller, bags, and groceries were gone . . . Alina made her way to the next house and the people there called the police.

The cops didn't come and search the house with Alina until it was night.

There was no one there. And no traces of life.

The quilt wasn't even on the trestle bed. Good thing they didn't steal her son.

She did have all her documents. Alina carried them in a large pouch on a thin cord at her waist, under her skirt.

That was where she kept her money, too. She'd been taught that at the trade office.

But the money wasn't at her waist now. Strangers' hands had checked the pouch after all. Good thing they didn't take her documents. That meant the robbers were experienced.

Stealing a passport is a serious crime, the police investigate those cases. But there's no name on money.

Alina and the baby spent the night at the police station. The ambulance came and bandaged up her head. It's a minor wound, the doctor said, superficial, thank God.

In the morning, she left the station shaky from lack of sleep, carrying the child.

Good thing she hadn't weaned him. The women at the trade office had told her this was the only defense against intestinal infection.

There was a puff of smoke, and the grass glittered with dew. Alina kept moving, oblivious to her destination.

No one had taken a statement from Alina at the station.

She walked through the village, came out into a field, and skirted a sparse stand of trees with a pond, all familiar places.

Here, at this pond, she and the little boys had caught gobies.

Up ahead was the train station, but she had no money, they'd stolen it all. Bandaged, a woman utterly alone in this world, with neither house nor home, she moved toward the station, toward Moscow.

Where no one she knew remained, everyone had graduated from university and was working somewhere, was married, had children, and had forgotten Alina a long time ago.

And where, according to the address in her passport, lived the mama of the real but deceased Masha Sertsova.

Her number one enemy in this world.

The boy was sleeping in alleged Masha's arms.

A person with a name and address, just not her own.

We'll leave them for now because new and very important acquaintances await us.

For at the address listed in Maria Sertsova's passport, on the same floor and behind the next door over, was the apartment of Evgraf Nikolaevich Shapochkin, a disabled veteran, holder of many medals, some of them stolen.

41

A Man Called Shapochkin

EVGRAF SHAPOCHKIN, known as Graf, a designer by profession, was so poor he'd started collecting empty bottles, while the organization where he'd been employed drawing horses, rabbits, and kittens (he was a "four-legger," his art being used in kindergartens, clinics, park and building playgrounds, and so on)—so here's the thing, that organization was shut down because the director turned out to have signed a bill of sale for the building to someone from Fiji, who'd immediately flipped it.

And now no one needed Shapochkin the designer, a small-time nobody in a world of big-time wheeling and dealing.

His cheerful brotherhood of colleagues scattered to their meager little apartments and would call each other and get together now and again, mainly for funerals.

Wretched buses and a handful of his former colleagues, talented people no one had ever heard of, would stand in the wind, in the rain, or under the sun's beating rays around yet another hole, and the gravediggers would stick a beloved friend you'd spent your whole life with in the ground.

Some left behind widows and children, but Shapochkin had neither wife nor progeny.

He had sunk so low that he told everyone about the circumstances of his current life, and once, after a long absence (which no one noticed), he called and kvetched to his old work friend, another designer, Lana (who they called Angel, because she drew them. That was her specialty. Except that for kindergarten murals she often took the Sistine Chapel angels as a model, and that made for problems with the higher-ups. At a meeting for one kindergarten design, when the director asked Lana, "And who is this modeled on?" she said, "It's Raphael." To which she was told, "Just what we don't need. Now they've dragged in Israel").

Graf was open about what happened. "You know, Lana, a bottle I found under the counter, they bashed me in the head with it, I had an operation, had a plate inserted in my skull. How was I to know they kept their secret stash there, under the counter?"

Lana commiserated and offered to come over and feed him soup, but doughty Shapochkin refused and at the end of the conversation bragged he'd been given group-one disability and was going to get a big pension, and soon! They'd promised an apartment, too!

In his former life, Shapochkin had been adored, forgiven everything, including his absences and naps on the bench in the courtyard in all weather, and his harangues against the bosses at meetings. He was a truth-seeker, a frontline veteran, a good-looker, a gallant ladies' man.

And all of a sudden he called his friend, that same Lana, and reported, somewhat embarrassed, that he'd finally been given an apartment as a disabled veteran. True, he was putting off the housewarming because he had to save a little money. You don't move into a new home with your old junk, you have to buy this and that. And then invite people.

Right now he had nothing to sit on.

But his old pals came anyway, and later in the evening his comrades ran out to the square and brought Graf a garden bench with a back and iron legs. The laughter was Homeric!

A month later, Graf's modesty got another and rather unexpected explanation: he now had a girlfriend and she wanted to get married.

"But where did you meet?" his friend asked innocently, and she did not have to wait long for the answer: in a store.

"What department?" Lana continued her interrogation, pretty sure she knew the answer.

"The liquor department!" the veteran replied dashingly. "She likes brandy, too, can you imagine? And she treated me! I only had enough for some cheap port."

"Where did she treat you?"

"What's wrong with you, don't I have an apartment? On the second floor, and with an elevator! As a disabled veteran! In a brick building, old construction, it needs repairs. She knows a work crew! We're getting it ready for the wedding!"

"What's wrong with you!" Lana, his faithful adviser, exclaimed heatedly. "Why are you doing that? She's using you!"

Then she bit her tongue. Shapochkin didn't need to know that no woman would take a shine to him for no good reason.

Especially since Graf was full of plans.

He specifically hinted that he and his wife were going to sell the apartment and move to the country, where they'd have a whole estate, he'd long dreamed of that. With a fish pond!

"Aha, and a bridge across the pond," Lana replied, citing her favorite Gogol.

"You'll come for a barbecue! But mum's the word for now," Shapochkin concluded in a happy, unsober bass.

"And how old is she?" Lana asked in a faint voice. She'd already come across a few stories like this, and they all ended the same way, with a group of comrades standing over a freshly dug hole.

"Oh, pretty young," Graf replied, squirming. Then Lana heard him ask someone in the room with him, "How old does your passport say you are?"

And that someone laughed a nasty laugh. A shiver went down Lana's skin.

"Forty-six, if she's not lying. But she looks fifty."

Another nasty laugh close by.

"And what's her name?"

A pause.

"Graf, do you know her name? Or not?"

"Basically she's called Galina. But that's a bad name, it's wrong for her. I call her Maruska. Maruska!"

The same laugh in response.

"And her last name?"

"What for?"

"Graf! Are you hiding something from the collective? Why?"

"Well . . . She's not my wife yet."

"All the more so!" an assertive Lana exclaimed. "Graf! What's her last name?"

"What's your last name?" Graf asked the someone again, and right away, after hearing someone's very soft answer, he repeated:

"Kukush-? Ku-what? Kumashkina? Give me your passport!" He thundered. "Give it here, I mean it! Or I won't marry you! So-o-o . . ." A crackling and grinding in the receiver. "Your passport! So-o-o. Well, what do we have here? Ku-by-tra-ta-ta . . . Well, what's so good about that? We'll change it, change your name. Shapochkina will be better. Galina . . . Aha!" A grinding. "Galina, you're Galina! And look! Fifty years old! Oh! That's it! And she's going to be Shapochkina! Don't poke your nose in again! Marusya Shapochkina! That's it, Lana, bye. I'm going to go live in nature!"

No one saw him again.

That is, it was spring, and then came summer, an important time for poor owners of dacha plots.

There and only there was the source of their further survival: their vegetable beds.

Lana left for her hacienda outside Tuchki, where first she tilled, then weeded, then harvested, and then canned.

When she came into town for her pension, Lana called Graf, but to no avail.

She collected herself and headed for Graf's place. She'd written down the address for the housewarming, when there had been a real celebration! Not for a funeral, not for a wake or the anniversary of a death, but for a housewarming—something this vanishing brotherhood hadn't seen in a very long time. When his comrades shouted, "We've brought you furniture!" and put the park bench in his kitchen.

Armed with his address, Lana set out.

She got there. She rang the bell for a long time, many times.

Someone was obviously there in Shapochkin's apartment, people were walking around, she could hear men's voices.

But they didn't even answer the door, let alone open it.

Lana left, sure they'd killed him.

The police didn't want to take her complaint, but later, on the evening of the next day, after nearly twenty-four relentless hours from this indefatigable senior citizen, they did take it and registered it.

"Lady," the investigator said, "what gang? Alcoholics often marry out-of-towners. All you like! Then they exchange the place and pay more on top to go to the country. That's the scenario. And the whole gaggle go running to the alkie, and they drink up that money, often take it. And finish off the owner. They're all monsters. The dregs of humanity."

"What dregs? He's a well-known designer! He made films!"

"So what? Don't go getting ideas. This case is a pure dead-end. An unsolvable case, I'm telling you. Especially since what reason do I have to mislead you? I'm quitting anyway. Resigning. What they pay here, it's a joke! Am I supposed to take bribes? No!" He suddenly growled at the corner, glared at an imagined interlocutor. "In parting, I might even agree with you, but the truth is more powerful. Actually, out of respect for you, I won't be able to open a case."

Everyone truly did appreciate Lana, they respected her and showed her every possible sign of attention, even this investigator. But she sensed that this older man, bald, grimy, and sweaty, obviously knew something, he kept hiding his little eyes too much. And why was he quitting his job?

People don't resign, they're fired.

42

Lana Goes on the Warpath

LANA HAD A magnificent memory. Especially aural.

For example, she was fantastic at repeating all kinds of gibberish in foreign languages, mimicking the pronunciation.

This was always one of her bits at the collective's drinking and skit parties.

One time, there was this bit where she recounted expansively about going to Riga, on a business trip, and her compartment companion turned out to be this swarthy blonde with bright blue eyes dressed perfectly elegantly, as if she were at Mariupol or something (a green leather jacket, orange high-heeled boots)—and who spoke approximately like this (at this point the group froze in anticipation of laughing):

"'Course I'm all tan, I'm comin' from Odessa, dontcha know. So what's yr'name? Ah, Lana. I'm Indya, s'nice to meet ya. Wanna see my passport?"

And Indya immediately dug into her boot and took out a slightly bent—to the shape of her leg, naturally—document.

In her passport, of course, she was listed as Zinaida.

Being shown someone's document meant they trusted you completely. And you could trust that person completely.

At that moment, the compartment door slid to the side.

There—like a framed portrait—stood a handsome older man, also tanned and dyed blond, who said something with a question mark (at that point Lana uttered a series of sounds clearly not in Russian with an obvious accent).

Then Zinaida replied similarly (another series of sounds) and, as Lana understood it, she said she still hadn't had a chance to raise that question.

The blond nodded. The door shut.

And then Lana (attention!) repeated Zinaida's statement in its entirety (at their skit parties there was always a repetition and a burst of laughter from the audience).

This Zinaida's eyes popped out of her head, and then she said something else.

Lana immediately repeated what she'd said, but with a rising intonation. If Zinaida said, "So you understand our way of talking," Lana would repeat the same thing in jest, exclaiming archly, "You understand our way of talking?"

After that, Indya made herself scarce.

Evidently, the older blond had asked her something about Lana. That is, was it worth having anything to do with her. And Indya had said it wasn't clear yet but we'd see.

And Lana had exposed all their secrets.

Now here she was, all set for the decisive burst, standing in front of the Kievsky Train Station, her purse half shut, a wide-open and perfectly clean kefir container poking out of it (containing vials of old mixtures and little medicine boxes, also not new), and also a fat wallet.

She'd come here because she'd heard a rumor about a certain Romani woman at the station, Sasha, who plied her trade at the Kievsky Station and didn't exactly tell fortunes but sometimes saw certain things. To the point, she'd told a distant acquaintance of Lana that HE was in a well.

She'd just said it as this unfortunate woman was walking past her from the Aprelevka commuter train.

No one had asked the Romani woman, by the way. She was the one who latched on, even walked alongside her.

"Let me tell your fortune, precious, he's in a well, your beloved, the one you're searching for," she'd said.

"You mean, he's dead?" the poor woman asked, on the verge of tears, and she took the silver ring off her finger.

"I don't know yet," the fortune teller answered.

"And what's your name?" the poor woman exclaimed.

"Her name's Sasha," the crowd of Romani women replied mockingly. For no one is a prophet in his own land. Yes, prophets are mocked. His own people haven't believed him since the dawn of time.

Grabbing the ring, Sasha immediately vanished among her fellow tribeswomen.

She was talking about a cat, of course, the cat the whole family had been combing the dacha settlement for for a week now.

After that encounter with Sasha, the neighboring wells were ransacked, and the poor darling, wet and mildewed but alive, sitting on an outcropping deep in the well, was scooped up in a bucket.

Well, not scooped up: the clever cat flopped into the bucket all by himself. A bucket swaying nearby, how could he not take advantage? Cats like to hide in whatever they come across.

That woman had been searching for this legendary Sasha for a long time in order to pay her for her prediction, but the Romanis, clearly, had migrated all over Moscow.

The only place where there was any hope of finding her was that same square in front of the Kievsky Station.

The Kievsky Station of the twentieth century's impoverished nineties!

Ranks of people lining the approach to the metro on both sides, like an honor guard, badly rumpled, holding out trousers-jackets-coats for sale, old women selling cigarettes by the block, the pack, and singles for young people, the flower mafia with their big plastic pots, and crazed cops with swollen pockets.

Well, and the Romanis.

They migrated from station to station, moreover these were obviously distinct groups who sometimes exchanged insults across the square, their howls easily outshouting the distances and raining curses down on the competing tribe.

Lana had gone to the trouble of breaking her money into small bills and filled her dead uncle's old leather wallet with them to bursting, slung an old purse over her shoulder, crammed it with brochures and rags, and posed that washed and dried kefir container stuffed with all those vials and boxes, so it was obvious who you were dealing with (a batshit crazy), added a dried-up half head of cabbage, and then on top of it all set out the wallet and fastened the purse, but counting on the fact that the zipper was constantly separating in the middle.

Lana threw a handsome, albeit torn, old shawl over her shoulders.

All these trappings were meant to speak to the owner's derangement.

Then, armed with these props, Lana exited the metro.

As it happened, the warring tribes were roaming around the square. Shouting threats at each other from a distance.

Lana cut through one family on the diagonal.

The crowd of kin immediately hailed her:

"Tell your fortune, lady, oy, your beloved, he'll come back, cross my palm, whatever metal you like, a ring, or a chain, don't be afraid."

Lana made an angelic face and exclaimed, "Oy, all I have is money!"

"Well, then put money there, precious."

Lana dug into her purse, opened it, and took out her fat wallet.

The tribe closed in around her.

Lana stopped with the wallet in hand:

"But tell me, my dear, I'm looking for Sasha."

The Romani relatives got worked up, and one older beauty shouted across the whole square:

"*Bambalimba kay yov isi Sasha?*" Evidently addressing the other tribe. At least, that's what Lana thought *bambalimba* meant.

Someone over there gave her the finger.

The details were hard to make out from far away, but they shouted some kind of insult.

"Sasha's gone," the beauty said bitterly, and it sounded like "Sasha's gone for good."

"*Sasha tampampararu, ey ugeya*," she explained to her people.

Lana laid a stack of bills on her palm. The Romani woman slipped them into her side pocket and began:

"Your beloved has gone, my dear. But if you put a little more money in my hand, I'll tell you when he'll return."

"Just a minute, I'll be right back. Oy!" Lana sang out, and she made her way out of the family unscathed.

Her path lay through the crowd of traders, but in the distance she picked out the grouping of colorfully dressed women hostile to the other group.

Lana walked into this opposing clan fearlessly and respectfully, like a tamer in a cage with tiger beauties. That was the only way to do it.

Women waiting to offer to find her beloved clustered around.

For some reason, they were sure Lana's beloved had left her.

Evidently, that's what her appearance said.

"*Sasha tampampararu, ey ugeya?*" Lana said shrilly.

"Sasha?" a stunned Romani woman, tall and beautiful, echoed, looking around at her people.

"*Sasha tampampararu kay ey isi?*" Lana said in pure Romani.

"*Bambalimba trr prr kay ey isi Sasha,*" the Romani woman said, and Lana repeated the same sentence after her word for word, but followed by a question mark.

The women started vociferating.

Lana immediately duplicated their loudest words. She gave the impression of actively participating in the conversation.

She was still holding onto the wallet.

Occasionally Lana even shook it, as an argument.

At last they brought her an elderly woman who shot a darting glance at Lana, interested and rather keen, and who immediately said, "Put something on my palm, a ring, a chain, and I'll tell you all about your beloved."

"I don't have any metal, Sasha dear, I have money."

"Well, money will do, though it looks pretty skimpy."

"Look, dear Sasha, people have told me you know a lot, you're different here, not like the rest. You're brilliant!"

The family's faces depicted a great deal—doubt, faint laughter, surprise, even contempt.

The principal in these events stood firm, her expression unchanged.

"Sasha dear, genius, find where he is, here's a photo of my beloved."

From her pocket, Lana pulled out a group photo with Graf standing in the middle.

"There he is, with the crutch. Graf. He's a veteran, with one good leg. He's gone missing."

"*O, bambalimba, lacho manush!*" Sasha said. "*Yov ugeya? Lacho manush? You need kay yov isi Graf?*"

"*Kay yov isi lacho manush,*" Lana agreed. "*Graf yo-yo ugeya. Tamparam.*"

"*Bambarda kay yov isi,*" Sasha corrected her. "*Kay yov isi.*"

"*Bambarda kay yov isi Graf?*" Lana said, nearly in tears.

The other Romani women, stunned by this woman speaking, looked at her and the photo curiously.

Some became thoughtful, as if trying to remember something.

Or just pretended to, the actors. A fat wallet was at stake!

Sasha treated Lana's speech with great respect.

It was as if she saw in her an equal, intelligent and clever. But her profession hadn't made things easy for her.

She had hungry children and a husband, also hungry, waiting at home.

"*Bambarda de mange, mek mishto*," she said, indicating the wallet with her chin.

"*Bambarda pararu, mek mishto*," Lana agreed, and she put the wallet in her nimble hand. "Here."

"*Kada na mishto. Pararam nane but lave*," Sasha said contemptuously, not even opening the offering.

"*Parara, nane*," Lana agreed sadly. "*No lacho. Nane but lave. Oy-yoy, tarara pam*. That's all I have. *Nane but lave*."

"Graf," Sasha thought, and she donned an otherworldly look.

The other women watched her jealously, laughing at her. Some turned away, and one even yawned demonstratively. Her fellow tribes-women were jealous, obviously.

"If I find him, I'll give you a gold signet ring," said Lana, all of whose family possessions had become KGB property—after her father's arrest, the apartment's confiscation, and her mother's suicide after they put her father back in prison when he'd barely come home from a seventeen-year absence. But after his second return, her papa had married her mama's sister, in Leningrad, who still had her belongings.

Sasha suddenly squinted, gazing over the Kievsky Station and the droning crowd.

Her friends also went on their guard when they heard about the gold ring. As Lana's papa, who came home alive after his second stint, used to hum in these instances, "People will die for metal."

(He'd mined uranium and buried friends in the permafrost of the Butugychag labor camp. All winter, their remains awaited burial in storerooms—permafrost is impenetrable—and when the warmth did come, the prisoners were driven out to dig a trench, where they lay the foot-tagged bodies and covered them with the same icy soil.)

Lana looked at Sasha with a desperate gaze. Sasha might save Graf.

Finally the woman said, "Wait, I'm telling you. Wait, don't go anywhere."

And she left, melting into the crowd of Romanis.

Her fellow tribesmen, newly intrigued by the gold ring, were still crowding around Lana.

But once they'd had a look at her kefir container, the half head of cabbage, and the brochures, to say nothing of her whole beggarly outfit, including the holey, fairly shabby shawl draped across Lana's tattered jacket, the encampment began fading away.

"*Shapochkin kay yov isi pararu?*" Lana yelled, and she started pulling the shawl off her shoulder, intending to pay for further information with it, but the women lost all interest in the client and melted into the crowd.

Sasha the brilliant Romani had raked in all her money.

And no one had any wish to answer this direct question for free.

"*Pararu, kay yov isi?*" Lana said loudly, preparing to leave.

By now the encampment was gone anyway.

Guided by a single thought, she rushed home for money, ran out and bought what groceries she could find (and what was offered on the shelves in stores was incredibly foul-smelling cans labeled "Tourist Breakfast," crushed black bread (only in the mornings), and three-liter cans of marinated squash (always), and if there was any alcohol, then it was the notorious and vomitous Solntsedar, but in every house women made a home brew from whatever they could get, while the men made moonshine).

Lana grabbed the last two loaves of black bread in the store and also asked her friend behind the counter for a packet of margarine.

Since last year, though, thank you Lord, Lana had had her own pickles, she hadn't given them all to friends: homemade, not the Bulgarian things you couldn't find: lecsó, eggplant and beet caviar, and also home-canned mushrooms, tomatoes, and cucumbers, and also black currant, strawberry, apple, and sea-buckthorn jam. People (even men) saved up sugar all winter.

The moment it was put out for sale, big long lines formed.

There were always dried apples, just in case (that year there'd been a harvest).

Lana was prepared to hold the line at her apartment and at her phone, which was exactly how she understood the words "Don't go anywhere."

43

Lana Awaits Word from Graf

GRAF DIDN'T KNOW her address, after all, so there was no point waiting for a letter or a message.

But Graf did know her phone number.

Any village, any hole, will have Moscow dacha dwellers and their children. Where else were they supposed to put the next generation? Pioneer camps had been scrubbed and no one had money for resorts.

So mothers and grandmothers went to the country, where there was a forest with mushrooms and berries, a river or brook with a pond, a place where local women still kept a goat and a dozen hens and you could buy eggs and milk, to say nothing of goat meat, and currants and raspberries, the best ever devised for feeding children and making jam.

They hoarded their sugar for the summer.

Old women are the foundation of the people's life, that's what the old woman Lana told herself, and she didn't leave her house for two weeks.

She even took the phone with her to the bathroom, like a poodle on a leash.

Lana hung up on her girlfriends' random calls. She'd explained everything to everyone. Not that many did call anyway—only in case of sickness or someone passing away. Everyone was staying at their dachas.

At the end of this period, there was a loud ring, long-distance.

"Moscow!" the distant telephone operator shouted, leaning hard on the first *o*. "One six one four six four one? Will you speak with Melenki?"

"Yes, yes!" Lana shouted. "Yes, I will!"

And someone's female voice said, "Is this Lana? This is for you from Evgraf Nikolaevich. He sends greetings, here's his address, write it down: Dubtsy village, Melenki District, Vladimir Province. Are you writing?"

"Just a minute!" Lana said. "I'll get a pen!"

"Got it?"

"Just a sec . . . Yes, now! I'm writing."

As always, at the last moment nothing is at hand.

Inasmuch as Lana had whiled away the time these two weeks painting watercolors of her balcony flowers, she wrote down the address with a brush in her album.

But what could she do? This person was calling from there and paying by the minute!

"Evgraf Nikolaevich sends greetings and his address, Dubtsy, Melenki District, Vladimir Province. You have to go to Murom and from there to Melenki. From there you take a bus to Panovo, hear me? And from there it's a kilometer and a half on foot to Dubtsy. Come, he's doing poorly here. I'm from Volgograd myself," the woman added. "Ask in Dubtsy for Nina Ivanovna. People there know. I'm from Volgograd!"

The connection dropped, and the next day, at six o'clock in the morning, Lana stepped off the train, waited for the bus to the train station square in the old town of Murom, and then waited for a bus to Melenki at the town bus station, buying her ticket at the ticket office but not in time to be among the passengers for the first bus.

Lana accepted this misfortune bravely. She'd miscalculated—people had gone a roundabout way to the bus station, whereas she'd rushed directly, as the crow flies, to where the bus was waiting, and stumbled on road work and a deep ditch that spread to both the right and left.

The people always know better, they're patient and know the way, while the intelligentsia tries to barge through. So Lana was left high and dry for an hour and a half, in punishment for her lack of faith in the native wit.

She couldn't imagine what awaited her—that's what she later said over the phone to her friend Struchok, another unemployed designer, a veteran of their combine whose slogan was "Everybody dances," because she masterfully drew the group dances of the peoples of the Soviet Union and the dances of animals, especially bears.

Struchok was a real veteran, her older son had already finished law school and was defending the poor, and she'd kept studying at the Isadora Duncan School of Dance started in the late 1920s by the famous Alexeyeva, where even Lana had, up until recently, danced in a tunic, barefoot, in this studio. Thanks to which she had retained her flexibility, slenderness, and urge to adopt antique poses. (In the studio, ancient Greek tunics were simulated by sheets bleached in caustic soda, under which the studio dancers wore gym shorts.)

In another system of coordinates, Struchok of the big nose, who was descended from princes and from time to time attended the recently created Assembly of the Nobility, where one other person from the design combine spent time, too, a man about whom a rumor had gone around the combine that he was a Romanov by his great-great-great-grandfather, his great-great-great-grandmother having been a palace maid.

Judging by his face, she was a charwoman, or so his colleagues in the combine believed. Emperor Paul looked exactly like that.

His nickname was the Heir, and he was distinguished for his public-minded temperament and for constantly signing appeals.

The Heir's signature was "N. Romanov," an exact copy of the tsar's (designers can do anything), and his first initial really was "N," but for Nikita. Both of these men are irrelevant to the story, but they were Lana and Graf's friends.

44

THE TWENTIETH CENTURY:

Lana and Graf

LANA HAD A long bus ride ahead of her, two hours sitting over a plate of cabbage soup and an ancient, incredibly gristly chicken leg with dark macaroni in Melenki's restaurant waiting for the bus to Lyakhi, and from there the bus to Panovo, and then the path through the forest and fields from Panovo to Dubtsy, rolling up her trousers and crossing the Chernichka River barefoot—and a straight shot uphill to the village.

Judging from the deep depressions on both banks of the Chernichka, a log had lain here recently but had been taken away. In Russia, nothing useful is supposed to just lie around like that.

And right then the designer's heart started beating at the surrounding hills in the fog, the pines' silhouettes, pure Hokusai!

Pick up your watercolors and weep.

But there was no call for weeping. That wasn't who Lana was. Soon after, though, she did feel like it, for a different reason.

Finding Graf's house was easy. The first woman Lana's age standing on the street in a line of other village women pointed it out.

"We're waiting for the herd," she explained, leaning on the letter *r*. "I'd take you, but I can't leave. One-eyed Lyonka the shepherd ate more than his fill again so he's sleeping somewheres, but the herd's on its way!"

Reaching the spot, Lana saw a prosperous little house painted blue, she saw unwashed, dim windows with handsome carved frames, a porch, and a door.

Doesn't matter, Lana told herself, *it'll come off. We'll wash the windows.*

She walked into the anteroom, pulled hard at the door, which was covered in torn canvas, all in good order, and stepped under an open sky.

There was no roof.

Except for a few rafters, that is.

Remnants of roof decorated the house, but only from the street side.

In a corner, under a remaining cornice, on a crooked stool, sat Graf.

Leaning on one crutch.

Next to him was a flaking stove, once white, and two pieces of plywood, evidently for burning.

Behind the stove was a lair that makes us queasy to talk about.

The floor was wet and dirty. It had rained recently.

Graf was sitting there equally wet and dirty, having grown a large gray beard. He was very skinny.

"Ah, Lana, you've come," he said, after a fit of coughing.

They greeted each other, kissed each other's cheeks.

Lana wiped away a tear.

On a shelf nailed crookedly to the wall lay his provisions: two potatoes, easily a year old, boiled, a pickle, and half a loaf of bread, already plucked at.

Obviously the peasant women's gifts.

There was also an old tin can of Hungarian peas with a crooked open lid—for drinking, evidently.

Graf looked at Lana proudly and independently, but his cheeks were wet.

Lana paid no attention to that detail, nimbly ran out, and returned with Nina Ivanovna and an armload of logs. Nina Ivanovna lit a fire in the stove.

Thick smoke gushed from every crack.

Coughing, Graf said, "I'd have puttied it, but you have to get the clay, I've just got the one crutch, I would've fallen flat. Thanks be she didn't bring me here in the winter. I'd have been done for by the morning. But there's no telephone here. This drunk, Olen, he cut all the telephone lines in the forest to sell them, there's a scrap metal depot in Lyakhi. He just left the electricals. Nina Ivanovna here went to Melenki and called you, thanks be to her."

"Come, let's go to my place," Nina Ivanovna said, whereupon she was renamed dear Nina Ivanovna.

They were all three coughing as they walked down the street.

It turned out she'd asked Graf to come stay with her, but he'd evidently decided to die right where he was. To spite someone.

Somehow they got there.

Sitting at the table in Nina Ivanovna's house was an even older woman, toothless.

"This is my sister," Nina managed to get out. "Pay her no mind."

And right then, without responding to Lana's hello, this sister said to Nina, "Brought a lover again? Aren't you ashamed to bring them into the house where your grandsons are sleeping? You prostitute. Floozy."

Lana quickly seated Graf on the first stool she came to and said, "Oh no, it's me, I'm the one who came for him. We're leaving."

"Where's that?" the sister asked with a grin. "Good riddance."

"Manya, calm yourself," Nina intervened.

"Oh, we're going to the States," Graf said, once he'd recovered. "The United States, America, we are."

"Jews?" the sister asked with a laugh. "So now the kikes are invading us. We haven't seen you for a long time, thank you very much. Do you have the money?"

"Yes," Graf replied. "How could I not! A whole lot of nothing and all kinds of squat."

"They ate their fill of Russian bread," Manya said, "and now they're running away."

"Yes," Lana agreed. "What should we send you from there? A warm blouse? Or medicine? You are seriously ill, aren't you?"

Manya opened her mouth to respond with some quip, but Nina intervened.

"Yes, she is seriously ill, this is my sister, let me introduce you. Manya."

"Pleased to meet you. Lana Alexandrovna. And this is Evgraf Nikolaevich. We'll be leaving soon. What is your diagnosis?"

Manya replied, "She's the one with the diagnosis, not me. Her diagnosis is schizophrenia, she doesn't wash the dishes, doesn't watch the children, they're out running around from morning on, she just brings her lovers here. She made currant jam but doesn't make strawberry and gives the berries to her lovers. All she brought me in the hospital was fruit leather and a cookie."

"They don't allow sausage there for the heroes of Shipka," Nina Ivanovna managed to say.

"You're for the heroes of Shipka," and her sister laughed. "You laid down for the heroes of Shipka three times. Not me, not once. In the nuthouse, yes."

Graf rasped out, "We have to go to the States immediately. They're waiting for us impatiently on the plane. Find a car."

Meanwhile, Nina Ivanovna was making sandwiches with something suspiciously brown, saying, "This is squash caviar, imported, I made it myself last year," she poured hot water into cups, added a few leaves ("this is mint, it grows here, under the porch") and blurted as she was running out, "You eat in the meantime and I'll go to the neighbors', they have a car."

"This is my caviar," Manya broke in. "Pay me money."

Nina Ivanovna stopped in the doorway.

"Enough already, for goodness' sake. Why frighten people? Don't be afraid, she's good."

"Only I don't have any dollars right now," Graf replied and bowed to Manya.

Manya started shouting, "So now you brought this lover, you're the one, Ninka, you bare-assed beggar, she can't make strawberry jam, and he's from the same seed. All right, we'll take it."

"That's okay, that's okay, don't worry, all we have to do is get to America, it's not far," Lana answered.

"Two hours all told," Manya said. "I know, they have a town there, Kishinev."

Nina Ivanovna nodded and slipped outside, while Manya went on.

"Kishinev has kishkes. Nothing but kishkes. They buried me behind an old black wall."

"Go on with you," Lana replied, serving Graf tea and a sandwich.

"I've had five whole jobs," Manya boasted. "I'm an old Bolshevik on my mother's side."

Half an hour later Lana took the now full Graf (a sandwich and two cups of mint tea) in the neighbor's Moskvich to Murom, to the station.

They had to drive through the forest, over potholes and ravines, over deep, washed-out ruts.

Graf and Lana, both skinny, reached Murom shaken in the literal sense of the word.

There weren't any tickets for Moscow at the ticket window, and when the train arrived, all the conductors stood in the doorways like gatekeepers prepared to block any goal.

Lana shouted up at them that this was a disabled vet and tried to find the train foreman, but in vain.

One conductor got distracted, though, standing in profile, looking down the corridor, laughing there with someone, and Lana quickly sat Graf and his crutch on the lower step, and he hopped higher, then clambered onto the landing, while Lana plumped her bag on the floor and stood close behind him, clutching the handrail.

Like a wall.

"Where are you going!" the conductor snarled when she turned around and tried to push the old man with her mighty body. "You're not allowed! There aren't any seats. I mean it!"

"This is a disabled veteran," Lana shouted. "I'll take you to court, I'll have you fired! You're an enemy of the people! I'm a correspondent, a journalist! He's on his way to the Kremlin, to give a speech! You're out of your mind, you idiot, pushing a hero! He has a bad heart! Call your foreman here this minute!"

But the train had already started. The conductor, cursing, stood like a mountain in the passage a little longer, but then let Graf and Lana into the corridor, pulled up the steps with a crash, closed the outside train door, locked it, spat in annoyance, and went to her room.

Lana opened the door to the first compartment. Totally empty.

She sat Graf by the window and strolled down the car out of curiosity. Not a single person.

The train to Moscow was traveling without passengers.

But they weren't selling tickets for it in Murom. Lana went to see the conductor to raise hell, she wanted to buy tickets, she demanded the foreman be summoned.

She threatened to write a complaint to the ministry in Moscow, saying, "They'll fire all of you immediately."

Sitting with the fat conductor was yet another fat conductor who obviously sympathized with Lana. She nodded, frowned, and in response to Lana's shout—about who here was responsible for all this and to whom she should write her complaint to the ministry—aimed her thumb at her boss.

In response the now quiet woman brought her and Graf each a glass of tea with sugar, a couple of crackers, and even pills on a saucer.

"This is for your heart. It helps."

And quickly left.

Graf looked at the pills and said, "This is clonidine. It knocks you out for a good seven hours."

Lana, who knew all of Moscow's terrible stories, objected.

"That's if you take it with alcohol."

Thank God no one else bothered them. Lana was bringing a war hero to Moscow, to the Kremlin, after all, but why the trains were running empty she never did find out.

Maybe this was happening everywhere, all over the country, a conspiracy of conductors not to let anyone on at the stations, passengers were nothing but trouble, dirt, and drunkenness. And even if one toilet is closed, the second one still has to be cleaned after them, and there's no money in it whatsoever.

Just a salary, which isn't going to be any more or less whether the car's riding full or empty.

Or someone may have hired the entire train for his own purposes. Who knows? An anniversary or his daughter's wedding.

Strange times had descended upon the country. No one ever explained anything to anyone about what was going on.

45

Graf in Moscow

LANA BROUGHT HER treasure to Moscow. They limped over to the long line for taxis, but then with a shout of "Let a disabled veteran through!" Lana led him past the many waiting passengers (Graf literally galloped on his one crutch, that was the only way that worked), and put him at the head of the motley row.

The thing was that when Graf had clambered onto the train car steps, and Lana was pushing him up, she'd felt sharp pieces of iron in his right pocket through his skinny side.

Before Moscow she made Graf fasten those medals onto his grayish jacket, which was fraying at the elbows and cuffs.

The lapels were a lost cause; they'd been all curled up for a long time.

Not a peep out of anyone.

An impoverished hero, and on a single crutch, aroused the line's unity, solidarity, and good humor (unlike those pregnant girls and mamas with seven children, who made up the permanent avant-garde and source of irritation for the line with the demand "next but one!").

(In those years taxi fleets were shutting down, and private cabs kept clear of Three Stations Square, where cops lay in wait and took bribes—fines, supposedly—from drivers. And then there was the hard-hit, pretty foul-smelling transport that scurried through the

Moscow streets, the migrants' domain, stopping at a raised arm, so dumbfounding the clientele that they waved the same arm to indicate "pass me by!" Transport like that was soon replaced by somewhat cleaner Zhigulis and, best of all, Toyotas.)

But at the station where Lana and Graf arrived, those at the head of the line, with multiple children and pregnant, kept quiet when a long-awaited taxi appeared and Lana, without a glance at anyone, but apologizing, sat her ward in the back seat.

By the way, besides his medals, Graf had retained his passport, his defunct lighter in the form of a pistol, and the keys to his apartment.

Which turned out to be useless. Graf and Lana got there and went upstairs but the keys didn't work; the door to his apartment wouldn't open. As if it were cemented shut.

It wouldn't budge when the handle was tugged.

Although inside there was movement and someone tromped past the other side of the door.

Lana took her hero to the police, having learned where it was from the grandmothers on the bench (Graf referred to them as "popular oversight in action"), sat him on a chair there in the corridor, wrote a statement (Graf signed without reading it), put the paper on the duty officer's desk, made him register this important document, and then went upstairs to see the department chief, Major Klopov (that was the name on the door).

For some reason there was no secretary, and Lana burst into his office shouting, "A war hero, a disabled veteran, is not being allowed into his own apartment by some"—here Lana slowed down—"out-of-town female pensioners! This is the limit! They've commandeered his living space! They're shouting that he married them! But they have no residence permit!"

Lana had chosen this incredible line on purpose so Klopov would understand there was no one to put up a fight there. Female pensioners may be quarrelsome, but they don't attack the police. And how's that? Married to pensioners?

Polygamy?

Graf sat on the first floor quietly cursing, jangling his medals.

He wanted to smoke so he hobbled on his crutch to the duty officer. Who gave him a proper cigarette and respectfully lit it, and Graf
finally, after months of quitting, smoked.

One floor up, Major Klopov, who was not pleased by this old woman's incursion (evidently his secretary had stepped out for a moment,
that happened with her, everyone's human), this major looked first out
the window, then at his pager screen, yawned, and drummed his fingers on his desk, but finally realized he'd lost, and then he got mad and
ordered to call in the patrolman who was responsible for that building
(Lana had to wait an hour and a half next to the secretary, with whom
she instantly hit it off).

The patrolman was sent with Lana and Graf to verify the living
space allegedly occupied by some out-of-town female pensioners.

Said patrolman went with great reluctance to carry out the order—
and Lana immediately realized he knew all about it, and not only that,
it looked as though he had an interest in this apartment, maybe they
were already paying him to live there illegally, or maybe he wanted to
move in himself.

Because when they were still at the station and in the corridor
upstairs, and at the exit to the stairs, he said to Lana, "And who are you
to him? Doesn't he have a wife? Where do you come in? What business
this is of yours anyway, I don't even understand."

"And how do you know?" she objected. "About this wife? What, are
you in on this with her? And are you aware that she took him out to a
village so he wouldn't prevent her from privatizing his apartment here?
To a village, to a hut without a roof? As if that were now his home!
For which she exchanged his apartment! She planted him by the front
porch and made off with one of his crutches, she only left him one—
him, a sick old man! So he couldn't go home! A war veteran, he has
medals, let's go see him, he's sitting downstairs, you'll see for yourself! Have you ever heard a more brazen statement? That that house in

the village belongs to him? Instead of his own apartment in Moscow? An exchange was supposedly made? That's not his home, and on top of everything, it doesn't even have a roof! I have the neighbors' testimony, they all signed!"

(At this Lana pulled out of her purse a few supplementary, already fairly well-worn sheets of paper and held them out to the patrolman. He brushed them aside.)

She went on forcefully.

"The roofless hut belongs to other people, two sisters there are the owners, one is housebound in Vladimir and the other takes care of her. They haven't lived in the village for more than two years. And the house—it's their uns', that's the testimony everyone gave, he didn't buy anything and didn't exchange anything for that house!"

(For authenticity, Lana used a local expression and shuffled her papers.)

"And what?"—she had a flash of insight—"this alleged wife, did she, what, show you his death certificate?"

"What certificate?" the now bored patrolman said.

"What certificate. His death certificate. She bought a forgery. He's alive, see! We'll go downstairs and you'll see, he's sitting covered in medals. A war hero at that!"

"So what do you need?"

"Clear the apartment for him! Let's go! Major Klopov gave you an order! It's Shapochkin's apartment. A war hero. They haven't called you from the veterans' council yet? They're drawing up a lawsuit. The lawyer is Struchok's son. About professional impropriety—yours, by the way."

The patrolman made a face. This was the last thing he needed, on top of everything else.

They went downstairs, where Graf was quietly cursing on his chair with his crutch. He stood up with Lana's help, and they had to stop a private car again—but cars won't stop for a cop in uniform, so Lana went around the corner and tricked a car into picking them up, and the migrant driver wouldn't even take their money, he waved his unwashed hand, slammed the door, and sped off.

(Lana had done the right thing going to the chief alone. Graf couldn't bear that breed and frequently resorted to obscenities in conversations with higher-ups from top to bottom, most often with their director—and was vindicated ultimately when this director eventually sold their building, the design goods combine, to a third party, and vanished into thin air. While here, at the police, Lana was worried they might lock Graf up for those kinds of colorful, extended obscenities.)

This picturesque threesome, worthy of Repin's brush—an overweight patrolman in a uniform that was tight on him, a badly rumpled and hastily (in the train lav) combed Lana (just before Moscow, after her twenty-four-hour trip to Murom), and a skinny Graf, dressed like a vagrant but with medals on his jacket—finally got off the elevator and headed for the door to Graf's apartment.

"Police! Open the door," the patrolman said lackadaisically.

Behind the door, the silence of the grave.

"Did they leave?" Lana worried. Graf rasped out, "Hands up. Surrender! Police! Come out one at a time!"

The cop shook his head in disapproval. Like, "Let's not get ahead of ourselves, it's all going according to plan without any help from you!"

Behind the door, people started running. Oh. That had hit home.

They started shouting (in some language) and swearing (in ours).

Finally, on the other side, they rattled something aside, a bolt, evidently.

There was a wail and twice something banged on the floor.

Without waiting for an order, characters straight out of the "Ali Baba and the Forty Thieves" cartoon started coming out on the stairs, albeit dressed in track pants and T-shirts, badly stained.

There was something rotten in Denmark.

The detachment's vanguard was armed with painters' rollers on long poles, paint buckets, and trowels.

Hanging off the shoulders of the others, though, were striped bags, the latest fashion craze from China. The bags were jam-packed, clearly very heavy, and the last person was also carrying an old suitcase.

"That's mine! They're taking what's mine!" Graf bellowed. "Hands up! Stop! Document check! I'll shoot! You're all going to jail!"

And he instantly pulled out of his pocket, the one opposite his crutch, the lighter that looked like a small pistol. His ever-present toy. He cocked the supposed trigger.

His pride and, evidently, his persuasion in disputes with his fellow bottle sharers.

The cop looked around at him with the same expression on his face, but the thieves ditched their bags and spilled down the stairs.

The rumble kept up for quite a while through the stairwell. The second floor—running downstairs was no problem.

The apartment gaped with its door wide open. Inside it stank. Vile.

The cop went in first.

When he saw the situation (scraps of wallpaper, newspapers stuck to the floor, cut wires dangling from the ceiling, that was in the vestibule, and beyond that there was a faint stink and filth, the kind you find around dumpsters, with trash and spills all around), the patrolman said, "Sort this out yourselves."

Lana and Graf stepped cautiously under the vaults of this cave, and the cop had pressed the button summoning the elevator (from the second floor!) when a young woman with a bandaged head and carrying a child literally bobbed up in front of him.

46

The Apartment Next Door

EITHER THE YOUNG woman had been hiding one floor up. Or she'd just gone unnoticed sitting on the stairs.

"I need to talk to you. I have to get into my apartment. This one here, next door."

"Huh?" The cop didn't understand. "Get into it? What's with you? Are you in cahoots here? My job's done, finished."

The young woman held out her passport, clearly she'd gotten it ready when she saw the cop.

"Look! This is my apartment!"

"If it's yours, why don't you go in? Go in. If it's yours."

"It's mine, here's my registration in my passport. Take a look." The cop reluctantly took the passport.

"It's not your photo."

"Yes, it is. Who else's? It's just from ten years ago. You don't look like yourself in your passport either."

The cop replied, "An old woman and her grandson live here."

"There, you see, I'm her daughter, only my last name's different. It's my husband's."

"Her daughter died. It's not you."

At this the young woman decisively took back her passport.

The cop lost interest. He'd had his eye on this apartment for a long time anyway.

According to his information, the apartment's official tenant, an elderly grandmother, was an alcoholic, and a sick one at that, on her way out, and the kid was little.

No other relatives.

If the granny kicked off, and the baby got sent to a home, who got the apartment? The state.

And the state was—the police, the passport desk, the housing department.

The young woman, this contused woman, kept talking.

"Oh no, it's me, this is me. Here's my passport. I've been away three years, I was working overseas. I came back and was attacked by robbers in a taxi, they took all my luggage, they beat me up, it was a good thing the child was sleeping in my arms. You see?" She touched her bandaged head. "I came home and rang, and no one opened. And a child's locked in!" She started shouting. "There, in the apartment! He's crying, he's moaning, he's alone! What a terrible thing to have happened, do you understand? He's locked in all alone!"

The cop walked toward the door to the next apartment, in no hurry. Stood there.

"It only seems like that, that's all. There's definitely something wrong with your head, lady. Go see a doctor. I need the court's permission to open an apartment. Sure, sure. It all takes time. We know what's going on. We keep up," he said significantly.

And he solemnly entered the elevator and descended into hell.

Alina sat back down on the stair.

Seryozha said, "Ma, I'm hungry! And thirsty! Mama!"

But there was this: the door to Graf's apartment was still open.

And, as always, Lana turned out to know all about it, she just hadn't shown her cards so as not to rile the cop yet again.

"What is it, little one," she said, walking toward the stairs. "Come in, come in, little girl. Everyone come in."

Ten minutes later Alina was sitting next to Graf on the park bench in the kitchen.

She and the child had already been to the fetid bathroom and washed up in the black bathtub.

And now, with Seryozha in her arms, she sipped hot water (Lana had washed and poured boiling water over the empty glass jars left by the former residents.)

And they were eating an old loaf of bread discovered on a shelf, one for all of them.

Not just the black bread, but didn't Lana find a skillet in the bags? Her own skillet, a gift to Graf!

So they ate slices of stale black bread browned in this skillet (Graf dunked it in his hot water). And they found the salt.

"My buddies brought me this bench from the park, for my housewarming," Graf explained for the umpteenth time.

"We remember," Lana said. "How you barely escaped getting picked up by the cops."

"There, in the next apartment," Alina said, "there's a little boy crying in that locked apartment."

"Let's go," Lana said. "Seryozha can sleep here, I've made up a spot for him. My jacket. There's no pillow, but I put down a bundle."

"Mama, I want to go with you," the little boy said.

"Then we'll all go."

Five minutes later they were standing and listening at the neighbor's door, but there was no sound.

"I remember when I came here and they gave me this apartment, I saw a grandmother and her grandson by the elevator. I said hello. She didn't answer but the boy did. She was very proud."

All of a sudden Alina started crying.

After that, she wouldn't budge from the door.

She kept listening, leaning sideways against the crack. Seryozha fell asleep in her arms.

Lana said, "Graf. You know I remember how you opened the door to Boyarsky's office. When he got drunk and lost his keys. You took a taxi home and brought back a bunch of hardware. Everyone said, 'So, Graf, you're a burglar. It's a wonder those painters didn't find your picks. Thieves treasure those.'"

"You have to know camouflage," a preoccupied Graf replied.

He stood there, listened at the door (he heard some kind of whining from there again), and Alina bobbed right up.

Graf nodded, Lana dragged over the suitcase he pointed to, and also helped him open the slightly rusty locks of this ancient, cardboard construction.

In the depths of this treasure trove, wrapped in newspaper, was a pile of keys and hooks, all on an iron ring.

Lana brought out a chair for Graf—but what kind of professional burglar sits down?

He went about his business cheerfully, leaning on his crutch, trying various keys, but the door wouldn't give.

Half an hour fussing with the lock yielded nothing.

Then all of a sudden they heard heavy, uneven steps on the other side.

Graf stepped aside just in case, and Lana pulled the chair back.

There was movement behind the door, a grinding, then a bang (the owner apparently had bolts, too), the lock clicked once, then twice, and the door cracked open—on a chain.

A woman's voice came through the crack.

"What are you doing here? Trying to open my door? I'm calling the police. Robbers! I was resting, why did you get me up?"

The woman was obviously not sober.

"Forgive me, I'm sorry," Alina exclaimed, "a child has been crying in there for a long time. We thought he'd been left alone."

"And who are you? What right do you have? Yes, the boy's crying, he's being naughty. He doesn't want to eat."

Seryozha woke up in her arms at this yelling.

He stared with his big eyes at the old woman shouting through the crack.

And started crying himself.

All of a sudden the chain was removed and the door opened. The old woman took a step forward and said, pointing at Seryozha, "This is who? What's his name?"

Alina replied, "Seryozha Sertsov."

"How old is he?"

"Three."

"What's his birthday?"

"March eighteenth."

"You mean you were in the maternity hospital with my Masha?"

Alina, upset, stepping back, replied, "What's going on?"

"You have mine! This is, I don't know, some kind of miracle! This is Masha's son, I recognize him! He's turned up! Give him back, you horrible woman! This is my Masha, this is her little! The spitting image! They misled me, tricked me back then, passed off one for the other! Give him back this instant!"

The woman grabbed Seryozha with a trembling hand, but he clung to Alina and hid his face in her T-shirt.

Lana immediately stepped in front of the old woman, walling off her people.

But the old woman kept tugging on Seryozha's shirt. Crying, she kept saying, "This is the living Masha! One of my arms doesn't work, have mercy on me! This is my child! It's a mistake, a terrible mistake was made! My mistake, I admit it now! Masha, come to me! Because of me someone died, I'm to blame, but only now have I seen my Mashenka, my real live Mashenka!"

And all of a sudden crying was heard from the other side of the door, from the apartment.

A little boy, skinny, tear-stained, his little face red, grabbed the apartment owner's skirt and pulled her back, repeating, "Mama, mama!"

"Wait, let go, leave me alone," the old woman shouted, not looking at him. "You've ruined my whole life, get away this minute, Sergei! Don't yell! You think I can cook for you with one arm? How can I turn on the gas when only my left works?"

She reeked of liquor.

Alina held tight to her frightened Seryozha and stared wide-eyed at the little boy standing in the apartment over the shoulder of Lana and this strange woman. A puffy little face, red from crying, big, screwed-up eyes, winglike eyebrows, a large nose.

She recognized him. The head of Antinoüs.

Lana said to the old woman, "You poor thing, what's wrong? What's happened to you?"

"I'm paralyzed, my right side! See?" She nodded toward her shoulder.

Indeed, her right arm was dangling like a vine. Lana tenderly took the woman by her left arm, gently detached her from Seryozha's shirt, and led the old woman into her apartment.

She kept mumbling, "I went and stole him. But that was a mistake! This isn't your little boy. Give me that one. I killed someone for him."

"Yes, yes, poor woman, we'll take care of everything right away, we'll feed you."

"No, buy me two half liters of brandy, please, I'm begging you on my knees. I don't feel well, I don't feel well at all. That's the only thing that helps, takes away the pain, lets me sleep."

She turned toward Alina, and, stepping shakily, holding Lana's arm, continued.

"That's my child, the one you have. What a coincidence! Things like this don't happen, do you understand? He appeared to me when I was already dead. I died in the night. He appeared so I'd get up. I don't feel well, not at all well . . ."

And she was drawn down, bent over, fell to her knees, and buried her face in her own skirt.

The little boy sat next to her, repeating, "Mama, mama!"

Alina leaned over toward him with Seryozha in her arms. Her son.

He was big already, but his exhausted, puffy little face, red from crying, his swollen eyelids—it was unchanged.

Little Avtandil. As his parents led him away and he turned around helplessly.

She had to keep her cool.

Seryozha suddenly slipped to the floor and hugged the new little boy, repeating, "Don't cry, don't cry."

Alina scooped them both up and carried them past the old woman doubled over on the floor.

Over whom Lana was leaning with a cup of water in her hand.

She tried to get her to drink, and the old woman took a sip and started coughing.

Alive.

Lana tried to help her up, but couldn't.

Alina put down the children and helped Lana drag the lying woman to the sofa and put a pillow under her head.

An inert body. What should they do?

No more than a body: it raised its head and mumbled, droned something.

"Are you thirsty?" Alina asked.

"Naturally," the body answered, and it lowered its head. After this began the procedure of giving her a sip, its head starting to cough, spilling everything, saying, "You have to know what you're doing. Where are you bringing the cup? Past my mouth. Why did you choose that one? That's a company cup. There are everyday ones."

They helped her drink.

Then the head said to them both, "What are you doing here? How did you get in? Who are you anyway?"

"I brought little Seryozha from Handia," Alina replied.

"You didn't bring any Seryozha, he's here with me," the head said. "Wipe my mouth, my whole chest is wet."

Alina went to the bathroom, found a towel there, fairly grimy, and wiped the sick woman.

She started in again. "Who are you, that tramp who gave birth next to Masha, that scumbag Sertsov took on as a wet nurse? To feed who knows who? You've got me soaking wet now. I have to change my underthings."

She tried to get up.

"I don't think I can move my legs."

She tried again, leaning with all her strength on her one palm.

"No. For some reason I don't feel a thing. I can't feel my legs."

"Call an ambulance?" Alina said.

It was like the Handian situation all over again: the mistress and her slave.

"Maybe you should. Call one." At that moment, Lana walked in with the children. "Alina, I put some hot porridge on for them. I found the rice there. And a can of condensed milk. Ah, hello, dear woman, how are we feeling?"

"What, have you all moved in with me here?" the sick woman asked.

"As it is you've had a child crying behind your door for a whole day so we had to open the lock," Lana replied. "The child might have died."

"You discovered the rice and condensed milk? Dug through everything, found everything?" the old woman asked coolly. "And who is this other boy? Who is this other boy? Ah! My God, my God! It's my Masha, my Masha has come alive!"

The previous situation repeated itself. Evidently, the ill woman had forgotten everything that had happened.

"Just like Masha at three years old! From Handia! Handia! I made a mistake! I stole the other one! What can I do? What can I do!"

She sobbed at the top of her voice, letting go completely.

She goggled through her tears and reached out with her one hand toward Alina's Seryozha. Who hid behind his mama.

Right then the second boy ran to his grandmother and buried his head in her robe.

She put her arm around him, held him close, and said to him, "We aren't giving you away to anyone, not to anyone. Don't be afraid. You're my little boy. And this is Masha's little boy. Come to me!"

Alina quietly said to Seryozha, "Go, say hello to your grandmother. She's taken ill."

You had to feel sorry for her.

Seryozha, a compliant and also hungry child, obediently went up to the old woman lying there.

She put her arm around the two children, pressed them close together, and commanded, "I can't die, I can't, understand? Have you called an ambulance? My Masha sent me her son so I wouldn't die. He told me to open the door to you, he came into my room."

The rice milk porridge was finally ready, the children were taken to the kitchen, Alina fed the old woman, earning several vitriolic comments, and then the ambulance came.

Alina led in a burly female medic. She was alone.

"So, what's wrong with you?" she asked wearily.

"Hello, what's your name?" the old woman asked in an authoritative voice.

"What's with you?" the woman repeated.

Alina intervened.

"Paralysis of both legs, evidently."

After an examination and telephone consultation the medic said, "We have to take you in. But who's going to carry you? Our driver's never lifted anything heavier than a bottle in his life, and I'm one big prolapse from carrying more than my share. Do your best, get your neighbors to help."

Alina said that all the neighbors were at their dacha.

"Well, I'm warning you, the hospital where they might take you doesn't have sheets. Or pillowcases. The laundry isn't operating. There's no detergent. Bring your own."

"Do they have doctors?" the sick woman asked.

"Oh, they're all on vacation. In practice it's med students from

Lumumba U. Blacks and slants from North Korea, third-years. They've been complaining to me in admissions. Asking me not to bring anyone else. They'll be practicing on you. But there aren't any medicines, either."

"So-o-o," the sick woman droned. "What am I supposed to do if I'm at home?"

"It's no skin off our backs. We can't know what's going to come of the stroke, the paralysis. All you can do is wait. Well, and massage, exercises."

"Do you know how to do massage?" the old woman asked Alina. Alina shrugged.

"What's there to know?" the medic grunted. "It's the same as with kids. Kneading, rubbing, slapping, tingling. Twisting, tapping. Picking up, letting go. Not that that will help. You'll get bedsores. We've been down that road, we know."

"Who did you call for me?" the old woman asked.

Alina shrugged.

"Zero three. The ambulance."

"I'm special contingent. What's wrong with you? There's a little address book by the telephone. Under *k*, for *Kremlyovka*. I'm a KGB lieutenant, my ID is in the lower left drawer, in the wall unit."

"What's the Kremlyovka?" Alina asked.

"It's the Kremlin hospital," the medic said energetically. "All the doctors there are hotshots. They take all the precautions. The specialists are better, too. Well, if that's the case, so long. You're sending people on wild goose chases."

But after the call to the Kremlyovka, the sick woman suffered another stroke, and she died before the Kremlyovka ambulance arrived.

In the morning, a doctor came, then that same patrolman checked in, peered in from the threshold, nodded, and left. In the late afternoon, the deceased was taken away, moreover they hinted at payment.

("There were lots of calls, but we dropped everyone else and came here, you know," the orderly said. The other nodded.)

No payment was forthcoming, so they demanded that Alina undress the body, then they lifted the unfortunate naked woman by her arms and legs on two sheets, tied the knots, and left with their cargo.

Alina upturned all the cupboards and desk drawers and found the documents for Masha's grave.

Along with everything else, she discovered in Tamara Gennadievna's documents her red ID with the letters "KGB" embossed on the cover. In her name. Turns out, she was a lieutenant.

Or she'd bought herself the ID somewhere in some underground passage. In those days, all kinds of covers were for sale everywhere, and you could order any diploma or ID in your name, even minister of health or university president. Even a general in the police.

All the money in the deceased woman's purse went to her burial.

But there was no way to pay to have her name chiseled on the marker. The gravediggers ended up leaving a plain stone.

The mother was put to rest with her daughter, though.

Alina burst into tears remembering her good-hearted neighbor in the ward. And how Masha had loved that scumbag Sertsov. Who cheated on her with a paid prostitute.

In the vilest moments of Alina and Sertsov's life together, he would bring up that Lariska and her little ways.

47

Alina's New Family

SOON AFTER, ALINA and the boys were brought to we-know-whose fazenda, to the garden association, where she and Lana put up food for the winter, Graf repaired the leaning shower and then spent hours tidying the shed, only to find, among the firewood, a book by an unknown author, people said. It was À l'ombre des jeunes filles en fleurs.

Graf liked the book without a title very much, and he spent all summer reading it in the shed.

The house was noisy, there were children running around, their own and the neighbors', and there was jam on the simmer.

Graf instituted cleanliness in the shed and the wonderful smell of firewood. His pal the Heir, who we all remember, would stop by.

All this happened far from Lana's eagle eye.

The settlement's male complement, the few luminaries left among the living, a goldmine of banned artists who'd earned their bread at the combine and in children's publishing houses, would join Graf in the shed.

He even set up two benches there and a kind of one-legged table.

The old cupboard, all dry and cracked, in the corner, had been there however long, and there were some wood sticks, an axe, a plane, chisels. A hammer and nails.

They reminisced about the past and treated each other to last year's stash of homemade liqueurs.

They discussed the children's lessons—right now Lana was teaching them to draw with a pencil.

Graf declared that drawing with colored pencils was a Vkhutemas idea.

He was supported in this: "Nikita Favorsky drew amazingly in pencil!"

Graf went on: "It's a rejection of recognizable local color. The task here simply is to build some kind of structure from this array of colors, six pieces, mixed. She's not teaching that. She just says, draw a dog. But that's wrong!"

"Oh, they're still little," the luminaries replied.

They reminisced:

"How we used to travel all over the Union, from city to city! Outside Vologda we found ourselves with some Old Believers, four sisters and their mute brother. He carved these duck saltcellars—*solonki*—out of wood for us, so we called the family the *Solonitsy*. Well, Borya Alimov bought them from him and got reimbursed by the Union of Artists. He went out, came back drunk, and all of a sudden said, 'I drove a tough bargain! I can send them all to hell!'"

He was supported in this:

"At the time, there were procedures for every enterprise—a portrait of Lenin for management, revolution, war, and history in the hallway, and pretty flowers and a still life for the secretary. They had money for that and they paid us in the combine. Not like now."

Graf interjected, "Animals were for the kindergartens."

"Forget about that, four-legger," the unemployed, long since impoverished master craftsmen told him.

"Hey," Graf objected, "these days the Impressionists turn out to have been realists."

"Let's drink to modern art," the Heir said in support. "Garbage is the theme now!"

"And Rousseau was a hack, churning out copies to sell," Graf said. "And *Hedgehog in the Fog* is badly drawn."

"You mean the horse? No, I like it, but you would've made it better, more expressive," the Heir said, and he plucked a stray mashed currant out of the jar.

To which Graf, who was overflowing with thoughts about art, expressed himself as follows: "Don't be afraid to make mistakes. Don't be afraid to screw up. Learn to wiggle out of any situation. The picture should resemble life, but you have to add something fresh to it."

"Otherwise it'll be like a photograph," a pleased Heir supported him, wiping a black currant smear off his face. "That's something to be afraid of."

Graf elaborated on his theme:

"The eye sees a great many things that a camera misses. There's something we see that can't be photographed. We may take pleasure in a precise line, but now, when it doesn't come out, we get our marching orders: something's wrong, don't change the situation. And you can't fix your old work. Our pictures are testimony to an era."

Meanwhile Alina's boys made friends with everyone straightaway through the gardening association, and the gang of dacha kids would run off to swim in the pond at the forest edge, catch small floating creatures with a net, put them in a three-liter jar with the same water, and admire their handiwork on the windowsill.

Alina started an English class and had half the settlement and their children attending—a social event.

Everyone memorized poems and the mothers brought refreshments.

It was free, after all.

As a result, through the preschoolers' efforts, they put on a performance of Marshak's *Attic* in English.

This was the dacha settlement for that same former design combine, so it was all their own people living there, artists and designers. And the costumes were exceptional.

Graf himself, the four-legged specialist, painted the sets, and all his animals were as good as, if not better than, Disney's.

His troika of horses painted on a piece of old wallpaper came out especially well. Horses were his passion.

But designers rarely had orders for them. Horses in a kindergarten? On a House of Culture wall?

48

Threats

WHEN ALINA RETURNED to the apartment with a backpack full of wrapped jars (from grateful parents) and her progeny, the impatient patrolman paid a visit.

He was sick of waiting. "Incredible, two months!" His monologue ran to the effect that the orphan was being removed to a care home tomorrow, and she had to empty the apartment of her things.

"Whatever you don't take will go to the dump," he said. "The vagrants there will sort it out fast. There's a line waiting. The deputy minister's family is coming from Semipalatinsk. His mother-in-law and whole family."

He went on to inform her, as if reading off a written page, that she shouldn't worry about the child, there was no need, because upon reaching fifteen years of age, this minor Sergei Sergeyevich Sertsov would leave the children's home with an eighth-grade education, would enter a technical school with a dorm, and a few years later would be given a room by the state meeting the standard of twelve square meters per person plus three square meters for being a responsible tenant.

To these ravings Alina replied that she'd been registered at this apartment since she was five years old.

"Passport," the cop demanded.

"I'll show it to you," she said. "You have no right to take this apartment away, and I won't give it to you. You have an interest in my apartment, after all."

"What's that?" the cop was indignant.

"I have information that you and the passport officer registered to yourselves two apartments of deceased pensioners, who were single but had relatives. Zakharov and Umnova. The relatives are filing lawsuits right now."

"Those went to the state! Second cousins twice removed! And now they're making claims! Writing! They've got a snowball's chance in hell! But I'm on the list. I have every right seeing as I'm police!"

"You didn't stand in line for the apartment, and people found out. You're from out of town, you've worked in Moscow for three years. You have no right to a separate apartment! You only have that right after ten years!"

"I'm not in the line! There's a word for people like you. Dissident! For human rights, get it! Free this space or I'll put you in Serbsky Psych!"

"I'm registered here. Take it to court, and it'll decide in my favor."

"This passport's a forgery. Maria Sertsova died three years ago. The passport officer has all the facts. We're going to drag you out of here by the arms and take away your children. The care home's been upset about them for a long time, with them running around here. They'll take your things out to the yard. And the next in line will swoop right in with their own furniture."

"Sertsov and I performed our mission in Handia as a married couple, understand? For State Security, understand? I'm a KGB lieutenant!"

The cop pursed his lips and shook his head with a grin.

Alina continued calmly.

"That's actually why he and Masha got married, although he had another woman. The baby was born exactly a week before departure, but Masha died in childbirth. She and I were next to each other in the maternity hospital and got to be friends. My fiancé was taken away to Georgia by his parents. I lay in the maternity hospital without a husband but with a baby. But the work Sertsov and Masha had spent a whole year preparing for, important work for the KGB's foreign department, was endangered. So after Masha's death they found me in the maternity hospital. I'd decided to give up my baby at the time, I had no home, no family, no money, a university student from the dorm, and I agreed to go to Handia."

"Listen," the cop spoke importantly, interrupting this useless rubbish.

"No, you listen. And I left immediately with Masha's son and Sertsov, I nursed him, I raised him for three years. But Captain Beryozin came from the KGB and he took me into intelligence work. I have five languages and I also learned Handi and Irdu there. Sertsov wasn't supposed to know anything about it. I duplicated all his reports and sent them off, I had my own handler, while Sertsov sent them through his own channels. His own hackwork. His goal was to make money. But I duplicated all his information and labored honestly for the agency. Then he went to escort two shipments of copper scrap, and both those shipments supposedly sank. There were huge insurance payoffs. Lloyd's, you've heard of them?" The cop raised an eyebrow and nodded, the idiot. "I had to leave Handia with the child. I took a taxi with my baggage to Skhodni, but my house there had been sold. I asked to spend the night with a girl I went to school with, and she took me to this house, where they tried to kill me as I was sleeping, I woke up, the baby's crying, I've got a head wound, my luggage is gone, and it's a good thing I had my documents hidden on myself as usual. They'd notified me in Handia through my liaison that I'd been promoted to lieutenant."

And now came the crowning moment.

Alina pulled out of her purse Tamara Gennadievna's red-covered ID, inscribed "KGB" and showed it to the cop. He was about to reach for it, but Alina said, "This isn't for you to examine. Haven't you been informed? I still haven't reported to Major Beryozin about my arrival. I have to call him in Handia. But according to KGB documents, the apartment belongs to me and my son. And the child who has lived here since birth and is registered as the son of Maria and Sertsov, he is also the apartment's owner. Why there is yet another child here, I haven't been told, but I'm not giving him up to any children's home. Is this all clear? I'm going to call Major Beryozin. I'm a KGB lieutenant. If anything happens, if you take any initiative here, you'll be fired. You'll lose your apartment and be taken to court for exceeding your authorities, is that clear?"

By the middle of this statement, the cop had begun to have second thoughts, check his watch, look around, and a few times he raised his hand, as if to reassure Alina, and by the end he was much diminished, nodded a few times to indicate everything was under control, not to worry, lieutenant, and he slunk off.

49

Life after Life

NEVERTHELESS, SHE DID have to go to the university with her own passport, sort things out with the fourth- and fifth-year classes she missed, and then take the state exams while also getting some kind of a job.

At first the little foundling cried terribly at the dacha every night, called Alina auntie, and asked, "Where's Mama?" but later, imitating the older Seryozha, he started calling her mama.

Later the younger Seryozha somehow naturally became Osya. Upon her return, Alina discovered a nearby daycare and started there as an aide, and put both Seryozhas there, that was her condition, and the reason she could make any demands was that soon afterward she started teaching English.

She was useful, an aide with two languages.

Both little boys called her mama, both Seryozha Sertsovs, and in their birth certificates, for both of them, the mother was Maria and the father Sergei.

It didn't matter, though, the director needed money and an aide, and with that kind of janitress (Alina's job title as the director put it), the daycare was besieged by parents, and the children recited English poems (and on Fridays sang French songs).

The daycare was no longer free. And soon not cheap.

Later it was privatized and turned into a dental clinic.

At that time, lots of daycares were shutting down, the birth rate in the country had plummeted, mothers were paid once a month a sum sufficient for one trip to the grocery store (much later, when the situation became truly dreadful—the country was losing several million people a year, and this in peacetime—the authorities came to their senses and instituted a multiple-child allowance, in order to salvage the situation).

For a long time, Alina couldn't find another job.

Her searches for money in the strange apartment led nowhere, and in order for everyone to get fed, she was forced to start selling editions of collected works.

These were all popular authors, a good selection, not Pushkin-Tolstoy-Dostoevsky, which were on sale everywhere, but Thompson Seton, Jack London, Conan Doyle, and even Dumas and Maugham, which the buyers in secondhand bookstores were happy to take.

In Soviet times, these collected works were not for sale to the public, by the way, they were subscribed to by Party district and provincial committee secretaries, diplomats, and directors of enterprises and company stores. Well, and some speculators had connections in book warehouses. The print runs of limited-run books were always rising. Otherwise what gain?

The people needed books in those days.

Vysotsky's poetry collection, *Nerve,* an entire train carload of it, was stolen one night. It had been standing on the tracks.

Ordinary people were offering trash fiction, kilos of old magazines, textbooks, and just books they didn't need, in order to buy works by the most beloved Soviet writer, Pikul. While bookstores had the works of Writers Union members who numbered in the thousands in Moscow alone. When those books expired, they were written off and taken away to be pulped.

But that's just by the by.

Then it came time for Alina to take the silver bracelets to the consignment stores and, in the end, a massive goblet, all of this pulled out from behind the glass of a lacquered wall unit, from the family treasure trove.

About the goblet, the buyer at the consignment store said respectfully, "This is a genuine Kubachi."

Alina didn't know what a Kubachi was and didn't argue when he wrote down a modest sum.

Graf later explained that Kubachi was a village in Dagestan famous for its massive, high-quality silver crafts.

"And very expensive," Lana added sadly.

One rainy evening, Alina crawled home from another lesson with the daughter of a rich TV anchor and graphomaniac (known for the fact that he had taken his daughter from her mother so he wouldn't have to pay alimony, an act many rich fathers had taken into their repertoire).

This particular father approached Alina with his monumental belly to suggest she take half as much for his daughter's lessons.

And that's how much money he gave her.

Alina shrugged, took the half fee, and said he should look for another tutor.

And went out into the rain to wait for a bus.

Which arrived half an hour later, crammed with people, at the overfull stop.

The apartment was quiet.

She could tell from the threshold that Lana had left.

Alina had a bad feeling. She walked in and immediately heard the little boys' muffled laughter and some kind of banging-knocking.

Entering her bedroom, she discovered the boys sitting on the floor. One was armed with scissors, and the other by his side had his tongue out, mentally helping, waiting for his turn.

Colored paper was heaped around the children. It was old money! Portraits and views of the Kremlin cut out from it were lying on a separate piece of cardboard with a tube of glue.

"Ma, we're making a collage!" the older Seryozha shouted, using Graf's term.

He called any children's drawing brought to him for praise a collage.

The younger Seryozha, aka Osya, casting a glance at his mother, hurried to keep cutting. He realized he'd done something bad and decided to go whole hog.

"What are you up to, people?" Alina asked.

"We found this folder behind the cupboard!" the older Seryozha exclaimed. "There were pictures there!"

"Money, you dunce," the younger Seryozha, aka Osya, corrected him. "It's going to be a very expensive collage! We're going to sell it!"

"Right. This has to stop," Alina said.

"Ma, is it okay if we cut the portraits out of these green pictures?"

"What . . . green?" Alina choked.

"We found them there in the folder, too. Show her, Seryozha."

And the older Seryozha pointed his mother to a stack of dollars peacefully lying in a pocket of the opened black folder.

"My ball rolled under your cupboard, and I saw there was something there, it was up against the wall, but I could see it. We took a brush and a stick and pushed it out. It had pretty papers in it. And these green ones."

Alina took the folder into her bedroom.

Five thousand dollars. Fifty banknotes.

That made sense.

Why wouldn't diplomats save up enough hard currency to last their whole life?

It was another thing entirely that Soviet people didn't have the right to do that.

People were sent to prison and executed over hard currency.

Suddenly Alina was afraid of everything. She didn't pick up the phone (who in the world could know this number?), didn't respond to the doorbell in the evening, and taught the children not to run up and ask, "Who's there?"

Lana, dear Lana, took it upon herself to exchange the first hundred dollars.

First of all, everyone in the combine knew her and loved her from their skit parties.

And there were some very well-off people working in their combine, mosaic specialists who designed hydro stations, metro stations, elegant banks, and private pools.

It was they who traveled all over the world, who had the money and needed hard currency.

And who could suspect Lana, an old woman, of speculation? She'd found the money at a payphone and that was that.

Someone had hung her purse on the hook, and all that was in it was dollars and no ID.

In principle, someone that absent-minded could well end up in concrete over the lost dollars (a barrel of wet concrete was the most popular form of execution in those days).

So Lana went to the payphone and stood watch next to it for a week (she was preparing an alibi just in case and really did stand there with a grave expression to make sure the lady in the newspaper stand and the ice cream lady saw her).

They made friends with Lana, actually, after all everyone in the neighborhood where Alina and Graf's building was, anyone who had spoken with her even once, was her friend.

True, by law anything found went to the state and the finder was paid a certain percentage of the amount.

But the mosaic designers said nothing, took the dollars, and gave her rubles.

This exchange of hard currency could have cost them seven years in prison camp.

So little by little, the dollars came into play.

50

The Committee of Our Women

EVENTUALLY, ALINA GOT a job with the Committee of Our Women, an international organization whose editors, for example, supplied cases of Kalashnikovs to struggling Angola.

One such colleague in that same Angola started having terrible belly pains while crossing a river's swampy floodplain (she was shouldering a crate of weapons).

The Committee's unfortunate, moaning representative was airlifted in the rebels' helicopter to a hospital, where they diagnosed her with an ectopic pregnancy!

A first for the military hospital.

Alina had been hired for the Committee's Handian department as a translator. Fine.

She'd already passed all her exams, defended her thesis, and received her diploma. Also thanks to those green portraits . . . everything in her life had stabilized, and the only thing she was lacking was men.

Men were kept only in senior positions on the women's committee, and they didn't condescend to staff.

In addition, Alina wore her hair in a bun, eschewed makeup, and wore skirts of the saddest length and Soviet shoes or, in the winter, Soviet boots modeled after military footwear.

They were good in the rain and wintry slush, and when she pulled her foot out—all dry.

She propped her boots up against the radiator to dry in an inconspicuous spot, to one side.

And since it was made clear that in addition to Handi, Alina also knew Irdu, and besides that English, French, and the languages of our brother Slavs, they were constantly dragging her to negotiations and took pride in her appearance. A modest Soviet laborer!

(Tereshkova herself had been such a woman, the best woman in the Soviet Union, a weaver-cosmonaut. They cut and curled her hair, dressed her, and gave her a European look, but you can't cover up hands and cheekbones, or an innate lack of facial expression, to say nothing of pronunciation.)

Once a week, that privileged international organization gave out groceries—Hungarian green peas, Bulgarian lecsó, Polish pickled cucumbers, three hundred grams of Sovetsky cheese, two packets of Jubilee cookies, a kilo of buckwheat groats, and two cans of pink salmon in its own juice.

That is, the family enjoyed a fabulous life.

And every so often there were parties at their house.

On Saturdays, ladies would show up with flowers, a bottle of sweet champagne, and a torte, and the men with we-know-what.

Lana even complained about her friends from the combine, who would make any excuse to visit Graf, and always with these presents.

"Graf will drink, though he shouldn't," Lana would repeat over the phone. "Don't bring any."

So she would have to lay out a spread for them. Bake potato and onion pies.

The younger family members would take advantage of the occasion and eat enough to last until Monday.

But Alina never stopped being afraid. Afraid that Sergei-*père* would show up.

Supposedly he'd died, but from time to time information would reach her from former co-workers in the trade office (everyone simmered in the same diplomatic soup, and a thing or two even reached the Committee of Our Women) that the disappearance of the two ships with the copper scrap intended for building a statue to Christopher Columbus (a gift from the Soviet land to some uninterested Latin Americans), whose insurance had been paid by Lloyd's—that this insurance case was still being investigated.

Some large sums had gone missing, too.

51

A Terrible Call

UNTIL ONE DAY she got a call—on her mobile phone, because the years had sped by and it was the twenty-first century—from an unknown number.

A man's voice, totally gangster, said, "Fucking Maria Sertsova?"

"Y . . . No. You've got the wrong number."

"No, I don't have the fucking wrong number. Alina?"

"What do you want?" she said, switching to the same tone of voice as the caller.

"We're wondering what condition Sergei Ivanovich Sertsov's fucking son is in."

"What's going on? You mean he's alive? Didn't he go down with that copper ship?"

"We want to pay for his fucking education, understand? He'll be seventeen soon. So he doesn't end up in the army. Fuck, that's as bad as prison."

"You'd know better than I would," Alina objected with a pounding heart.

"Did he fucking graduate from high school?"

"Yes. The English-language one."

"And he speaks it?"

"Perfectly," Alina boasted for some unknown reason.

"Let's cut to the chase. He's being sent an invitation to go to Montegasco."

"Ah. Lots of people hiding out there."

"That's none of your fucking business. We fucking have the ability to give Sergei Sergeyevich Sertsov an education in England."

"And who are you?"

"Me? I'm the fucking lawyer. And bear in mind that you living in someone else's apartment under someone else's passport isn't risk-free, either. When Sergei Sergeyevich Sertsov leaves for Montegasco, his apartment has to be sold and the money has to be transferred to the account we tell you."

"And when will he come back?"

"He won't."

"Into a barrel of liquid concrete and to the bottom of the sea?"

"You bitch. A tongue like that can be cut out so it doesn't wag too much."

"Naturally, Seryozha isn't going anywhere. Until his father calls me. Who has been officially ruled dead."

"Alina, let's talk seriously. Seryozha's father was fished out of the ocean in an unconscious state by fishermen, he lived on an island for a long time and didn't speak. Then he moved to a certain Latin American country, where he acquired a fortune."

"Yeah, that insurance from Lloyd's."

"That's all a myth. And Sergei Ivanovich had no desire to return to his country of residence."

"Oh, they've been waiting for him here for a long time." And Alina surprised herself by joking, "Two with a stretcher, one with a shovel." Alina had used one of Sergei's sayings. What can you do? Live with a wolf, howl like a wolf. Three years of those speeches, it was like doing hard labor. Prison.

The voice replied, "We've got that all sorted."

"Yes, they haven't called me in a long time."

"You don't call from the next world." The lawyer thought that was funny.

"And what, you think I'm going to send my son to a papa like that?"

"He's not your son. And very soon he's going to be fully informed. He himself, he alone, will control the money from his apartment. And every boy wants to know his father. Think about it. And don't let it get out of hand. As to the second Seryozha, the pretender, in the event of your resistance, we'll send him to a certain republic, to a village in the mountains, to a cellar, where they'll castrate him and sell him to men. It's all arranged."

At this the connection dropped. Alina finally sat down.

The fact that both Seryozhas dreamed of knowing, each, his own father, was the truth.

And these threats were real, too. But not in Montegasco.

In Montegasco you could warn the police, moreover on the day of arrival, that a kidnapping was in progress.

The next day she made some inquiries with some people she knew, and not just any people but from the former Committee of Our Women.

They all recommended Montegasco as a country with a ferocious and meticulous police system.

Someone from the Foreign Ministry, a friend of a friend, said that the fact that Sergei Ivanovich Sertsov was living there was a mistake by the local agencies, now irremediable. He'd come to the country as a victim of Soviet terror, after jumping into the open ocean and being fished out in an unconscious state by fishermen, and the reason he'd jumped was that in the Soviet Union he was threatened with the Gulag (a word the whole world knows).

Now he'd surfaced for some reason in Montegasco, far from the Pacific Ocean, shown up and gone to all kinds of trouble to marry a Montegasco citizen, a Russian moreover, from an old noble family whose descendants long ago, in the terrible year 1918, had fled from

Crimea to Turkey, from there to Yugoslavia, and from there to Belgium, winding up, finally, in Montegasco in the person of a fairly young woman of thirty with a child.

Three years after marrying this citizen of Montegasco, our personage was granted provisional citizenship and purchased a half-hectare estate with a villa and, naturally, a gatehouse.

It was here that this victim of the Red Terror learned from this wife of his that he had to adopt her son. So that after the owner's decease the estate would go to his heir rather than the state.

According to Montegasco law, only children could be heirs, not widowed spouses.

Interested parties in Russia had made futile efforts to get Sertsov to return to the homeland, since, under Montegasco law, as a victim of the Red Terror, he was not subject to extradition to any other country.

This law had been passed back in the 1920s, when everyone was fleeing Russia—over the hills and far away.

Every individual deemed to be a White—nobles, doctors, professors, officers, lawyers, philosophers, bankers, artists, writers, composers, singers, and merchants—all the country's best people had fled.

Characters out of Chekhov plays.

They'd abandoned it for fear of execution.

Alina's own great-grandfather, a trustee of grammar schools in Kostroma, had been taken away—and that was the end of him.

But she also learned that Sertsov was being watched in Montegasco.

The police and prosecutor's office had traced all his contacts and the movements of his immense capital.

This is what Alina's friends in the Committee of Our Women were told at the Foreign Ministry.

That is, the boys would be safe there.

Whereas here, in Russia, should she fail to obey, Sertsov's pals and accomplices would kidnap the boys and confiscate the apartment.

The next evening, she told the boys that finally the father (without specifying whose) wanted to see his son, that he was living in Montegasco, and that he had a plan to send his son to England to study.

And she asked who wanted to go.

"No question. We'll both go," Seryozha senior said. "We'll say we're twins and can't be separated."

"But there's only going to be one invitation."

In short, no invitation turned up in the mailbox anytime soon.

Soon after, a call came from someone calling himself a lawyer.

"No, nothing's come from you," Alina said. "What do you mean?"

Evidently her sarcastic tone convinced her experienced interlocutor.

Finally the invitation arrived. The younger Seryozha brought it to his mother respectfully.

A little while later, both Seryozhas started packing and asked their mother to buy them good backpacks, T-shirts, and shorts.

"So," she said. "Why are you both going?"

"We took one invitation out of the mailbox and waited thinking maybe another would come."

Both of them well knew the story of their time at the maternity hospital, only they didn't want to know who was who.

Why should they? They had Mama and they had Grandpa Graf and Grandma Lana.

52

NIKOLAI:
Guests in Montegasco

MOREOVER, THEIR MAMA had officially changed her full name; it was more convenient for her to be M. V. Sertsova.

She changed her diploma, too. Mama is Mama.

Nikolai the driver drove them both to the villa.

Well, they shook hands, and the host stood there stunned, not expecting two. "Why don't we get acquainted? So. Two came, only one was expected. Which of you is Seryozha—Sergei Sergeyevich?"

One said, "Both of us."

And they started laughing like idiots.

The host said, "I don't get the joke."

They both started digging around, got out their passports, still laughing, and showed them to him. The host's jowls started flapping and his teeth grinding. He put the passports in his pocket and said, "What're you trying to pull? Should I call the police? What twins? What is this, a setup?"

They were too upset to say a word.

Kolya's boss was a tough guy and had cracked much tougher nuts than these here. Kolya had witnessed that on occasion but hadn't told a soul.

"That's why you wrote you hadn't received the invitation? So you'd get a second one? You're putting me on?"

They were too dazed to say a word.

"Well, which one of you is my son? I'm asking seriously. I have forces in motion here that you'll find formidable. They'll get to the bottom of this. So, shall I call them?"

"But why do you need a son?" one asked.

"Why is my business. Any other questions?"

"But what if the truth is unknown? We don't know ourselves. Neither does Mama."

"What Mama is that?" At this he swore. "My son's mama, Maria Valerievna, died in childbirth! And that's that! She was my wife! But this one . . . where did she crawl out of? What's her name?"

"Maria Valerievna."

"Maybe to you, but the hell she's Maria Valerievna! I buried Maria Valerievna in the ground! And put up a tombstone!"

They were silent for a while.

"So," the owner said weightily. You could tell he was dying for the truth. He'd drag it out of them.

"Are you hungry?"

"No, thank you," one said.

"Tea?"

He'd found his move.

Nikolai understood that, and he understood what that move was.

They exchanged looks.

"Okay," the same Seryozha replied.

"Sit here for now."

They exchanged glances and sat down.

One talked, the other didn't.

The other, actually—Kolya could tell—he was the boss.

You can tell who's boss by who talks the least. Bosses bide their time, don't show their cards right away.

And the first one, who replied, he was the errand boy. That's what Galina said, and she was a smart cookie. The boss had called her on the intercom.

"So, Galina, some Babylon tea."

And to them: "Would you like a cookie?"

"No, thank you," the errand boy said.

"Delicious cookies, also from Babylon."

"All right, then."

"From an ancient recipe, with cinnamon and amphibra root."

They agreed.

53

Kustodiev Eavesdrops

THEY ATE THE cookie, cinnamon, nothing special.

But why were there two of them?

Kustodiev couldn't stand it. Her boss had been expecting his son, and madam had cleared out for London in short order so she wouldn't see him gloating about her not being the only one who had a son. He had someone in this wide world, too. And not just the two Japanese girls with the mobile Japanese bathhouse, with that barrel thing, Japanese girls who came to bathe the owner for half a day and giggle in the bathroom. While he roared with laughter.

What family life did they actually have?

Before you knew it madam was going to file for divorce and demand half, if not more.

He was bound to end up giving her a black eye. The rest was obvious. We call the police, they call the ambulance, we already know this from the neighbors.

The wife of that tennis player raked in ten million for a bruised cheekbone and he was barred temporarily from getting within a kilometer of her, and did he need that?

Ahead lay divorce. Another hundred million!

Kustodiev went into the kitchen.

Whatever they said there, she could hear.

"So why are there two of you and who's who?" Her boss said.

"Who's who?" He repeated it as if smiling. But him smiling boded no good. Galina knew that.

Right then laughter broke out in response. Those two were laughing?

Her boss flew into a rage.

His chair creaked.

"So. Which one of you is Sergei Sergeyevich Sertsov?"

One of the boys answered with a laugh: "Actually, we're both Sergei Sergeyevich Sertsov. We were born the same day."

The other one: "It's a soap!"

"What the hell? I don't get it." This was her boss.

"You know, a soap opera. The plot about the switched babies."

"Ah." The chair creaked again. "Switched. We'll sort this out later. What about your mother?"

"Our mother is Maria Valerievna Sertsova. Daughter of the diplomat Valery Ivanovich Dolinin and Tamara Gennadievna Dolinina. Who by her maternal line was Princess Georgadze."

"And where does she live, your mother?" At this the owner positively leapt up. The chair nearly fell apart.

"Where we all do. You know our address."

"Maria Valerievna Sertsova, just so you know, I buried her myself and threw sand on her grave!"

"Yes, we know."

"And Alina stole my child! The con artist! The skank! Took him away! Alina Rechkina! She's living under someone else's passport? Well, she's got prison camp in her future. I'll do my utmost. You see what details have surfaced. Now you do this, you show me your passports."

They stamped their feet.

The chair creaked once more under Galina's boss.

"So-o-o . . . Everything's identical in this one and that one. Interesting. It's a fraud! A fake! People go to jail for this! For producing forged documents!"

"Oh no, they're not forged. We have birth certificates."

The host said, "I'm holding on to the passports for now."

"But you have no right . . ."

"I know what I do and don't have. No, we need to wash this business down with tea. My mouth is parched. Galina!"

She responded instantly from the kitchen, glanced into the room.

"Galina? Organize us some real Russian tea, from the heart. My tea! From the blue box! And those cookies. And a glass of milk for me."

Galina knew what he meant by "real Russian tea."

She put the blue box on a tray, along with a glass of milk from a farm, special Japanese teacups with saucers and antique spoons, a silver sugar bowl with a coat of arms, and a pitcher from the same tea service. She walked in with the tea on a cart, just as madam had taught her, all very elegant, the mistress herself having brought the tea service from Italy, from Penne.

Linen napkins, genuine, from Vologda. These, Kustodiev had bought in Tula, at a souvenir shop.

Her boss said to the two boys, "Give me your mobile phones."

"What for?"

"Because I told you to!"

"No . . . We can't give you our mobiles. You never know."

"Fine, then. Galina?"

She set everything on the little table.

"You run along."

But Galina zipped downstairs without making a sound through the service entrance at the back of the house, got down on all fours behind the bushes, and crawled into her own crawl space, where she knelt on a cushion.

Galina had realized that this hole had been specially thought up by a previous owner—you could easily hear what was going on in the bedrooms, the bathrooms, and the dining room. None of the utility rooms or kitchen fell into the surveillance zone.

Inasmuch as at the present time there were just two residents, two bedrooms, Kustodiev could listen all she wanted to their telephone conversations at night, but the madam didn't speak Russian, and the owner only expressed himself loudly in obscenities, whereas in business he spoke very quietly, covering his mouth.

Only once over the phone did the owner not try to hide and start yelling so that Kustodiev heard everything just standing in the kitchen.

He'd been given citizenship, that's what.

"What's the matter with you? You fucking moron! Have you gone completely deaf? I got citizenship! Fucking yeah! What the hell? Citizenship! Shit. If you only knew how much"—then he whispered—"but that's strictly between us. Now, she can't fucking inherit anything, her and her asshole degenerate! Damn it! Only my own son has that right! Only him! Yeah, she's going to kick the bucket before me, ha ha ha, I have a man of my own." Whisper. "I found two more afterward through friends, called them here, and they talked such shit about him that I realized it was a sign of competen . . . competence, you know, that he had a better handle than anyone on this project of ours. I'd called for that guy from Handia, but he understood everything and fit right in. I can't take one step anywhere, these people of mine, shit if they've tipped off Interpol. Not that I have it so bad here. I'm not exactly dreaming of birches. I'm from Krasnodar myself, and they don't grow there, not a one! I'm not going to leave a fucking will, one way or another everything will go to my son. And not her. Unless she bites it by then. It'll go to my Sergei Sergeyevich, who I raised from diapers without a mother, she died, I got no sleep . . . I can't believe it, fuck, these shitty genetic tests supposedly, they swab your cheek, what good's that? Only blood tells. You have to draw blood first, and then."

But that conversation was long ago, at a time when Galina had started making long-term plans about how much she and Kolya could earn in another ten years.

So now Kustodiev listened from her hiding place very attentively to all the rustles and voices in the living room.

It was quiet. They were drinking tea.

Now, in a few minutes, something was going to happen.

Yup. One crash, and then another crash.

Both fell. Both boys had ingested the sleeping powder.

"Kolya!" (The boss on the telephone to her husband, quietly.) "Come over. Do you still have that sharp knife? You know, that penknife. What do you mean you don't? Right. Doesn't matter. Come over. I bought it for you back in Moscow, so you'd have it in the car . . . What expiration date for a knife? Did you get scared? Well, you're a sap. Fine. I'm waiting."

Galina was waiting, too.

Someone's steps. Yes, Kolya. The boss was using him now. He was going to stitch him up for this. What should she do? What should she do?

"Okay, Nikolai. Go to the kitchen, look in the drawer there, in your hippo's drawer." (Hippo, eh? You're the hippo.) "There's that sharp knife. For steak, I think. Why are you standing there? Why are you mumbling? Lost your nerve? Okay. Fine, this doesn't have to be done right now. We'll carry them onto the lawn. Grab their feet. Off we go. Heavy as an elephant, my kin. As skinny as he looks. He was born skinny like that, too. He was small, his mother was ill. Gave birth and died. I felt sorry for her, even though I loved someone else. Oh, how I loved her! I spent all my money on her, and she wasn't shy. Lend me some more, give me cab fare."

Galina couldn't hear what came next. They tromped around a little and went out. Kolya was already in deep, and no good was going to come of it.

If she called the police, they'd arrest him as an accomplice. And her as well. Time to get out.

Galina sat there, petrified.

They'd arrest them, put them in prison, and give Angelka away for adoption.

"But hey, I was at home, ironing. I don't know anything. I didn't see or hear anything."

Time to run.

But she didn't budge.

And again they came tromping in, two heavy guys.

Kolya had pigged out on the three squares and beer here. While she was practically doing hard labor, it was like a roadside café here, from dawn to dusk.

She didn't think this but somehow her insult blocked out everything. It wasn't too expensive for them to buy prepared food. All the wives here had it easy, not a one of them cooked, they took a package out of the freezer and popped it in the microwave. Or, Rimka used to tell her, if someone here lived alone, all she took from the refrigerator was water. They were all skinny.

The boss's voice: "Oh! He's heavy. They grew up!"

They grunted, trudged along.

That was it. Kolya was going to prison.

They had to get out of this, do something. But she'd run out of steam.

She was dazed.

Galina managed to crawl out of her hidey-hole.

She dragged herself upstairs to the living room.

By the time she got there, by the time she looked out from behind the drapery, she could see it all there—below, on the lawn, on the grass. Two bodies.

Green grass, dark heads, white T-shirts. White arms, bare feet flung every which way. Like dead bodies.

But they'd taken off their shoes at the door. Lord. Lord.

Over them was that fool Kolya and their boss holding a knife. The biggest knife from her drawer. A meat cleaver. Just the ticket.

Her boss held the knife out to that fool Kolya and said something to him. Shouted at him.

Kolya looked to the side. Shook his stupid head.

He was already grimy, from carrying them, the two bodies. He was looking at a prison term.

His boss was shouting, pointing to Galina behind the drapery. Galina ran back and sat on the sofa, hunched over.

Kolya tromped through the living room, banged something, a window rattled.

Walked out.

Galina returned, stood behind the drapery, watching. She had to know everything.

Kolya held out three shot glasses to his boss.

His boss shouted and again pointed at Galina. Well, at the living room windows.

More hide-and-seek, Galina crouched behind the sofa, Kolya walked by, banged something, rattled a window, then went crashing back downstairs, and Galina jumped up and stood at her post behind the drapery.

Kolya held out three shot glasses to his boss—red, blue, and white.

His boss nodded, took the glasses, set them on the grass.

What for?

Held out the knife to Kolya.

Kolya stupidly shook his head, looked in the other direction. Crossed himself? What's that?

Obscenities were streaming from their boss, you could tell, it looked like he was chewing something hard.

He spat it out, leaned over one boy, Galina couldn't see anything, just her boss's back, he was making a small movement, the elbow with the knife was barely moving.

He was cutting one boy's finger.

He grabbed the white glass, leaned over, straining.

That's what it looked like. He'd cut the boy and was squeezing his blood out?

Kolya took one look and collapsed.

Fainted.

That meant it really was that.

Kolya used to say that whenever they took his blood in the army, he would turn away or else he'd faint, like at the enlistment office. When he collapsed there at the sight of blood, the enlistment office doctors for the construction battalion said he was mentally ill.

The boss shook his shaved head. Evidently he wasn't getting much.

He brandished the knife, as if plucking up his nerve.

He took the boy's arm, pulled it to the side—Galina had a good view of all this—ran the knife over the crook of his arm, and immediately brought the glass up to it.

He filled it, crawled over to the other boy, took the blue glass, and wielded the knife again.

Kustodiev was already racing to her house and dialing the police.

She dialed, told them the address, shouted, "They've killed someone here!" and hung up.

She took the remote for the gate from the drawer. Grabbed her bicycle and raced off with it as fast as she could.

She opened the gate.

And right then a tiny old woman squeezed past her and the bicycle onto the grounds.

The forbidden territory of the boss's villa. Kustodiev grabbed the woman by her jacket collar with her mighty hand.

With her other, though, Kustodiev kept a firm grip on the bicycle handlebars.

Because of that she messed up. She was left holding the old woman's jacket in one hand while the other was on the bicycle, even though it was propped up by her strong knee.

Meanwhile the jacket-less old woman, wearing a white T-shirt, had already hightailed it toward the house.

Galina swore angrily, Tula-style, at length and with major exaggerations.

She carefully set the expensive bike on the path and was about to speed after the woman, but!

As if they'd been standing guard right around the turn, a police car turned on its siren at the gate.

Galina turned back and buzzed the gate open.

Quickly picking up the bike, she climbed on and started off ahead of the police, gesturing to show the way.

Just like Delacroix's Liberty on the barricades (Kustodiev had studied all her boss's art books, looking for people like her. There were scads of them, like in Rubens, or that one of Delacroix's with the tits).

And after all, the police had come at her call!

Galina had her speech all ready.

How did you say "It was my plan"—in Montegascan? "My thought? My idea? To call you."

And, "I was afraid of my boss and his knife, he could kill you for interfering."

Just so that fool Kolya didn't come around too soon!

Galina swore again. They were in the car anyway and didn't understand a damn word of Russian.

When the police spilled out of their cars (there were two of them, and also an ambulance perched behind them out of which doctors and medics with stretchers climbed, too), the scene on the lawn was awful.

The knife-wielding murderer was kneeling—drenched in blood—over the three dead bodies.

A bloody murderer! Cameras started clicking. Where had the reporters come from?

Also kneeling, her head pressed to the heart of one of the bodies, was that little old woman, also in a blood-stained T-shirt.

She raised her head and started shaking her fist at the knife-wielding murderer.

And shouting in an incomprehensible language.

Actually, what she was shouting—Kustodiev immediately translated for the reporters, who were holding out their cameras toward her—was this:

"Their hearts are beating! He failed, the pig! Vile creature!"

The police worked quickly and handcuffed the man with the knife and the old woman.

They wanted to handcuff Kustodiev, too, but she held out her Nokia and shouted, "I was the one who called the police!"

And then, more quietly now, she told the reporters, having fluffed her hair, raised her eyebrows, and puffed out her lips (as if they'd been botoxed, but that was just a dream): "This old woman"—in Montegascan, "not young lady"—"only just got here! She's not to blame!"

They photographed everything.

"I work here as a gardener. This is my dead husband, he was the driver."

She went over to him, got down on her knees, and leaned over the body, ready to start sobbing.

At that moment her murdered husband opened his eyes and raised his head, and Kustodiev quietly swore. "Lie there and close your eyes, fool!"—and he returned to his original position and closed his eyes tight.

They picked up the dazed boss and led him in his bloodied T-shirt to their car.

They found and spent a long time photographing the murder weapon, a big scary knife, then wrapped it up in plastic and took it away.

The doctors worked on the three bodies.

The medics had a lot of wondering ahead of them as to why all the deceased had excellent cardiograms and one even opened his eyes and waved to the TV reporters from his stretcher.

"Fool!" the beautiful Rubenesque gardener—soon to be the main heroine of all the TV reporters' evening newscasts and also to appear in photographs in every morning paper—shouted at him in a foreign language. The woman who had averted death!

The murderer hadn't had enough time to slaughter his victims!

As for the old woman, she calmly slipped out of the handcuffs, which were too big for her (the police hadn't brought children's handcuffs, assuming there were any in Montegasco, a peaceful country where each child was a national treasure).

She told reporters first in Russian and then in Montegascan, "This is a mistake! These are my grandsons! I flew here from Moscow!"

She spoke very well but made no sense.

That is, it was clearly Montegascan, but those words didn't exist in it.

Galina told the representatives of the press the same thing, but normally.

They wrote everything down and then also were present at the questioning of the old woman, the murderer, and the beautiful gardener, the wife of the murderer's driver, who had nearly died of fright.

The morning newspapers also ran the story of the Russian citizen Lana, who had adopted the two grandsons, fraternal twins but not from the same family, not brothers at all, as it came out, and she had followed them to Montegasco, afraid of the consequences of their visit to a representative of the Russian mafia, who was once the father of one of the twins (but not both! some kind of Russian genetic peculiarity!).

Before leaving the scene of the crime, Galina locked up the villa, the garage, her house, and the gate.

And heroically, stashing the key ring in her bag, went to give her statement to the police.

There she started sobbing, saying she couldn't do this, she had to pick up her daughter from school before she could start talking.

And if that was impossible, then they at least had to question the driver, Angelka's father, since he'd come around.

He'd been lying unconscious throughout the crime.

He hadn't seen and didn't know anything.

They had to release him so he could take Angelka home.

True, they couldn't even question her right away, they had to call in an official Russian-Montegascan interpreter.

The country had only one, and at that time he was vacationing in the distant town of Serpukhov, where white bears roam the taiga.

As a result (Montegasco laws are strict), the police picked up the child at school and took her to a care home that had sat empty since World War II—so that she could later be put up for adoption if her mother and father were arrested.

At the care home they asked the child what the little girl wanted for dinner, and at her request they took the poor little thing to that dreadful McDonald's (which exists for American and Chinese tourists, the natives wouldn't be caught dead there, for fear of the fat and salt, which brings on swift and incurable obesity), and then, also at the poor child's request, they took her to the Disneyland in the next country, where Angelka had a blast on the rides.

Everywhere she went, the little beauty was accompanied by reporters, and there was even a film shot about the poor dear.

Which ran one night on television, and in the morning forty families had declared their desire to take her in and raise her in order to subsequently give her an education at the best university in Europe.

By the evening of that insane day, the interpreter had arrived in Montegasco from Serpukhov, and the girl's father had been questioned and kept in a jail cell on suspicion of complicity (he'd brought the knife and helped carry the bodies).

Nikolai told them he hadn't known anything, his boss had told him to bring him the thin penknife his boss had bought him a long time ago.

Back in Moscow!

"There," they wrote in the newspapers, "where bears roam and there's permafrost in the Kremlin!"

Nikolai hadn't given him the penknife, he'd said he'd lost it.

But the knife was still there in the glove compartment. You can check, I didn't give it to him.

Then his employer told him to get him a big sharp knife.

By that time both boys were already stretched out on the living room floor.

Nikolai thought they were just worn out from their flight.

These things happened with his employer's guests, they flew in, had dinner with him, drank tea from the blue box, and then lay there as if they were sleeping.

Then the guests had to be taken to the hotel and carried to their room, and sometimes they were very heavy, too heavy for one person, and often at the hotel the staff there helped carry the guests from the car.

You can check with them, they'll confirm it.

They had guests who weighed a good hundred kilos.

Or whatever that sleep-inducing tea the employer has is, the tea in the blue box, that immediately knocks them off their hooves (the interpreter changed "hooves" to "heels").

His boss was always ("constantly" in the translation) taking and checking the sleeping men's phones and writing down numbers and names.

The driver thought everything was going to go as always ("as a rule, as usual" in the translation).

The driver thought they were taking the boys out of the house and onto the lawn to get them fresh air. So they'd feel better.

The sleeping powder lasted twelve hours.

But then, when the driver saw what his boss was up to and the blood flowed—he didn't remember anything after that.

The sight of blood made him dizzy, he fainted, they found that out back at the enlistment office.

Instead of "enlistment office," the interpreter said "military headquarters."

Which was why they took him into the con-bat ("construction battalion," but untranslatable, according to the interpreter newly arrived from Serpukhov, so he left that part out).

After questioning, the driver was kept in jail for the time being.

The latest-model lie detector (with three simple lights: "lie," "truth," and "half-truth") lit up the "truth" light.

Under questioning, Galina wept copiously and broke down over what the criminal had done to her, and the story with the sperm was brought up, and new tests were done.

"Truth" lit up this time, too.

Galina's employer was questioned after her and after his driver.

The Serpukhov interpreter, who was a little under the weather, having flown in from the taiga, where they survive on nothing but Russian vodka, laid out the following story, leaving out the criminal's untranslatable obscenities, as best he could: "Me?! I wanted to do a blood test! To find out who's who." The interpreter repeated this English expression in the original. "Which of them is my son! Why there are two of them is a total mystery! How two of them could come! I sent one invitation, but two times! And that's it! And I didn't know how to take a sample! How to take blood! My driver advised me to do it this way and brought me that knife! And he was the one who suggested carrying the boys out on the lawn! He carried them out himself! And slit their veins! And then went soft!" The Serpukhov interpreter hesitated, and not knowing the right word, blurted "impotent." The investigators maintained an unperturbed expression but twitched simultaneously. Did this mean there was also a sex angle to these recumbent boys?

"And I collected the blood! Just collected it! To have it tested! That's why I was covered in blood! I don't trust those cotton swabs they use for genetic tests. Only blood tells the truth."

"Lie" lit up on the lie detector.

After questioning, the Russian-speaking citizen of Montegasco was issued sheets, pajamas, a matching cap, slippers (all striped), and a card with Wi-Fi info.

And led to a two-room cell.

Soon after, though, the arrested man had his next interrogation, on the other case, in which figured the facts concerning Galina.

He was led in in full uniform, all stripes, after the traditional five o'clock prison tea (Montegasco being under the jurisdiction of the Queen of England).

The prisoner gave his statement:

"She was the one who asked me into the house I'd given them, other servants rent a halupa"—a separate cabin, the interpreter said—"in the suburbs, but I gave them all this! And later, when I'd already started leaving and hadn't paid her any money, this happened. She was the one who wanted to fuck"—in translation, "he did something rather indecent to her." "That was when she pulled out some of her hair, smashed her head on the floor, and started threatening me so that I'd give her money and an apartment. I refused and left. That's when she called the police."

"Lie" lit up.

An unhappy, humiliated, and vindicated Galina was given a police car and motorcycle escort, and her daughter and husband were escorted to lodgings in the most expensive hotel in Montegasco (which the locals called the "Emirates' Dorm"), all at the president's expense.

This event landed on local TV news and all the evening papers (two).

Naturally.

Elections were coming soon.

Alina flew in from Russia, her car was escorted by motorcycle police and a cavalcade of reporters' cars.

Nothing of the kind had happened in this country for a very long time!

Victims of the Russian mafia!

Fraternal twins with identical passports!

Switched babies, the crime of the century!

They questioned Alina and then all of them—the now awake Seryozhas, Lana (who, so she wouldn't worry about Graf, had left him in the care of her sober friend, Struchok, with instructions not to let in any women with wine and cake), as well as Alina herself, the matriarch—and they were put in the same hotel with the family of Nikolai the driver, where bearded brunets wearing white dresses to the floor and white scarfs with hoops on their head stood in groups chatting in the lobby.

Sporting Swiss watches with diamond bracelets, too.

What comes next points to the future, as one orator quipped.

In any case, many in Montegasco considered deportation to their homeland, Russia, an excessively cruel punishment, tantamount to a death penalty.

White bears in the streets, a Gulag at the Lubyanka in downtown Moscow, permafrost, KGB everywhere, starting from the very top!

Which punishment would automatically lead to the inheritance of his capital and property by the criminal's children.

Of whom there were two, one his own, the other basically adopted.

But who was who—that they didn't try to clarify.

So as not to traumatize the minors' psyche and at their request.

However one other difficulty arose. The wife of Nikolai's driver, upon examination by a doctor, turned out to be pregnant, which brought with it further investigation as to whose child it was. If he was the descendant of a Montegascan citizen, then the child was a

Montegascan citizen with all the rights of a Montegascan citizen. Not only that, according to a recently passed law, this minor citizen of the state could not be removed from his biological mother, who also became a citizen. But this was if she vindicated this right by her irreproachable conduct (following this came an enumeration of all the sins listed in the Bible and in the country's criminal code, with the addition of the sin of a round-the-clock presence on Instagram with pictures of her baby!).

Long live the queen!

Moscow – Tarusa – Arugam Bay

Thank you all
for your support.
We do this for you,
and could not do
it without you.

DEEP
VELLUM

PARTNERS

pixel ||| texel

EMBREY FAMILY
FOUNDATION

ADDITIONAL DONORS, CONT'D

Mark Haber
Mary Cline
Maynard Thomson
Michael Reklis
Mike Soto
Mokhtar Ramadan
Nikki & Dennis Gibson
Patrick Kukucka
Patrick Kutcher
Rev. Elizabeth & Neil Moseley
Richard Meyer

Scott & Katy Nimmons
Sherry Perry
Sydneyann Binion
Stephen Harding
Stephen Williamson
Susan Carp
Susan Ernst
Theater Jones
Tim Perttula
Tony Thomson

SUBSCRIBERS

Margaret Terwey
Ben Fountain
Gina Rios
Elena Rush
Courtney Sheedy
Caroline West
Brian Bell
Charles Dee Mitchell
Cullen Schaar
Harvey Hix
Jeff Lierly
Elizabeth Simpson

Nicole Yurcaba
Jennifer Owen
Melanie Nicholls
Alan Glazer
Michael Doss
Matt Bucher
Katarzyna Bartoszynska
Michael Binkley
Erin Kubatzky
Martin Piñol
Michael Lighty
Joseph Rebella

Jarratt Willis
Heustis Whiteside
Samuel Herrera
Heidi McElrath
Jeffrey Parker
Carolyn Surbaugh
Stephen Fuller
Kari Mah
Matt Ammon
Elif Ağanoğlu

AVAILABLE NOW FROM DEEP VELLUM

FORTHCOMING FROM DEEP VELLUM

KIDNAPPED